Other Titles b

The DEAD Series:

DEAD: The Ugly Beginning
DEAD: Revelations
DEAD: Fortunes & Failures
DEAD: Winter
DEAD: Siege & Survival
DEAD: Confrontation
DEAD: Reborn
DEAD: Darkness Before Dawn
DEAD: Spring
DEAD: Reclamation
DEAD: Blood & Betrayal
DEAD: End (October 2015)

DEAD Special Edition

DEAD: Perspectives Story (Vols. 1 & 2)
DEAD: Vignettes (Vols. 1 & 2)
DEAD: The Geeks (Vols. 1 & 2)

DEAD: Snapshot— {Insert Town Here}

DEAD: Snapshot—**Portland, Oregon**
DEAD: Snapshot—**Leeds, England** (August 2015)

Zomblog

Zomblog
Zomblog II
Zomblog: The Final Entry
Zomblog: Snoe
Zomblog: Snoe's War
Zomblog: Snoe's Journey

That Ghoul Ava

That Ghoul Ava: Her First Adventures
That Ghoul Ava & The Queen of the Zombies
That Ghoul Ava Kick Some Faerie A**
Next, on a very special That Ghoul Ava
That Ghoul Ava...on the Lam!

Blood & Betrayal

(Book 11 of the *DEAD* series)

TW Brown

Portland, Oregon, USA

DEAD: Blood & Betrayal
Book 11 of the *DEAD* series
©2015 May December Publications LLC

Printed in the U.S.A.

ISBN - 978-1-940734-42-2

The World of the *DEAD* expands with:

*Snapshot—**Portland, Oregon***

(Available now!!!)

To see your town die in the *DEAD* world, email TW Brown at:
twbrown.maydecpub@gmail.com

The World of the *DEAD* expands with:

*Snapshot—**Leeds, England***

(Coming August 2015)

To see your town die in the *DEAD* world, email TW Brown at:
twbrown.maydecpub@gmail.com

A moment with the author...

The fear of being a disappointment!

Any *Sopranos* fans out there? How about the riveting show that was *Lost*? If you fall into either of those groups, then you might know a little something about feeling like you went on this amazing journey that ended up with a great big kick in the naughty bits. Sure, there are those who will profess to be just fine with how two of the most epic television series ever came to a halt, but judging by the responses at the time, I am guessing that those people are in the minority. *X-Files*? Hell, even *Rosanne* and *Seinfeld* get grief from anybody who vested any serious amount of time watching a sitcom for anything other than the humor. And don't get me started on *How I met Your Mother*, a sitcom that started off with a supposed end game.

Give me the ending to *Breaking Bad*...or either of my personal faves, *Friday Night Lights* and *Quantum Leap* (the song "Georgia on My Mind" garnered some serious meaning for me after that QL finale; it still almost brings a tear to my eye when I hear it). The finale is the reward to the fan. It is that last image that they will cling to for eternity. It can be the toughest episode to create because it is going to have the greatest impact. Nothing that came before will mean squat if the finale sucks. (See *Lost*.)

So, what the hell does any of that have to do with me? Well, as many of you may very well know, the proper *DEAD* series is coming to a conclusion. I expect to release *DEAD: End* (Book 12 of the *DEAD* series) on Halloween of this year. I am currently cobbling book 11, *DEAD: Blood & Betrayal* and am experiencing some tremors of nervousness as the book wraps. (I believe I have set a record for the lack of zombies in a zombie novel with this one.)

I intend to go directly into the writing of *DEAD: End* immediately. This book has gone through so many possible conclusions in my head that I could write five "alternate ending" books. One of my earliest ideas was to give each major character a final chapter. Too bad most of them (major characters that is) did not survive to have a final chapter.

I think I have settled on one story line's ending. I am not certain how I will get there, but that is half the fun for me as a

i

writer. Still, even though I think the ending is kinda cool, that by no means carries over to how it will be received. I have learned over the past few years that things I see clearly can often be cloudy at best for my readers. (I thought I dropped enough clues when I began the Emily-zombie story line to explain the behavior of the child zombie...umm...NOPE! I still have folks asking what the deal with the child zombies is after book 9.)

To say that I am feeling the pressure would be an understatement. You, my loyal reader, have embarked on this journey with me and trusted that I would take you to a satisfying conclusion. I have almost reached a point where the last paragraph has Pamela Ewing go into the bathroom where Bobby is taking a shower. Once she tells him about her "crazy dream" he says, "Wait until I tell you about mine! Spoiler, it has zombies in it!"

I guess I am just saying that, like anything in the world of entertainment, not everybody is gonna love it. My biggest goal right now is to avoid comparisons to any of the shows mentioned in the opening paragraph.

Oh well, I have until October before the calls rise up for the villagers to assemble with their torches. Right?

"Do you have any tattoos, Janet?"
TW Brown
March 2015

Thad and Scotty
Still my friends after all the crazy stuff

Contents

SNEAK PEEKS

1

Vignettes LXI

Juan felt himself slip from consciousness. His last memory was seeing a pair of legs coming his direction. He wished desperately that he could see Mackenzie's face as it was before she died, but the only image was that of the sallow-faced, tracer-riddled eyes that had consumed her beauty in those last days.

The next thing he knew, Juan's eyes were struggling to adjust to the flickering light of a fire. Through slitted eyelids, he could make out the log walls of a cabin. He was trying to decide if he was in a good place, or maybe this was a new and horrible basement scene like the one he'd endured at the hands of a crazy woman all those years ago.

"You thirsty?" a man's voice asked. It was rough, and sounded awkward.

Great, Juan thought, *zombies have finally learned how to talk.*

"Daddy!" a familiar chorus of squeals brought him fully awake, and Juan was now suddenly frantic. He was bound and unable to move. He began to squirm, desperate to come to the rescue of his daughters, Della and Denita.

"Easy, mister," the awkward voice warned.

A shadow fell over Juan as a coarse-spun shirt filled his entire field of vision. Juan looked up and could only see a dark

1

outline against the light of the fire. There was a moment where he wanted to scream as he felt hands fumbling for him, but then he was suddenly free to move.

"Just take it easy, mister," the voice whispered. "The girls don't need to see you all frazzled. Took them a mighty long spell to get comfortable here."

Juan tried to sit up and found that his head swam the moment he got less than halfway upright. He lay back down and took a deep breath to try and get his nerves settled. That was also just enough time for two small figures to climb up and on top of him. Both girls began talking a million miles an hour, not a single word managing to make sense as both talked over the other and neither relating a similar part of the story. Then he heard something that got his attention.

"Wait!" Juan groaned, getting his elbows underneath him and easing up just a bit. "What was that 'bout the deaders?"

"The Grizzly Man came in and chopped them all down just in time to save Keith and the horses and Brianne. Then he talked with Keith and they said they would meet you in Ankledge," Denita spoke with amazing surety.

"Actually, my name is Gerald, but your girls think it is fun to call me the Grizzly Man." A hand that looked as if it could engulf both of Juan's at once came forward and waited to be clasped in greeting. Juan shook the man's hand and accepted the help to a completely upright position.

Juan's eyes had finally adjusted to the light, and he took in the figure that spoke. His daughters had chosen well in their nickname. The man was taller than any human being that Juan had ever met in his life. He was wearing a heavy shirt that was partially unbuttoned to display more hair on the man's chest than most men had on their heads, and then there was the beard. ZZ Top in their heyday could not compare to the thick and massive beard that climbed the man's cheeks to the point of almost hiding his eyes, and hung down low enough to settle on the solid but ample belly.

"Juan Hoya," he said absently as his eyes drifted around an open cabin that looked like the setting for a really cheesy horror movie.

The walls were adorned with the heads of bears, wildcats, moose, and a variety of other animals that all stared back with empty gazes. One shelf had a variety of smaller animals. This was where his gaze lingered. There looked to be a squirrel or some such creature on a tiny unicycle. He saw a skunk reading a newspaper while seated on a miniature toilet, and then there was an arctic fox wearing glasses and leaning against a light post checking his wristwatch.

The man noticed Juan's gaze and made an embarrassed cough. He started for the shelf and then stopped as if realizing that he could not cover anything up as the cat was already out of the bag so to speak.

"Alone out in the Alaskan wilderness, you come up with some…interesting ways to bide your time." The man reached over and adjusted the fox so that it was easier to see the fact that it appeared—above everything else already apparent—to be smiling down at a mouse that was standing beside him in some sort of jacket.

Juan made a grunt as his eyes now shifted to the arsenal of bladed and spiked weapons adorning one entire wall. One sword in particular looked to be taller than his daughters. The gleam from the firelight and the few hanging lanterns gave away that the edges were finely honed. Juan had no doubt that every single blade on that wall was sharpened to a razor's edge.

"So, as your daughters already told you," Gerald rumbled, "your friends went ahead to Anchorage." He made a point to enunciate the word as he winked at Della and Denita.

"How long have I been out?" Juan asked cautiously.

"In and out for over a week," the man replied.

"Grizzly Man had to clean your butt!" Della snickered, and then both she and Denita were giggling uncontrollably.

"You have been taking care of us this entire time?" Juan gave the man a curious look.

"He killed the deader wolves before they could eat you," Denita said around the last of her giggles.

Everything came flooding back for Juan. The horse falling,

the pain in his leg…and the wolves. No matter how many times he encountered those horrible things, he didn't think there would ever come a time when he would not be totally creeped out by them.

"You took a nasty fall," Gerald said with a nod. "All that noise distracted the wolves from their original target."

"Huh?" Juan shook himself clear of the memory and focused on Gerald again. "What target was that?"

"Me," the big man said with a sigh. "Damn things had me dead to rights. Already took down my bear. I'm gonna miss old Walt."

Suddenly, the nickname was making a lot more sense.

***

Vix moved down the long walkway. Below her, a sea of undead faces looked up. That was not the scary part. The really scary part was how many of those heads did not even regard her passing. There were more zombies here than she had ever imagined could gather in one place.

It had taken twelve days since that mob was spotted for the first of them to begin arriving at their shore. No telling how many were swept away in the currents of the waters of the River Medway and sent out to the sea. It did not seem like nearly enough as the waterway was now a slurry of parts that had come free and no sign of an end to the mob that was still pouring in from the far shore across the river.

"Beacons alight!" somebody cried.

Vix paused and turned to her right. They were being surrounded. This was the third beacon towards the direction of Warden. Already, in the direction of Queenborough, the beacons were burning as far as her field of vision would allow her to see. They were basically being cut off. The one thing that they had going in their favor was the wall.

So many people had complained against the hard, back-breaking labor that had been required. She would do her best not to rub their noses in it later when this crisis was averted. It was

4

far too early for her to gloat.

"It looks like the entire population of the bloody country is here," a young man hissed as he moved past Vix on the walkway.

Vix looked out across the water at the horde that were following their brethren into the surf and across the waterway to what had once been their peaceful refuge. It still did not make a great deal of sense. In all the years since the first days of the zed rising, the abominations had not made it a point to just walk out into the water.

"Something caused this," Vix grunted as she thrust down with her spear.

Her shoulders were starting to protest. Her shift was not even a half hour old, and already she was feeling the muscles start to ache. After three shifts of an hour each yesterday, and this just her first one today, she did not look forward to what she might feel like in a few days.

For the next thirty minutes, she put her body on auto-pilot and let her mind drift. She considered all of the choices made in the past decade and fixed on every single one that she now viewed as a mistake. The first one was actually in relation to the walkway and wall system that she was currently using.

The meetings had been worse than the old days of Parliament with all of the hissing and shouting that took place. The people were divided on three lines: first was the group that believed that only a section of the island needed to be walled off; second was the group that wanted the entire island walled off; and last were those who felt no need for a wall at all. The third group was the smallest, and quickly pounced upon by the other two as each side sought to secure the majority vote.

In the end, most of the island had been walled off. The wall proper was set inland about fifty to a hundred yards depending on location as some ground was more stable in certain places. However, Vix only brushed over that for a moment; currently, her biggest regret was the fact that she had allowed herself to settle in a location that had no ready escape.

She felt a tap on her shoulder and breathed a sigh of relief that her shift was over. After a brief exchange of pleasantries, she headed down the stairs and made her way home. She wanted to just flop on her bed and sleep until the knock came at the door that would signal it was time to start over, but she could not relax until she'd washed up.

After dumping the basin out, Vix was finally prepared to get some rest. Her eyes had not closed for more than a minute or two when a knock came.

"Impossible," she growled as she got up to answer.

"You need to come with me right away." It was Chaaya. She was in full gear for a trip off the island. Two others were with her, both also dressed for the field.

"What is going—" she started, but was not given the chance to finish as a hand came up and covered her mouth.

"Not here, and not now!" a man hissed. Even in the hushed tone, she recognized the voice of Gordon Richardson.

Gordon was average when it came to height, and even by the new standard, he was a bit skinny for a bloke. However, it was his voice that made you remember Gordon from the first time you met; it was deeper than you would expect by a considerable amount. His fair hair and blue eyes were pleasant to look at and he always had a bit of a lopsided smile on his face.

The other individual was Marjorie Burns. Marjorie had been an up and coming snowboarder on the extreme sports circuit as well as an Olympic hopeful when the world ended. She had lost none of her attitude or daredevil outlook in all that time. If there was a trip to be made, she was always a volunteer, if not a leader. Marjorie was also a bit of a scrapper. Her round face was highlighted by a flat nose from the frequent scrapes the woman seemed to find; and she did not care if you were man or woman—in more ways than one. Lately, she and Chaaya had been an item.

"Suit up." A satchel was thrust at Vix by Gordon. She opened it, not really surprised to discover the full field compliment inside.

After a brief internal debate, she shrugged and did as she was asked. Ten minutes later, she was moving along the wall, headed towards what had once been the Elmley National Nature Reserve. Now, it was pasture and open grazing land for sheep, cows, and chickens as well as a few horses.

It was an hour later when she noticed that none of the danger lanterns on the wall towers were lit in this area. That was a good thing, she decided as she walked in silence with the others. Twice she had tried to ask what was going on; both times she had been unceremoniously hushed and told that she would be told everything in due time.

They stopped suddenly and Vix heard a jingle of keys. She felt the hairs on the back of her neck stand up. Nobody was allowed to have the keys with the exception of the roving patrol assigned to that area. The day that the zombies had been sighted across the channel, all of the keys had been collected and secured. There would be no excursions. This was one of what Vix called "The Horror Cinema Rules." This rule in particular was enacted simply because somebody had mentioned that somebody always left a door unsecured in the movies, and that is how the monsters got in and wiped out the humans. In the event of an assault from outside the walls—living or undead—all keys were secured until the threat had been dealt with and declared null.

"Okay," Vix snapped, folding her arms across her body and planting her feet in the ground, "I'm not budging until somebody tells me what the bloody hell this is all about!"

The nervous looks that passed between the trio did not go unnoticed; there could be no doubt that something was seriously wrong. At last, Chaaya gave Marjorie a nudge forward. "Tell her what you saw."

"But we can't be sure." Marjorie shook her head. "I told you that I didn't want to involve anybody else in the first place. You tell her!"

Chaaya looked over at Gordon who nodded his agreement. All this did was annoy Vix further. It was bad enough to be woken up after a shift on the wall. Then she had been basically shanghaied into coming on this secret little journey for who-knows-why.

"Just spit it out, or I am going back home." Vix glared at

Marjorie, her eyes flicking down to the woman's clenched fists. "And don't think you can threaten me, girl. You aren't the only one who knows how to handle herself in a scrap."

Chaaya began to explain. As she did, Vix found herself slowly shifting from annoyance, to disbelief...to all-out anger. The story she was hearing was madness; that is why she believed every word of it.

"And you say these people are over towards the area of High Halstow?" Vix finally asked when the tale was told.

"That is where I spotted their man. I followed him just north of there to a keep they built up in the woods of the old reserve," Marjorie said in uncharacteristic nervousness.

"So why did you keep this to yourself until now?" Vix asked.

"I actually had forgotten about it until something from a few days earlier when I was out on that run popped into my head."

Vix felt another chill course through her as Marjorie filled in that final detail. Without further argument, she followed the threesome through the door, making sure to give the iron-bound oak door a good tug to ensure that it was locked...just in case.

***

The trap door opened and there was a second of near silence before the rope came to its abrupt halt. The body at the end jerked a few times and was eventually still. There was another moment of silence, and then a few spontaneous cheers erupted from the gathered crowd.

Chad shuddered and turned to the man beside him. "You guys sure don't waste any time."

"You say that like it's a bad thing," Butch chuckled as he reached out to shake Chad's hand. "Way I see it, the courts had it all screwed up back in the old days."

Chad kept his mouth shut. He was not a gambling man, but if he were, he would be willing to bet he'd probably had more exposure to that system than this gentleman. Instead, he shook the man's hand.

"I guess me and the ladies will be heading on our way."

"You sure?" Butch asked, hitching his pants and turning his head to spit; a gesture that never ceased to repulse Chad.

"We haven't had the best of luck with groups," Chad replied with a shake of his head.

"Well, just remember, if you do well this season, you can always bring down any meat or hides and trade here. We like staying friendly with those of you that choose to rough it. Now, if'n you'll excuse me, the corpse should start kicking pretty soon. We always like to take the heads prior to that unpleasantness."

Chad gave a nod. He watched the man join a handful of others. Sure enough, they brought the body to the ground and severed the head. He imagined that it would be adorning that twisted version of an "unloving" totem pole that stood in the center of this small fortified town. Butch explained that it was a sort of deterrent to crime.

Chad shook his head and strolled up the narrow street to the inn where Caroline and Ronni would be waiting. He had actually been surprised when Ronni had declined to witness the hanging considering how vehement she had been in regards to this young woman and her so-called attempt on his life.

"Ready to go?" he asked, coming up behind the two women who were both flipping through a stack of various bolts of sturdy looking cloth.

"Like, an hour ago," Ronni groaned. Caroline only nodded and gave the store one more appraising look before following the father and daughter out the door.

By the time the sun set, they were almost home. None of them cherished the idea of being out overnight as clouds had begun to roll in and threaten rain. The first rain drops began a short time after it was fully dark and made the ground all that much more treacherous.

Since Caroline was walking in the middle, she was the one carrying the lantern. It allowed everybody to see well enough to try and avoid twisting an ankle on an exposed root or large rock.

Each of them let out an audible sigh of relief when the cabin finally came into view. Chad set to getting a good fire going so that everybody could get warm and dry while Ronni and Caroline changed clothes and then put out a dinner of dried meat and oat bread.

With the fire blazing, Chad joined the other two at the table once he'd changed clothes. A jar sat in the middle of the table, a thin wrapping of cloth around it preventing him from seeing the contents. Both women looked like they would burst at the seams if he didn't hurry up and make mention of the jar; that is why he picked up a piece of meat and tore free a chunk of the bread.

"Oh, my God!" Ronni exclaimed, snatching the jar and untying the string that held the cloth in place.

"Problems?" Chad said around a mouthful of meat and bread.

"You are gonna regret taking that first bite," Caroline said with a mysterious smirk.

"Honey!" Ronni exclaimed, holding up the jar so that the amber contents could catch the light of the fire and take on a yellow-orange glow. "We traded for it back while you were out watching that hanging."

Chad almost wanted to spit out the mouthful of food that he was chewing so that he could spread a dollop of the sweet nectar on it. He refrained and was content to smear some on the rest of his chunk of bread. The remainder of the evening meal was a chorus of "mmms" and "yums" from each of them.

At last, Ronni said goodnight and gave her dad a hug before climbing up to the loft. Caroline and Chad sat in silence for a while before Caroline finally broke it.

"So why exactly did they hang the girl first?"

"According to Butch, they do it more as a way for people to really witness the punishment. Also, it is more of that deterrent system they seem so fond of using. Folks know that they will be executed in this way and then there is the whole creepy totem pole thing," Chad explained.

"And they've been doing this for how many years but people apparently still commit crimes under the death penalty umbrella?" Caroline quipped.

"I didn't want to point out the obvious," Chad said with a shrug.

They were quiet again for a few minutes. This time, it was Chad who broke the peace.

"We need to move."

"But we just got settled," Caroline protested.

"Yep. And it sucks, but I don't want to be anyplace near that settlement. I'm not suggesting that they would do anything, but here are the facts. We killed some of their people."

Caroline glanced up to the loft where Ronni was supposedly sleeping. "And what about her? You think that she will be happy with this idea?"

"I'd rather her be a little unhappy than a lot dead."

"You really think that it will come to that?"

"You are asking me to make that call based on a small outpost that has an undead totem pole in the town square where they mount the heads of all the people that they execute."

Caroline sat there for a few minutes, sipping on some lavender tea sweetened with just a hint of the honey that they had been so excited to find. Chad stared at the fire and let her come to her own conclusions despite having made his already.

"Crap," Caroline hissed.

Chad nodded. "You see?"

"They made it a point to say that they had the heads of every single person that they have executed on that totem, didn't they?"

"A number of times."

"I guess we start packing."

***

"They took Alana!" Selina wailed.

Jody ran out the back door to where Selina stood on the porch, one hand outstretched and pointing to the empty swing. He eased past the woman who was nearing hysterics as she began to call their daughter's name over and over in between ragged sobs.

Walking across the yard, he kept his eyes on the ground. It was still early in the morning and there was a hint of dew on the grass. He had no trouble following his daughter's footsteps as she hurried out to her swing like she did almost every morning. He had joked that she would be out on her swing in the pouring rain.

At least it was a joke until the morning he went outside to find her doing exactly that as thunder boomed and the sky dropped buckets of water in sheets that were almost too difficult to see clearly. When asked why she had done such a thing, Alana looked at her mother and father like they were crazy.

"It's warm outside. You say we should save water and so I was swinging while I took my shower," Alana had explained as if that might be the most normal thing in the world.

As he neared the swing set, he felt his heart leap to his throat. The back gate had been opened. However, it was the second realization that chilled him to the core. Alana had walked right over to whoever this mystery person was and left willingly.

"She knew you," Jody whispered.

Unfortunately, that did not honestly eliminate that many people. The community was still small. However, Jody had a hunch that Alana knew this person very well. She would not walk away willingly with just anybody. That shortened the list considerably. It also gave rise to a very frightening question.

How far out of touch had he become with the people?

Spinning on his heel, he walked back to Selina and put his hands on her shoulders. "I want you to go inside and stay here. She might have run off after a..." His voice faded as the lie turned to ash in his mouth. He knew damn well that was not the case, and so did Selina.

"This is because of that trial, isn't it?" she sniffed.

"We can't be sure—" he started, but she cut him off.

"Don't try to lie to me, Jody. It is all anybody talked about for months. And then to have the verdict come down to you making the final vote? It was almost like the jury set you up to be the fall guy."

"Those men did something horrible. I could not simply buy

into the 'our-word-against-theirs' argument. I saw with my own eyes what had been done to that one young lady, Angel. Jan was within her rights to demand that she and her people be compensated for what we did." Jody felt all of the turmoil resurface.

It had been several months since the trial had concluded. Yes, it was true that Danny had been mutilated. Hell, it was unlikely that he would ever walk without the use of at least a cane. Still, his people had stormed in and not only killed several individuals, but then there had been the animalistic beating of the woman by Margarita. Later, it was additional testimony by Bill Pitts stating that George Rosamilia had joined on the beating in addition to cheering and inviting others to "get their licks in before somebody like Rafe shows up and spoils the party."

It had been for that reason alone that Jody had cast the deciding vote to exile the pair. In truth, he had believed it long overdue. But that was another thing that he was struggling with at the moment. He had been feeling for some time that George had replaced him in Danny's life as a friend. Could it really be something as simple as his petty jealousy that had caused him to cast that deciding vote that sent the polarizing couple outside of the walls?

A knock at the door interrupted his thoughts. Jody gave Selina a squeeze and then went to answer it after telling her to stay put. He opened the door and was momentarily puzzled when he did not see anybody. Then he spied it. On the bannister of his porch was a small box with a red bow.

He stepped over to it with caution and found that he could scarcely breathe for fear of what he would find if he opened that box.

Holding it in his hands for several seconds, he finally gave in and peeled back the wrapping paper. He could hear Selina's sobs from where she remained on the back porch. Looking up and down the street, he noticed that it was strangely quiet and devoid of any activity. For a sunny morning like this, that was more than a little peculiar.

Holding his breath, Jody opened the lid of the box. He was slammed with a simultaneous rush of relief as well as the crush of dread. He'd expected something horrific inside that box; something that would likely send him plunging into stupidity and despair in equal measures. He could be honest with himself and admit that he had figured to discover a finger or something of that nature.

What he found sent a message equally clear, but without him having to consider the possibility of the pain and torment that his child might be experiencing. Jody plucked the lock of hair from the box and tucked it into his breast pocket.

Then, without a word to Selina, Jody walked upstairs and began putting on his gear.

***

The following is an excerpt of a diary found in a small trading outpost just south of Old Seattle.

Entry One—
My name is Adam, and I hunt the living. I am an avenger of those who fall prey to the dregs of humanity. In a world stripped of almost all law and order, the pecking order is often established painfully and with no regard for those who are not deemed strong enough to fend for themselves.

In the Old World, women fought for decades to reach some semblance of equality. The zombie apocalypse erased all of that in a very short time. It is like the implosion of a building. A few charges in the right spots can erase any memory of the past in the blink of an eye.

I don't imagine that I will ever be recognized for what I do. Honestly, I don't care. If I am even more honest, I will guess that there are those who think I am as much of a monster as some of those I hunt. After all, I debase and commit acts that most would call torture.

I know that this man that I have hanging upside down from an old pine tree would think that. He is bleeding out slowly. About an hour ago, he begged for me to just kill him. I wonder if he heard those same words from his victims. I wonder if he cared as little as I do right this moment.

The man hanging from the tree looks like he has been painted blood red from about his shins all the way to his recently shaved head. I had to shave his head because it gave me more surface to work with.

I should probably clarify at this point. The piece of human waste hanging from the tree used to get off by kidnapping young girls and bringing them out to his cabin where he had quite a harem building. He was one of those guys that you used to see in the Old World that ended up on the news because some poor girl that he abducted and then raped until she eventually became pregnant would escape. Then the cops would raid the house and find three or four other poor girls that had been missing for who-knows-how-long all kept in a basement.

This guy might have been doing this since before the zombies and never got caught. I know that one of those poor women was close to thirty and didn't even know that the world had ended. She was kept in a shed all by herself and will probably never be able to adjust.

I took all of the girls to a village on the edge of Lake Sammamish and dropped them off. I don't deal in rehab, just rescue.

Anyways, by the time I got back, the guy had finally woken up from the dose of poison that I'd hit him up with when my arrow punched into his thigh. He was smart enough to keep quiet since I basically left him tied upside down and naked from a tree.

Once I searched his cabin and found his food, I sat down to a nice meal. Every so often, I would get up, walk over to the guy and just cut a slice into him with the straight razor that he had on a shelf. This is probably a good time to explain that this was apparently the method this creep used to discipline the women if they stepped out of what he considered to be the line. This is also what he used to end the lives of any male children that these girls gave birth to during their captivity. I know this because of what is under the cloth on the table in the cabin. It was that discovery that made me choose how this creep would die.

15

It didn't take long for him to start answering me when I asked him to tell me everything that he has done with every single victim he has kept in this cabin. However, it took him a while to admit to the murder of those poor babies.

I had to make him stop talking at one point. It wouldn't do any good for that bastard to see me in tears. But seriously, how can you not hear something like that and not feel that lump in your throat grow? It took all I had in my power not to just slit the guy's neck and be done with him. However, that is not my way of doing things.

Don't ask me why, but I think it is vital to make them speak their crimes aloud and hear just how vulgar they sound when not being done in secret. I have no idea if it really matters or makes a difference, but with as many of these creeps as I have ended after reducing them to tears as they recount the horrors they inflict on others while simultaneously getting a little of that dropped on their own heads, I sleep easy at night.

One of these days, somebody will get the drop on me and I will be gone. But until that day comes…the victims have one person who is out there trying to make the world a little safer one piece of human filth at a time.

2

Missing a Geek

Catie stood in front of the metal surface that had been polished to an almost mirror-like reflective surface over the years. It was still a bit blurry, but not so much that she could not see a bit of her reflection. Her hand immediately went to her belly where the child grew within her. The slightest bulge was just starting to make itself apparent.

Her naturally curly blond hair was hanging limp, mostly due to not having been washed in several days. Her blue eyes were starting to dull and she had to attribute that to the fact that she was surviving on a very minimal diet. It was enough to keep her going, and that was about it. She needed to find a place to stay...soon. Looking around, she had to consider that perhaps this might be as good of a place as any. There were definite signs of the living occupying this area that she could spot with little effort.

There had never really been anything significant about the town as far as Catie was concerned. She had not spent her life wondering what it might be like to walk the streets or famous train tracks. Yet, for no reason other than the name had been on a dilapidated and bent sign one day, Catie now stood in an overgrown turnaround drive that had likely once been a destination for field trips and family outings.

"So, this is the Chattanooga Zoo," Catie said with false cheer as she patted her belly that was just now starting to show a bump where the child inside her grew.

In response, a dried husk of a zombie lifted its head from some weeds and opened its mouth in a pathetic mewl. With hardly a glance, Catie drove the metal spike-tipped end of her walking stick into its head and continued on to the shade of what looked like an old watch tower or stilted hut. She reached the cool of the shade and began to question her plan to head south as she sought someplace to settle in so that she could have her baby and give them both a decent chance of survival.

She knew very well how brutal even the mildest of winters could be if a person was not well situated to deal with it. Add in the fact that there would be nothing to scavenge like there had been in the old days. She needed to get situated and scour the area for any sorts of the numerous edible wild growing plants as well as bag a few animals and get the meat cured and dried. It was a lot of work, none of it glamorous, and certainly nothing she wanted to attempt when she was deep into her pregnancy.

She held out the slimmest of hopes that she might find a nice little community, but her experience was that people had settled away from anything remotely resembling a major population center. And while Chattanooga would never be mistaken for New York or Los Angeles, it had still boasted enough people to merit heavy military response and a massive but losing war against the undead back when the scales had not yet tipped over to offer the world she now knew.

"Pssst!"

The sound came from behind her and to the left. On pure instinct, Catie spun and hurled one of the throwing knives she kept in little notches across her vest. She had the second one out and was already in the process of refining her aim when the girl threw up her hands and dropped to her knees.

"I ain't holding no weapons!" the girl yelped.

Catie paused and examined the stranger. She guessed the girl to be in her early teens. Her dark skin was set off by the red shirt and pants she wore. Her head was shaved and shone in the sun as it reflected the light sheen of perspiration that coated her skin. She had dark eyes and full lips that looked cracked and ragged in stark comparison to how pretty she was.

"You need to get out of the open before the patrol comes," the girl hissed, waving Catie to where she stood at the edge of what had probably been a manicured hedge, but was now a tangled mess of new growth and old death.

She was about to decline when she heard a loud whoop and the sounds of shouting coming from—Catie glanced at the sun and oriented herself—the south; it was to the south of her current location. She wanted to be cautious, but something about the girl made her think of somebody she knew and suddenly missed.

Rose, she thought, and just as quickly, shoved the thought aside. Hurrying to the dense but scraggly foliage, Catie had to twist and turn to work her way into the towering and dense bush. She was just about to ask the girl what was going on when a dozen men came on the run across the cracked and overgrown asphalt that might only last another few years before it was absolutely covered by the unchecked vegetation.

She clamped her mouth shut and held her breath as the closest of the men jogged by no less than ten feet away. With as little actual new growth as this particular bush offered, any real inspection would absolutely reveal her location and that of the mysterious young girl.

At last, the men were gone; their ruckus indicating that they were now on the trail of something…or someone. Catie turned to the girl and used an arm to clear a few of the brown, dried branches from between them so that she could get a better look. There were a few scrapes and cuts on her face from having dove for cover so hastily. Also, now that she was this close, she could see a single thin scar that ran diagonally across the top of the girl's head.

"What are you doing out in the open?" the girl broke the silence. However, it was the way she spoke that piqued Catie's interest. It had been a while since somebody had talked down to her. Also, now that she was speaking in a tone above a whisper, her deep drawl was very noticeable.

"Not from around here," Catie said with a weak smile and a shrug.

She wanted to play the poor damsel-in-distress role for the time being. There was no need to advertise that she was a more than capable killer who could be almost as lethal with a weapon as without.

"No kidding?" the girl scoffed.

"Who were those guys?" Catie ignored the sarcasm.

"They call themselves the Beastie Boys."

"Not very original," Catie muttered.

"They run all the territory from the tracks to the west up to Ridge Road and from the old Parkridge Hospital on the south to where the Montague Village compound takes over," the girl explained despite Catie having already told her that she was not from around this area.

"That's fine, so then why are you here?" Catie asked.

The girl opened her mouth and then shut it with an audible click. She eyed Catie with a suspicion that had not been there a few seconds ago. After a moment's pause, she pushed back a few steps and planted her hands on her hips.

"Who are you really?" the girl asked.

"My name is Catie." She let that hang in the air for a moment before she decided to ask a question of her own. "And what is your name since we have not been properly introduced?"

"Kalisha."

"Well, Kalisha, I guess I am going to ask you to point me in the best direction out of here."

"You might want to wait until closer to dark. The Beasties don't usually run around much at night."

Catie considered the thought, and then shrugged. "Not like I have anything to do or anyplace to be. Maybe you could fill me in on why exactly you are out and about in this area if it is such a no-man's-land."

The girl dropped her gaze and some of the defiance slipped from her shoulders, causing them to slump just a bit. When she looked back up, the last thing that Catie expected to see were the tears brimming over the cusps of Kalisha's dark brown eyes.

"They took my little brother."

***

The shadows had joined from the surrounding buildings, casting the entire area in gloom. As the day passed, Catie had listened to Kalisha's story. It was nothing she had not heard or even witnessed before. It was the way of the world now.

Something Kevin had said a number of times popped up in her mind at one point while Kalisha was recounting some incident when her brother had climbed a tree and gotten stuck, crying until she had come and plucked him from the branches; basically, the run-of-the-mill big sister stuff.

"People think that humanity is in some sort of tailspin. I think we are simply returning to our more natural state. We were a tribal culture for much longer than we have been domesticated city dwellers."

"Did you hear anything I just said?" Kalisha's harsh whisper snapped Catie out of her daydream.

Catie looked around and realized that it was now almost completely dark. She shook her head to clear it, but could do nothing for the renewed ache in her heart that existed where Kevin had once filled her with love and contentment.

"You were dreaming…kept saying a name over and over. Ke—"

"I know whose name I was probably saying, let's just go!" Catie snapped a bit more harshly than she intended.

If her feelings were hurt, Kalisha didn't say a thing; she turned and waded out of the brush that had been their cover for the majority of the day. The pair crept along, moving over to a partially crumbling wall and hugging it as they made their way. After a while, Kalisha held up a hand to signal a halt. She tugged Catie's sleeve and then pointed to the left. Coming up the avenue were a dozen or so undead. The zombies were clustered close together and heading towards the two women.

"They probably coming from Warner Park. Folks was saying that one of the cells broke up near the cemetery of all places.

21

Can you believe that? Kinda funny when you think about it." Kalisha snickered and then ducked down low.

Without a word of warning, she bolted across the street to a destroyed storefront. She hopped into the gaping blackness that had once been a display window, and then vanished.

Catie sighed and stayed hunched down as she made certain that there were just the dozen or so. It would be nothing to take down twelve zombies. She shot a scowling glare of disapproval in the direction that her so-called guide had vanished. If she couldn't handle a little pack of zombies like the one currently limping her direction, then the girl had no business being out; and it was seriously a stroke of luck that the young lady was even alive.

Once she was satisfied, Catie stood and headed in the direction of the oncoming zombies, moving on a track that would come from the side. They were not yet aware of her judging by the way that they made no alteration in their course. She figured she could get at least a few of them before they could react. She was raising her walking stick up so that she could spear her first target in the head when a massive clatter came from just past the zombies and to her left—in the direction that Kalisha had vanished only moments before.

"Son of a..." the words trailed off as Catie drove the point of her staff into the head of the first zombie.

Great, she thought, *now this has to be a rush job so I can go rescue that stupid girl from whatever nonsense that she has gotten herself into.*

Catie made short work of the zombies and then took off at a cautious trot in the direction that the noise had been heard. She reached the end of the building and discovered a narrow and nearly pitch black alley.

"Yeah, I'm not going in there," Catie breathed.

"Why would you?" a voice asked from over her shoulder causing Catie to let out an uncharacteristic squeak of fear. It also caused her to spin and lash out, connecting with a solid punch to Kalisha's face.

"What the hell did you do that for?" the younger girl managed around hands that were now cupped over her nose.

"Are you that stupid?" Catie snapped, and then quieted her voice when a distant moan answered on the night breeze. "You're just lucky that I didn't run you through with my staff."

"I motioned for you to stay put," the girl retorted, shoving Catie back with a bloody hand.

"I never saw you do any such thing."

"Look, we can stand here and argue all night, but we both heard that moan. We gotta beat feet."

Catie cocked her head to the side and considered Kalisha for a second before she asked, "What are you not telling me?"

The girl's eyes opened wide and she instantly gave away the fact that Catie was on to something. Now it was Catie's turn to plant her hands on her hips and give a level stare.

"Listen, there ain't been no walkers in these parts for over seven months. Not *one!*" Her emphasis on that last word was harsh. "Now you show up, the Beasties are out snatching kids again, and we got undead crawling all over the place like it was the beginning of the apocalypse."

Catie bit her tongue. This girl had no idea what the early days were like. Chances were more than high that she had no real recollection of the Old World beyond stories. If she thought that a dozen or so were big numbers, she should have seen that herd back in Wyoming.

"...Dean wants us to just ride it out, but I say we are gonna end up either kidnapped or used as zombie lures by the Beasties if we don't hit them first."

"Wait!" Now this girl was speaking in a language that Catie understood. "Are you saying that your group or whatever is deciding on whether or not to get into a war with this other group?"

"Glad to see you were actually paying attention," Kalisha snorted. "You had that look on your face again like you were ignoring me."

Catie wondered how the girl could see her face so clearly in the dark, but she had bigger fish to fry at the moment. This place had bad guys, and it had people who were considering the option of taking the fight to them. Maybe she had just found the spot to camp for the winter.

It was in that moment that Catie realized what it was that she had been looking for as she wandered aimlessly these past few weeks. She needed a good fight to get the rest of the poison of anger from her system. Sure, she might actually be backing the wrong horse; there were always two sides to every story. That was of little consequence at the moment.

Catie would stay if these people would have her. She would undoubtedly be the outsider, but she knew her stuff when it came to a fight. Maybe she would get lucky and somebody would challenge her. Nothing moved you up the social ladder like punching out the leader of a group.

If she could get accepted by these people and help take the fight to these Beastie Boys, then maybe she would have a place to stay until winter passed. After that, she already had her mind made up. She would go back home. The others deserved to know how Kevin had died. After that, it was anybody's guess.

One thing at a time, Catie warned herself.

Falling in behind the young girl, Catie listened intently as she was given what she considered to be way too much information. After all, she was still basically a stranger. Yet Kalisha was now reciting life stories on resident after resident of her little clan.

"We need to be careful now."

Catie slowed and took in her surroundings. They had just finished crossing a large overgrown park and were coming to some sort of interstate. Up to this point, she had been doing her best to catalog all that she was being told. If she stayed with these people for any length of time, this would be one of the first things she addressed. Information was power, and this girl had all but given up her entire community in the span of a couple of hours as they walked.

One other thing that Catie had noticed were the glows of what had to be campfires—or the modern day equivalent, which, as Kevin always liked to say, were simply fires. Some were several stories up, burning on the upper floors of surrounding buildings that were now obviously homes to a surprising number of people.

"There are four other settlements all within a mile of each other here," Kalisha explained; once again the girl showed no restraint in divulging information. "We all mostly trade with each other, but there is a rule about passing through each other's territory without permission."

"What kind of rule?" Catie asked as she craned her neck to look over the guard rail of the overpass that they were now scrambling across in a crouch.

"You don't do it."

They were crossing train tracks. Catie fought to keep the chorus of that infernal song out of her head and did her best to look for landmarks. That was when she realized that daylight was within an hour or so of breaking. They had been walking all night!

She figured out their destination as they altered course just a bit towards a complex of buildings. She could see light from more than just a few towers. That was a good sign. She was even happier when they stopped at the edge of a clearing that was basically scorched earth for at least a hundred yards. Nobody was just going to stroll up to this place and take them by surprise.

"Now we wait," Kalisha flopped down on the ground and crossed her legs.

"Wait for what?" Catie asked.

"Daylight."

"Don't be skimpy with the details now, missy."

"The standing orders are to take down anybody that approaches at night."

"What if it is some poor person just out and about?"

The girl looked up at Catie, her face readable in the gray of pre-dawn. She was incredulous. "Who would just be...out and about?"

"Umm...you were when we met. As was I if you think about it."

"No, I was looking for the jerks that took my little brother," Kalisha insisted. "And you..." Her voice faded as she realized that, in all her talking, she really had not gotten any information as to what Catie was doing in the Beastie Boys' territory. "Hey! You never did tell me why you were here."

"Maybe when we get to your camp, I don't like the idea of having to do this a hundred more times." Catie started to her feet as the first rays of the sun were creeping over the tops of a few of the buildings.

"Now I won't know for a week," Kalisha sighed as she jogged to catch up.

Of course, that comment made Catie stop suddenly, which then caused Kalisha to run into her and knock them both over. On reflexive instinct, Catie threw out her hands and twisted her body so that she landed mostly on her side, and her arms absorbed a majority of the shock.

"What do you mean you won't know for a week?" Catie grunted as the two untangled themselves.

"Quarantine," was all that the girl managed to say before a loud gong sounded from the direction of the compound that was to be their ultimate destination. "They see us."

Any thoughts that Catie had of changing her mind and running for it vanished when a large gate swung open and a trio of individuals on horseback came out at a full gallop. Cursing herself for not having anything in the way of a backup plan, Catie did the only thing she could considering the circumstances; she raised both hands above her head and waited.

***

"You say that yours is the only community in the area that you know of?" Eldon Lindsay asked for what had to be the sixth time during this apparently endless interrogation.

"You might not have been all that familiar with the Dakotas back in the day," Catie leaned forward and gave the man her coldest glare, "but there weren't all that many people in those parts before the zombies."

The door opened and a slender woman with gray hair walked in. "You've bored this nice lady enough, Eldon," the woman said. She made a show of keeping the door open until the man got up and limped out. "You'll have to excuse him, he doesn't trust anybody. The last community he lived at was taken down by a bunch of them immunes."

Catie did not say a word. Her scar had been spotted right away during her strip search. As was her current condition of being pregnant. That had started the first line of questioning.

"Did you know the father?"

"Was he immune as well?"

"Did he die after conception due to infection?"

Seeing no reason to lie, Catie had answered their questions with: "Yes...Yes...No." Of course that had also been the extent of her reply.

"So am I to be killed as a heretic? Experimented on like some alien species? Or simply killed out of hand?" Catie asked once the woman had sat down across from her.

"Heavens, you have met some interesting people in your travels if those are your first three questions for me," the woman laughed.

Catie studied this woman's face, making it a point to hold eye contact. While it was true that most sociopaths could look you in the eye and lie with no problem, Catie still felt that the eyes would be the best indicator if there was something to worry about.

The woman had a pleasant enough face. It was showing the signs of age with a few lines and wrinkles. However, there was a natural upturn to the lips as if a smile might be a real and regular thing with this woman. Her eyes were a shade of blue that verged on gray, just like her hair. She was dressed in a set of denim coveralls and wore a tan shirt that looked like it might be made of some sort of cured animal hide.

"And you haven't met those sorts?" Catie tried to hide the sarcasm, but failed miserably.

"Oh yes. More than I would have ever imagined." The woman's expression darkened. "I have met some of the vilest examples that humanity has to offer since this craziness began a lifetime ago. But I have also met some wonderful and beautiful people as well."

"So then, what is going to be done with me?" Catie asked. She could have taken the woman's bait and started sharing stories of people and experiences, but she wasn't going to give up anything until she felt she was safe.

"Not one for small talk, are you," the woman said with another good-natured laugh that sounded absolutely genuine.

"You will forgive me if I am not ready to just spill everything like little Kalisha."

That was the second time that Catie witnessed the woman's features cloud over just a bit. She was not sure whether it was something to do with the girl in general, or the fact that Kalisha had not only walked a complete stranger to the gates of their community, but also apparently spilled a plethora of information.

"Kalisha is..."

"In big trouble?" Catie finished when the woman seemed to hang up on her next word.

"You could say that."

"Well, don't be too hard on her. She was only doing what she felt was right. Apparently your people are content to sit back and let some rival faction snatch up your kids without doing anything about it." Catie saw something flash across the woman's expression. She wasn't sure; however, when the woman's eyes flicked to the right where the two-way mirror was mounted on the wall and then back with just a slight raising of the eyebrows, she was pretty sure she was being signaled.

"We haven't actually been introduced," the woman spoke with what Catie saw and heard as a false cheerfulness. This put her on an even higher state of alert. Yet, she felt that there was something about this woman that she wanted to trust.

"You already know my name," Catie said, sitting back in her chair and folding her arms across herself as she regarded the older woman across from her with an arched eyebrow.

"My name is Denise DeCarlo."

"And what is your role here besides coming in as the good cop in this interrogation."

The woman twitched at the corners of her mouth as if she

was about to smile and quickly decided against it. "You are quite the cynic."

"No, I am a realist. In this world, that requires a degree of cynicism. Maybe you have been behind these walls a little too long and have forgotten what is out there."

"Yes, I understand that you came all the way from South Dakota? That must have been quite an adventure."

"So, how long am I going to be kept in this quarantine?"

"Actually, since you are immune, you will be allowed out today." Catie heard the condition coming in Denise's tone. "You will have to submit to one little thing."

"And that would be?"

"Nothing dark or sinister, I can assure you."

With that, Denise DeCarlo rolled up her sleeve and revealed a metal device. It couldn't be called a bracelet. It was about three inches long and seemed to be a solid device that could not be simply slid off. The woman rolled her arm over so that Catie could see the underside of this contraption. It had some sort of crimping and what looked like a weld or solder line as a final measure to prevent the red tinted piece of metal from being removed without serious work.

"You?" Catie glanced up at Denise. "You're immune to the bite?"

"I worked as the manager of a grocery store. I was working the night that a mob of people came and just cleaned us out. I pulled all of my employees up into my office for protection. We waited out the riot, and once it was quiet, we crept out to get a better look at the damage. They had run through the front entrance with a flatbed truck and when they left, well, that allowed the zombies to just wander in. It was still so early, that doctor lady from the CDC hadn't made the admission yet that these people were the walking dead."

Catie found herself leaning forward and listening with rapt attention. This was not part of the interrogation. The tears that were welling up in the woman's eyes came freely, and the sorrow that suddenly filled Denise's expression convinced Catie that this was a very real experience being shared.

"The little girl couldn't have been more than four or five years old. She was just wandering down the aisle by herself. She was wearing a little pink hoody top with some Disney princess on it, but the blood...so much. Her face was shrouded by the hood, but honestly, I don't know if seeing the eyes would have mattered at that moment. All I saw was a child that was in need of help."

The two sat in silence for a few moments. Finally, Denise pushed away from the table and got to her feet. She waved to the two-way mirror and then turned back to Catie.

"You are free to go. You will need to go to the indoctrination building. If you choose to stay, you need to get one of the bracers. If you choose to leave, then you will be given all of your things and will be allowed to stay a maximum of three days. There are restrictions as to where you are allowed to go without the bracer."

"Segregation?" Catie almost laughed.

"We prefer to call it safety. While we are still small enough of a community where most of us know each other by face and a stranger is easy to identify, we still do what we feel is important to maintain the health and safety of all our residents."

"Call it what you want."

"So, will you be staying?"

"Do I have to make that choice right this second?" Catie asked.

"Absolutely not," Denise replied with obvious relief. As they reached the door, she leaned close like she was opening the door, but whispered, "You would have been under even greater suspicion if you'd said yes right away."

Catie allowed the woman to open the door, and then she stepped through to find four armed men and women in the waiting room. They were doing a poor job of trying to act casual. There was a door to the right that she figured must lead to the two-way mirror viewing area, and there was a door just across the room with a single small window. One of the armed women rose and went over to give a rap on that door.

It opened to reveal what looked like every doctor's office

reception room that she'd ever seen. There were a couple of people sitting in the chairs that lined the walls. One was actually reading a book. Nobody seemed to pay them any mind at all as Catie was escorted to the reception desk where a young man around the age of thirteen looked up and opened the ledger before him.

"I will be escorting Catie to the dorm." Denise reached down to turn the ledger her direction and scribble something on one of the lines.

"Did you really come from way out west?" the boy asked with obvious astonishment.

"Yeah," Catie said with a smile.

"Did you see a lot of the walkers?" The young man leaned forward, his expression one of obvious amazement and curiosity.

"You say that like it is a big deal."

The young man's face flushed. He looked around the room and then to Denise like he was waiting for permission or approval. "I've never seen one."

Catie followed Denise out of the reception room and into the bright sunlight of a beautiful day. All around her, the hustle and bustle of people going about their business made her suddenly homesick. Why had they ever set out on Kevin's fool quest? He knew damn good and well that they would not find anybody alive.

As they wove through the people, Catie's mind flitted from one memory to the next. She could hear Kevin's voice whispering in her ear about how she needed to be paying attention, but she didn't care at the moment. Her mind had found a special memory from their trip. They were at the lip of some part of the Grand Canyon. The sun was setting and everything looked as if it were on fire. The colors were unlike anything that she had ever imagined.

Kevin sat with his legs dangling over a precipice. He was just gazing out over the vista and his smile was big and broad. He glanced over his shoulder at her and winked. Only, Kevin was one of those poor souls who could not control his eye muscles very well, so it was more of an awkward blink than anything else.

She had walked up and sat beside him. Together, the two of them waited until the sun slipped below the horizon. They did not say a single word, and Mother Nature rewarded them with a near perfect silence. Even the insects had grown quiet, almost as if they wanted to drink in the majestic spectacle themselves.

That night, they made love under the stars. Afterwards, with the glow of the campfire pushing a small circle of the darkness away, Kevin had sat up. He had laughed. When Catie asked him what was so funny, his answer had been simple but honest.

"This is more than I deserve."

She had sat up beside him and wrapped her arms around his waist. With her head resting on his shoulder, she had drifted in and out. She woke the next day with his arms wrapped around her. She remembered how bad she had to pee, but she did not budge. She wanted that moment to last as long as possible. At this exact second, she was thankful to have made that decision.

"And this is where you will be staying," Denise said, opening the double-doors to a non-descript, three-story brick building…mostly.

It was obvious that the top floor had been added on, post-apocalypse. The third floor was a wooden structure, and the workmanship was such that Catie had serious doubts as to how it had lasted any length of time.

The first floor was a wide open area, and it took a moment, but Catie finally recognized it as a gymnasium. There were rows of wooden walls that were just high enough to allow a small degree of privacy.

"Take your pick," Denise said, gesturing for Catie to lead the way.

Walking down the first aisle, she saw cubicle after cubicle, each looking identical with a small bed, a dresser, a desk with a chair, and a small foot locker. She also noticed that each appeared empty as each one had the thin mattress rolled up and situated at the head of the bed with an uncovered pillow.

"Yeah, we don't get many visitors," Denise answered the questioning look that Catie shot over her shoulder.

"I would be in here alone?" Denise nodded. "Seems like a real waste of space. You have all this room and an additional floor just vacant?"

"When we started planning this place, we wanted to allow for growth. We over-estimated. Add in the fact that some of the other communities have differing views and have set up accordingly."

"Different views?"

Denise looked around nervously and then leaned in close to Catie as if somebody might just appear out of nowhere and listen in on their conversation. "We are the only mixed community in the area."

"Mixed community?" Catie had a feeling that she knew what the answer would be, but she wanted to hear it for herself.

"Immunes. We are the only community that allows both immune and the unknown."

"Unknown?"

"Can't very well know until you get bit or something and then don't turn. Not many folks all that anxious to simply find out voluntarily."

"So the other communities don't allow anybody who is known to be immune?"

"Yes," Denise paused and then added, "well...the Beastie Boys. They are all immune."

"Kalisha is immune, isn't she?" Catie asked, suddenly starting to get her mind around the situation.

"Born to immune parents, as was her brother."

"And you people are okay with this sort of thing?"

"We don't have the numbers. There are more here who are unknown than are immune. We have petitioned the town council, but they have rejected every single time," Denise explained.

"How much?"

What?" Denise asked in obvious confusion.

"How lopsided are the numbers?"

"The unknowns have about a thirty person advantage. We have had a few of the first generation children reach voting age, thirteen in case you are curious. But we remain in the minority."

Catie dropped her backpack inside the cubicle that she had chosen. It was in the very center of the massive "dorm" that had once been a high school gymnasium.

"And none of you think it is odd that the children keep getting snatched by these Beastie Boys?" Catie asked.

"We aren't stupid," Denise said with a touch of anger in her voice. "But we don't have any proof. We can't just up and leave. None of the other communities will take us, and starting from scratch is a romantic idea until you realize the work involved. We have farms, crops, and livestock here. None of which would be allowed to be taken if we left."

"So every single animal and farm belongs to one of these unknown types?"

"Immunes are not allowed to be the sole owners of any property."

Catie opened her mouth to ask what the hell Denise meant when the doors to the gymnasium-turned-dorm flew open and hit the walls with a loud clang. On instinct, Catie's hand went to her hip where a machete should be but was suddenly very noticeable in its absence.

"Denise, come quick, they took Kalisha to the administrator's office!" a man shouted.

The older woman did not say so much as a farewell. Turning on her heel, she ran for the door. By the time Catie had recovered and tried to follow, the doors had swung shut. She opened them and stepped out onto the little avenue. People were still going about their business like nothing in the world was wrong.

"That was what I was seeing," Catie whispered to herself.

She went back inside and returned to her cubicle. As she walked through the empty dorm, her mind began to mull through the possibilities. By the time she reached "her" cubicle, she had an idea as to what she was going to do. She didn't know if it was the smartest idea, but she became more committed to it with every step.

"I sure do miss you, Kevin," she whispered.

3.

Hunter

I slid down the embankment and came to a stop in the shallow creek. My feet were now soaked, but that was the least of my worries. So far, I had managed to stay in the brush. Add in the fact that there were a few hundred thousand of the undead less than a mile away and headed straight for us, and I was the lowest of the priorities.

I peeked through some of the branches that made up my cover and sighed. So far, I had come up empty. I thought that I had a good idea where Jim and Jackson were being kept. I figured it would be easy to make my way to where they were being held prisoner. Of course, from there I had not even the slightest clue as to what I was going to do.

It wasn't like I was heavily armed or some sort of badass like Jackson. I couldn't scrounge together a few common items and make them blow up like Jim. Nope, I was flying by the seat of my pants. I was also trying to reason with myself by mentally preparing for the serious possibility that I was going to have to run for it and leave them both behind.

Staying in the tall grass, I got down on my belly and started crawling up the hill. When I reached the top, I wanted to cry in relief. Just ahead of me, I could see the grates over the holes in the ground where I knew Jim to be held. At least that was where he was when Suzi had brought me to see him that one time. I shoved away the thoughts of how he might be gone or even dead.

Scanning the area, I was relieved to see that only one person was currently posted as a guard here. Sure, that was a bonus, but the guy was almost as big as Jackson, so once more, I had no clue as to what I thought I might possibly be able to accomplish in the way of pulling off a rescue.

Meanwhile, the camp was a buzz of activity. However, I had to pause for a moment to be sure that I was not imagining things. Sure enough, I could hear the sounds of children laughing! How could that be possible? Also, I moved just a bit and could see between a row of tents. People were walking! One couple in particular stood out as they strolled by holding hands like nothing in the world was wrong...like there was not a sea of the walking dead coming right for this place.

"So?" the voice came from right behind me. I would have screamed if a hand did not clamp over my mouth. "What do you think you are doing?"

Whether it was because my attention was focused in front of me and I'd just been careless, or the person crouched right behind me had been that quiet, I have no idea. In any case, I could feel the person's body now that he had moved up right behind me—while the whisper made the voice unidentifiable, I had no doubts that it was a male.

"When I take my hand away, it would be a good idea not to scream. That would bring the guard and then you would probably end up in big trouble," the voice warned.

I nodded and felt the hand move away from my mouth and then grip my shoulder, turning me around. I was only a little surprised.

"Hunter?" I mouthed.

He nodded and then pulled me back down the embankment. Once we reached the creek, he returned his attention to me. It was obvious that he was angry.

"Are you trying to get yourself and those friends of yours killed?" Hunter hissed. I opened my mouth, but he cut me off and kept talking. "Suzi is tolerant of a lot of things, but if you run, she will have you hunted down and killed. And trust me when I tell you, she would find you. She has some of the best people working for her in that department."

"People like you?" I sneered.

"Yes."

Wow, he didn't even try to hide it. That actually caught me off guard enough so that I just remained hunkered down with my mouth open.

"She is not evil, but she is pragmatic to the point of being dangerous to any that she feels *might* be her enemy. She actually is still holding out hope that your people will come in and join the fold," Hunter explained.

"Why do my people have to do anything? Why can't they just stay where they are and be left alone? We never wanted any trouble to begin with. We were down here looking into why a large community like Island City got torched along with those college kids that, as far as I know, committed the crime of growing vegetables in their little commune."

"It is hard to understand the big picture when you focus on something small. There is a lot more going on than you might be aware." Hunter paused, but when I opened my mouth, he held up a finger to stop me so that he could continue. "And when I say you, I mean your entire little community up in the hills."

It took me a second to register what he'd said, but when it sank in, I felt my stomach churn. He never broke eye contact with me, but instead nodded his head as my own understanding was obviously painted on my face.

"Yes, Thalia, we are very aware of where your people are set up. We know all about your leader. Billy Haynes? His name is actually spoken with great respect." Hunter looked around and then returned his attention to me. "And you might be happy to know that you have passed a number of tests as well in these few days that you have been with us. But we can discuss this more later. We need to return you to your tent before Suzi finds out that you are gone."

I was too numb to resist. I got up and followed Hunter.

Nothing made any sense. How could he…they…how could these people know about us? We did not range far from the compound, and we had not brought in any new members in at least a couple of years. In fact, Island City was as far as any of us had been as far as I knew.

Of course that was the real key to unlocking this mystery in my opinion. I was not in on any of the details when it came to missions outside of the fence. Hell, I'd just been promoted to these things in the first place. My experiences up to that point were confined to within a mile or so of the walls.

If I got home—

No! *When* I got home, I was going to find out what the hell was going on. Did we have a spy? Did this Suzi person have people embedded in little communities all over? Is that how Island City fell?

Only, that didn't make sense either. There were too many loose ends for that to tie up all nice and neat. Additionally, there had been a few things that she did not know about. The biggest that came to mind was this mysterious "Skins" person that had simply vanished.

Then something hit me. While it was true that there had not been any new citizens to join our little community, there had been that one man who'd been captured just before all of this started. I'd been part of the detail that had escorted him into the interrogation room. And that was the last I'd heard of him. In fact, right after his arrival, I'd been tasked to my first field run and simply forgotten he existed.

That was extraordinary in and of itself. A new person, whether it is a simple traveler or somebody from one of the surrounding areas stopping in to trade or just use our place as a layover on their way from one place to another, that is always big news.

How had I forgotten that guy? I tried to recall everything about his arrival as I followed Hunter back to my tent.

***

"We found this guy down by the stream. He won't give his name or anything," Jim Sagar said to Billy and Dr. Zahn.

I was still shaking from the excitement. What had been just another boring perimeter patrol had turned into something a lot more exciting in a hurry. I was simply thankful that Jim had come out today to find me with a list of some items he wanted me to keep an eye out for during my patrol.

I'd been so intent on Jim's list that I'd forgotten one of the biggest rules when you are outside the walls. You always kept your eyes open for trouble. While zombies were rare, they still managed to find their way up here to our neck of the woods.

And then there were the living.

That was why Jim noticed the man first and had to grab me by the shoulders to stop me from walking out into a clearing where this guy was sitting on a fallen tree, sifting through (presumably) his back pack. From the looks of him, he had been out in the wild for a fair amount of time. He had a scraggly beard and his face was a mixture of dirt, grime, and over-exposure to long periods of sun that gave him a ruddy, brown-ish complexion.

We flanked the guy, and when Jim came out and told the man to raise his hands and step away from the pack, the man had done so with little more than a drooping of his head; sort of how my brother Stevie did when he got caught red-handed doing something he knew he shouldn't.

We escorted the man back, and once we arrived at the gates, I was given the honor of escorting the "prisoner" to a holding room. Of course, he wasn't technically a prisoner yet; he was simply going to be questioned. (Since we had not experienced any serious problems with raiders in such a long time, I guess we just got lazy.)

The problems started when this guy refused to say a single word. Not to me when I was just trying to be friendly and let him know he wasn't in any serious danger, not Billy who had gone in shortly after, nor Dr. Zahn who joined Billy after over an hour where this guy had done nothing more than stare straight ahead, hardly even blinking.

39

I knew this because Dr. Zahn had asked me to bring in the cart with all of her tools. It was a scary collection of some of the sharper and nastier things she used as a doctor. They were just for show as far as I knew. They'd never failed to get a person to talk simply by being set out on display in front of the prisoner...at least until this new guy.

***

I sat in my tent for a long time as I mulled over the possibilities. None of them were pleasant. Eventually, I reached a conclusion that I had to start eliminating all of the doubts swirling in my head. I also knew where I needed to start.

Getting up, I had to force my feet to move to the flap of my tent. I knew Hunter was still outside. I could hear his voice. I also knew why this place was not showing any serious distress when it came to that sea of undead that had been heading our direction.

About thirty minutes after Hunter had deposited me back inside my cloth jail cell, I heard the most annoying and continuous wail that I'd ever been witness to in my admittedly sheltered life. That was the current topic of discussion outside my tent as Hunter and a few others were sharing the most recent report.

"The riders have the herd redirected to the southeast. The majority of the body has turned and now we are trying to divert some of the stragglers," one voice was saying.

As soon as I stuck my head out of my tent, Hunter gave the men a gesture asking for them to hold off. He came to me and ushered me back inside with a gentle shove.

"I think you have used up your outside privileges today," he snorted.

"Actually, if you want to get technical, I haven't," I retorted, and then pushed ahead before he had a chance to object. "I want to see Jim."

Hunter gave me absolutely no emotion. His face could have very well been carved from stone.

"I figured you would want to know about how we had diverted that giant herd of zombies."

"Noisemakers, sure. I get it. I heard you talk about it."

"Not just any noisemakers. These things seem to be able to draw even the largest herds and re-direct their course. And in case you didn't hear, we have this particular herd moving southeast. That would be away from not only this valley, but also your settlement as well." Hunter made one mistake as he rambled on about this most recent event.

"Our settlement is well off the original course of that herd. And if you knew exactly where we might be, then you would know that." The only thing that I didn't do after opening my big fat mouth is cover it with my hands. Sure, I was moderately certain that this group did have somebody feeding them information about us, but that did not mean I had to hand them anything on a silver platter.

"Thalia, I don't expect you—" he began, but I cut him off.

"You are doing a great job at changing the subject."

"What subject was that?" he asked, his expression reverting to one lacking any emotion.

"I said that I wanted to see Jim."

"The prisoner?"

"Sure. If that is indeed what he really is."

The slightest twitch of a smile tugged at the corner of his mouth. I was prepared for him to refuse my request. He would make an excuse and then, if this suspicion I had brewing was correct, they would dirty Jim up once again and then put him in his little pit.

"What else would he be?"

"Take me to him." I folded my arms across myself in what I was hoping might be seen as defiant and not viewed as just being a petulant child.

"Let me go check with Suzi."

"Nope. Now. And if he is like I last saw him, then you can take me to Suzi and I will answer any question she throws at me."

"Just like that?" Hunter asked, the skepticism dripping from his words. It was clear that I had taken him by surprise.

"Mostly," I said with a shrug.

"Okay."

Now I was the one surprised. I had expected a denial and then an eventual trip to see Jim. Of course, that would not exactly prove my theory, but it would take me a step closer.

Hunter escorted me out of my tent. The entire time, I still could not get over how calm everybody seemed to be considering the fact that a wave of undead had been heading right for them less than an hour ago. This told me that these people were accustomed to such things and had become adept at whatever methods they employed.

I knew about how zombies could be distracted by sound; everybody did. It was Zombie 101 stuff. So, why hadn't our group come up with something like this? Also, now that I thought about it, those noisemakers had to be pretty damn loud for me to hear them at the volumes that I was still getting from as far away as they had to be.

Eventually I recognized the area of camp that must be their detention section. My eyes scanned for signs of anything that might be important. I could not help but feel a lump grow in my throat as I spied the metal boxes. Inside one of them was Jackson; it was easy to identify by the fact that two men were stationed outside of it instead of just one. I also realized that this indicated there might be three more of those boxes with somebody inside. That was worth noting.

At last we came to a stop and Hunter kicked the top of the grate with his booted foot. "Hey, Jim, you have a visitor."

"And me without a thing to wear," a voice that sounded sort of like Jim but not quite came from the pit.

I edged closer and peeked over the side. I was hit with a mixture of relief, confusion, and annoyance. Jim was right where I'd left him. If anything, he looked worse. One of his eyes was either very dirty or completely swollen shut; I was willing to bet on the latter. He showed no signs of having been allowed to clean up since the last time I'd been here with Suzi. And if Jim was this bad off...my mind shoved aside images of what Jackson must look like by now.

"Jim," I finally managed to gasp.

"Hey there, cupcake," Jim said around a mouth that was obscenely swollen. "You come here to tell me that I need to cooperate? If so, that is a dirty thing that these people are trying to make you do. I want you to forget all about me and focus on yourself and keeping your mouth shut."

I felt sick. Not only had I been somewhat cooperative, not only was I prepared to give these people more information, but I had actually considered Jim to be the most likely person to be a possible mole.

In my defense, he was often going out unaccompanied despite that being a big no-no. He had a way about him that made it impossible to really know him as a person. Unless, of course, he was really this much of a nut.

"You okay, kiddo?" Jim's voice cut through my growing wave of self-pity. "If they are doing anything to you, then I will make it my life's work to level this place around them and litter the ground with their burning corpses."

"Your friend has guts, I'll give him that much," Hunter muttered.

"And I will rip yours out first, you freak," Jim said in the coldest, level tone that I'd ever heard come from his mouth. In that instant, I could not remember my Jim, the clown and joker who never lacked a dirty joke or funny story when things got a bit too serious.

"Take it easy, hero," Hunter warned as he stepped up beside me and stared down at Jim. "You getting all emotional isn't going to help Thalia here at all. She has not been harmed in any way since her arrival."

"Arrival? You make it sound like we just strolled in here on our own for a little coffee and cookies," Jim scoffed. "Your people attacked a pair of innocent kids and would have killed us if we hadn't done what we needed to do to protect ourselves."

"We did no such thing," Hunter said, but his voice was a tight whisper like he did not want anybody to hear him except for me and Jim.

"So...what? You saying some other goon squad came in

43

and roughed up that couple?"

"I'm saying that it wasn't us," Hunter insisted as if he were the one being held in the pit.

This struck me as odd. Why would Hunter just give Jim information like that?

"Jim…" I started, trying to work up the courage to tell him why I'd just insisted on seeing him. As I struggled for the next words, Hunter took me by the arm.

"You've seen him, now we have to go. I already put my ass on the line by bringing you here without permission."

As the man led me away, I now turned over all of the stuff bouncing around in my brain. Nothing was making sense. Nothing added up to give me any answers. I was still trying to sort things when I realized where Hunter had brought me.

"We need to see Suzi," was all the man said as he pushed past the pair of sentries and through the tent flap to the relative gloom beyond.

"This better be very important, Hunter," the woman said through clenched teeth when she looked up from her desk.

"I believe that the prisoner is ready to talk."

"Is that right?" And just that fast, the dark-haired woman's features smoothed, returning her to the exotic beauty that I bet she used almost as much as her apparent ability to be ruthless. "And what would bring on this sudden desire to be cooperative?"

"I think there is more going on around here than what you or my people might be aware," I suggested.

"Is that right?" Suzi answered with a bemused smile.

"Figure out who those men were that Jim, Jackson, and I had to deal with yet? Or how about that young couple that we rescued?"

Suzi just stared at me. I could not tell if she was interested, bored, or annoyed. I wanted to hit her with a few more questions, but I decided that I would try something else. If I was wrong, then this would be a disaster all of my own doing.

"You supposedly know about my people up in the hills. You know about Billy Haynes." I felt Hunter stiffen beside me; that confirmed my suspicions that he was not free to divulge that information. I could worry about that later. "You say that you are here on some mission of peace? Fine, then let Jim and Jackson free. Send a team with us and we will escort them back to our place. They can meet with Billy and give him whatever message that you want to have delivered."

"And why would I send a small team of my people to your community? Then they end up captured and—" Suzi began to argue, but I was feeling bold and cut her off.

"You have us seriously outmanned. We wouldn't stand a chance and you know it if your intel is correct. And do I need to mention the whole thing about you obviously not being afraid to use the infection as a weapon?"

Suzi was silent for several seconds, and I was pretty sure that I was going back to my tent if I was lucky. It was entirely possible that I would be in a pit beside Jim before the day was done.

"Jim Sagar goes with you. The other gentleman stays as collateral," Suzi finally said, leaning back in her chair with a smile. "And if I don't hear from your people within…" she paused as if considering things. "Three weeks sound good?"

It took me a few seconds to realize that that was an actual question and not a rhetorical one. I nodded and eventually remembered how to use my words. "Yeah, that should be plenty of time."

"I am pretty sure you are being straight with me, but I haven't survived this long by being hasty or foolish." Suzi stood up and walked over to me, sitting on the edge of her desk. "I saw how fond you are of those men. I bet it would absolutely kill you to imagine one of them being injected with our serum that induces contamination and then maybe led to your doorstep."

I just stared at the woman. I had no doubt that she was being completely honest. If we did anything other than what was agreed, she would have Jackson injected and escorted to our gates. After that, she probably rolls in with her army and wipes us out like she did the folks of Island City.

"What if I offered to stay and you sent Jim and Jackson?" I

asked.

"No, I think it best if we send you." Suzi shot a look at Hunter before she added. "And I believe Hunter should come along as a..." she paused and her voice got sort of creepy, "escort? No, that's not it. He will be coming with you, let's leave it at that."

She said that like it should upset me, but I was actually happy about it. At least there would be one face in the crowd that I felt I could trust a little bit—excluding Jim of course.

"When should we leave?' Hunter asked with way more stiffness in his tone than I expected.

"Why wait?" Suzi turned her back and went to her desk. "I will have the team assigned and assembled by morning. That should also give your friend a chance to get cleaned up for the trip. Plus I have one thing to handle first."

"Yeah," I sniffed, "wouldn't want folks to think we'd been mistreated." Honestly, I thought I had kept that remark to myself, or at least quiet enough that she couldn't hear me as we exited the tent.

"Oh, Thalia, you have no idea what real mistreatment is like, but if you fail to return with my people, I assure you that your friend Jackson will be able to act as a shining example."

I shuddered at her words and followed Hunter back to my tent. I wasn't surprised that he did not say a word to me on the way there. I was a little surprised when he deposited me and left in silence. I don't know what I had expected him to say, but I was at least hoping that he would let me know things were going to be okay and that I'd made the right decision.

I sat in my tent the rest of that day with my mind turning over everything. I was no closer to figuring out anything when morning came. I was shaken awake by a woman with a crewcut and a nasty scar down the left side of her face. The woman did not offer her name and I didn't ask. She told me to get dressed and be ready to move out in an hour. I could tell when she left that it was still dark.

I was a little surprised to discover most of the gear that I'd had with me when we got nabbed. The obvious and notable exception was the lack of a bow. However, an equal surprise came when I discovered my machete in a sheath of hard leather.

I put on my gear and headed outside. The detail was already forming up. When I saw Jim, I had to keep myself from running to him and wrapping him up in the biggest hug. Besides not wanting to put on such a public display of affection, I also had my doubts as to if he would be able to withstand such a thing. Now that he was out of that pit, I got a really good look at his condition.

It was clear that he'd taken more than a few beatings. With the dirt washed away, I had to assume all those dark splotches were bruises. He was limping enough that I wondered if he would actually be able to make the trip. When he saw me, he gave a wave and that huge grin just about split his face. He hobbled over to me, making no effort to skirt our escorts. That was fine except for the fact that his bumping into them was obviously having a worse effect on him that it was on those he careened off of as he waded through the assembled group of Suzi's goon squad.

As I waited for Jim to reach me, I took in and appraised the people that would be accompanying us on this journey. My assessment of "goon squad" seemed pretty accurate. Besides the woman who woke me, there were two other females in the group. Neither looked very womanly. They all sported the same sort of high and tight hair style. They had hard expressions and faces that looked as if they might shatter if something as foreign as a genuine and happy smile dared to try and creep across their lips.

The men—there were ten of them—all had basically the same expressions as their female counterparts. I did notice that the genders stayed pretty separate and in their own little subgroup of goons. It was almost as if they were afraid of each other. The only thing missing now was Hunter. I did not see any sign of him.

"Hey, cupcake," Jim greeted me. I let him instigate the hug, and then I sort of used his own response as my personal gauge for the degree in which I returned the gesture.

"Glad to be leaving this place?" I tried to make myself say that with a laugh, but I think it just sounded strained, tired, and fake.

"I take it they ain't letting the big man go with us?" Jim asked as he studied the people gathered around.

"Nope, I even asked if they would let you two go and me be the one to stay behind, but Suzi shot it down."

"So what did you have to do to broker this little deal? What are the conditions?"

I gave him the full rundown. I also told him about the zombie herd and the noisemakers. I tried to be as detailed as possible. The one thing I left out was my suspicion that he might be somehow involved and how that had been the reason for my visit yesterday. As I spoke, I continued to watch our escorts. They were obviously waiting for something.

To add to my apprehension, Hunter was still a no-show. That, from what I could guess, had to be the reason that we had not started off for home. Apparently Jim picked up on my emotions.

"What's the problem, Thalia?" he whispered.

"Hunter." I glanced up and realized that Jim had no idea who or what I was talking about. "The guy that brought me to you? His name is Hunter, and Suzi was adamant that he come with us."

We stood around for another stretch of time that seemed to last an eternity. I did not have any idea what might be the reason for the delay, but the longer it went on, the worse my apprehension became. I heard a few gasps and that is what caused me to jerk my head up.

"Greetings, team," Suzi crowed. "Sorry about the hold up, but some things can't be rushed."

She stepped fully into the light of the big fire. She had two men with her and they were each holding what looked like a length of chain. My eyes followed the length slowly, unable to make sense of things at first. Hunter was shackled and manacled!

A split second later, the whole picture came into focus. His head turned in a jerky fashion that told me what he was before I could see his eyes. When I was finally able to look at his face, I was not surprised by the white film and dark tracers.

"Why?" came out of my mouth before I had a chance to bite it back. "Why would you do that?" I lunged towards Suzi, but Jim must have expected my reaction, because he had a grip on my arms that seemed improbable considering his condition.

"I want to make my point very clear." Suzi stepped around Hunter, or the thing that used to be Hunter. "We require each and every settlement in the area to send representatives down to us to negotiate how things are going to work. In addition, your group has a young man named Billy Haynes. I want him to meet with me personally to finalize this situation."

"That still does not explain why," I snarled. "Why would you do this to Hunter?"

"I had concerns regarding his loyalty. Why he would lie to protect you, I have no earthly idea, yet he did."

"What!" I exploded. To say that I was incredulous would be seriously understating my feelings.

"You tried to escape, he did not report you. You were taken to see your friend here without my approval. There are several smaller infractions, but those would be the main ones and the reason that I had to make things very clear to the men and women who will be acting as your escort." Suzi turned and faced the group that was no longer separated into their gender specific clusters. "If you fail me, if you allow this girl and her friend to escape, if you think of doing anything other than what I have instructed you to do in a very specific set of orders, I will ensure that each and every one of you joins Hunter in his fate. Is that clear?"

There were nods and mutters of "Yes, ma'am" given. I almost expected Suzi to pull some drill instructor crap and bellow about how she couldn't hear them. Instead, she gave a curt nod and drew a sword from her side. With one swing, she lopped Hunter's head off at the base of his neck. It was a clean blow that severed the head and sent it rolling towards me.

I wanted to scream when it came to a stop. As luck would

have it, the head came to a halt on its side, but the eyes were looking directly at me. Jim yanked me back and put himself between me and Hunter's head.

"Let me just tell you that I don't care what happens, you and I are gonna deal with this one day in the future." I was at a loss for words, and hearing Jim like this was even more disorienting. I simply stood there like an idiot.

Like a girl.

All my life, I prided myself on being tough. I wasn't afraid of anything or anybody. I could handle myself in a fight. Unlike girls like Kayla Brockhouse, I was a force to be reckoned with.

In this moment, I was the farthest thing from fierce. The tears came before I had the chance to even try and shut them down. Considering the volume, I doubt I would have had any success.

Ten minutes later, we were marching out of the camp and heading home to Platypus Creek. It would take us a few days to get there. Hopefully, I would regain control of myself enough to get my mind back in the game. Right now, the only thing that I knew for certain was that I wanted to see Suzi die a terrible death, and I wanted to be directly involved in that fate.

4

Vignettes LXII

It took a few days, but eventually, Juan was able to be up and about with the help of a handmade set of crutches. His leg throbbed, but each night, Gerald (he refused to call this guy Grizzly Man no matter how much his daughters begged) would whip up this pungent concoction and have Juan drink it.

Juan did not have the desire to know what it was made from; the taste told him that he would probably be better off lacking that specific knowledge. But whatever it was made from, it knocked him out cold each night and allowed him to sleep.

As the days crept by, Juan did what he could to help inside the cabin. He was no fan of scrubbing pots and iron skillets, but he was not much good for anything else. Meanwhile, Gerald sort of just came and went. Sometimes Juan would wake up to find the man had already left for the day. But no matter what, the man was always back by evening.

"Not much longer before we won't be getting any darkness at all," Gerald said over dinner one evening in particular. "Soon as that happens, I have to make my trip into Anchorage. If you like, I can check on your friends and get them any message you might want to send."

By the time Gerald was set to go, Juan had a letter written explaining that he and the girls would be there hopefully before

51

the end of summer. However, if not, then certainly as soon as the next thaw. He also asked them to do something nice for Gerald as a token of gratitude.

At last it was time for the big man to climb up onto his cart; Juan was more than a little surprised when the girls both started to cry. They made Gerald promise to come back as soon as possible and to be extra safe.

The next few days felt strange. He'd been so focused on getting up and about as often as he could that he realized it had been days since he'd dwelled on the loss of Mackenzie. That realization put him in a funk that carried over to his daughters. Juan realized this when Della came to where he was sitting, her eyes welling with tears that were on the verge of spilling.

"I'm sorry, Papi," she whispered, wrapping her arms around Juan as much as she could. A few seconds later, Denita joined.

"Sorry?" Juan leaned back so he could see the girls' faces.

"Sorry for whatever we did that made you upset," Denita mumbled, plunging her face back into Juan's chest and now starting to bawl.

"Whoa!" Juan put his hands on his daughters' heads and eased them up so that he could look them in the eyes. "You two haven't done anything."

"But you look unhappy," Della insisted. "And nobody else is here to make you sad, so it has to be us."

Juan frowned. He scolded himself for being so selfish and then cleared his throat to push down the lump that had grown.

"Tell ya what," he said, making an effort to put some levity in his tone, "why don't you two help me go down to the creek. I think it has been too long since we did any fishing."

The girls both squealed in delight and began to scurry about the cabin. Apparently they knew exactly where Gerald kept everything because every time that he opened his mouth to say where they might find one thing or the other, either Della or Denita would dash over, grab whatever it was and then add it to the carry bag that they had placed on the table.

An hour later, all three of them were beside the bank of a fast moving creek. Juan warned the girls about the water at least a dozen times in the first twenty minutes before he opened his mouth to do it again and got his own words parroted back at him in sing-song unison.

By that evening, they had more fish than the three of them could eat in a week. The girls skipped and danced ahead of him as he made his way up the path on crutches. He was enjoying their laughter so much that he was caught off guard when they both froze and went instantly silent.

The soft moan of a deader carried to his ears. Juan did not have time to scold himself for being so careless. Before he could engage in any such thing, a single zombie stumbled out of the tall grass to the left of their path.

How had he been so thoughtless? How could he drop his guard even for a second? And now it would cost him one, if not both, of the most precious things he had left in the world.

Those thoughts all hit Juan in the blink of an eye. However, he never truly had the opportunity to wallow in a single one of them. As if they'd been practicing for just such an occasion, both girls rolled away from each other in a blur of arms and legs.

Della now stood on one side and Denita on the other. Each of them held her belt knife in her hand. Denita struck first, darting in and kicking the deader behind one knee. The pathetic thing crumpled and fell to the ground in an uncoordinated heap. Just that fast, Della swept in and drove her small blade into the temple of the downed zombie.

"Stupid deader," Denita scoffed, giving the body another kick for good measure.

Juan was awestruck. While he had certainly done what he considered to be the parental duty of the times and teach his children how to fend off a zombie attack, he had never taught the girls anything like this. They had acted as a team in a very calculated and apparently practiced manner.

"Where did you learn that?" Juan asked, not making any attempt to hide how impressed he was with his girls.

"The Grizzly Man taught us," Della said with a smile. "He said that if you got sick and went to live with mama, that we would need to know how to take care of ourselves if we were gonna stay here with him."

**

Getting off of the island proved to be easier than Vix was comfortable with. In the first place, the simple fact that these people did it with so little effort was cause enough to be alarmed. She been living the life of blissful ignorance it would seem. She thought that this community was unified and that there was none of that funny business going on that always brought these sorts of groups to ruin.

As the sound of the oars dipping in and out of the water came in their steady rhythm, Vix had to wonder what else she might not be privy to when it came to the inner workings of their tiny community of New England. Couldn't people see that this was likely part of the cause that the bloody zombies got the upper hold on society in the first place?

Well, that could not be helped now. At the moment, they had something very peculiar to look into that might very well mean bigger problems than apparently the entire population of London walking into the water and coming to the walls of her little village. Leave it to the living to flub up a zombie apocalypse.

Dawn was just starting to break as they ground into the shore. She had no idea where they might be. While she had made runs across the channel when her rotation came, the days were long gone when they paid that much attention to where they might land exactly. Who could tell the difference anymore between Hoo, Chattenden or Cliffe Woods?

After they pulled the boat entirely clear of the water and even took the time to cover it with some branches, they fell in as Marjorie led them inland. As they moved down a mostly overgrown road, Vix marveled as she always did at how Mother Nature was making short work at something that the British Empire had spent centuries creating.

The one thing that was very noticeable was the complete and utter lack of anything resembling a zombie. They were simply gone. Not one sole walker or halfie (her term for those missing their lower extremities) could be seen, heard, or smelled.

"We will be making for the top of that ridge," Gordon said, pointing out the top of a long inclined slope. The ruins of a farm house sat there. It was two stories high and, if it somehow managed to be safe to enter, would provide an excellent view of the surrounding area.

Vix was so intent on taking in what was actually a rather stunning countryside that she ran into the back of Chaaya. She instantly went on the defensive, her hand going for her weapon. The woman placed a hand on hers and shook her head, her free hand bringing a finger to her lips in a shushing gesture. After Vix nodded that she understood, her eyes followed to where the other woman was pointing. On the opposite side of this narrow road was just another field, however, it was what was in that field that had the entire group so captivated.

A herd of horses were grazing on the grassy slope. They were all of different colors; some black, some bay. However, it was the pure white one in the middle that immediately drew the eye. The majestic animal was walking amongst the others, its head held high and proud, its long mane ruffling in the gentle breeze.

The animal froze and then craned its neck in their direction. Vix could almost swear that the creature was looking directly into her soul. If it was afraid, it gave no sign. More likely, it was just as curious about these recent intruders into its territory as she and the others were fascinated by its beauty.

Vix had no idea how much time passed until they resumed their trek, but she walked away feeling like she had witnessed something special. Wild animals were a common sighting on field runs, but horses were a rare treat. This herd easily numbered over a hundred and was by far the largest that she'd ever seen

At last they reached the top of the hill and the farm house. After Gordon pronounced it safe to enter, they all made their way to the upper floor. None of them were even the slightest bit inclined to snoop around. It was obvious that the place had been gutted and stripped of anything that might even be remotely useful ages ago.

The view was all they could hope for. It showed nothing but empty English countryside as far as the eye could see...with one exception. Far to the north, a single spiral of smoke twisted skyward. It looked pencil thin from where they stood, which meant that it was likely quite a large fire at the source. It also seemed to be in the general direction that they needed to travel.

They now had a general location for their target.

As the day dragged on, the group talked about what they hoped to do once they reached their destination. Vix took part in the conversation; however, she kept mum on making any specific offerings to the plan. In her experience, plans were best left as an outline. As soon as you put one into motion, something was bound to come along and ruin things.

They stopped for the evening at a roundabout. They could travel further, but there was no sense creeping along in the dark. Clouds had rolled in and there would be no moon to see by this evening. The world would be plunged into blackness. They would simply have to wait.

After a very brief debate, the notion of a campfire was finally agreed upon. Vix remained the lone voice of dissent. She was chilled, but her bed roll would be adequate. If the bad guys were close at hand, she saw no need in announcing their presence.

Her eyes had just closed after her standing the first watch shift when a scream jolted her awake.

***

"How many days since she spoke to you?" Caroline asked as they hiked along what had once been Interstate 5.

"Well, we packed and left five days ago, so I would have to say five," Chad answered, casting a glance over his shoulder.

Ronni was keeping pace, but she had put about a quarter of a mile between herself and her dad. Chad had stopped early the first day when he realized how far back she had fallen, but when he stopped, so did she.

"You are going to get yourself killed!" he shouted, his voice echoing off of the canyon walls.

"Tell my dad that I am not a baby and can take care of myself!" had been the reply.

"She does know that I can hear her, right?" Chad had asked, glancing at Caroline.

"I think this is more symbolic," Caroline had sighed, turning to resume walking and tugging at Chad so he would follow.

Every single day, Ronni made it a point to somehow wake up before either Chad or Caroline, gather her gear, and then put her distance between them for the day's journey. After the second night, Caroline had taken Ronni aside and asked if she intended to keep this up forever.

"Just until we find a settlement, then I am done. If you and my dad want to just roam the country for eternity, feel free. But I am sick of moving. I want to wake up in a bed, do things like talk to *other* people," had been the girl's response.

The problem was that Caroline could understand where the girl was coming from. She hated moving almost as much. However, she could not deny the peculiar vibe of that last group. Add in the fact that they had a thing against those who were immune—which would include Ronni—and the recipe for trouble was already in the pot and simmering.

Once she took more time to think about things, she realized that she had noticed people eyeing Ronni suspiciously. Her arms were a mess of hideous scars. Oddly enough, those were not even the bite marks. Those were from her self-inflicted injuries when she had done something drastic to try and draw zombies away from some children.

Chad, as always, was putting the best interests of his daughter ahead of everything. However, if Caroline was being honest with herself, he had a tendency to overdo it. He could find an excuse anyplace they went. Just because somebody eyed his daughter (or herself for that matter) did not mean that they had some hideous designs churning in their mind. The problem was that Chad had spent a good portion of his life in prison. That had clouded his outlook on humanity perhaps worse than somebody who had never had the misfortune to ever be locked up. Add in some very unsavory business from one of the first settlements he and his daughter lived in, and he was overly gun shy.

"Hey," Chad said, yanking Caroline out of her little ruminations. She was surprised to realize that he had come to a stop perhaps a dozen or so steps back.

"What's wrong?" Caroline's hand went to her hip and her machete out of reflex.

Chad pointed and she turned to look to the right. A sign was off of the road and up in a rocky crevice.

It read simply: Emigrant Lake-Survivors welcome!

"Seems pretty straightforward," Caroline finally said after it was clear that Chad was going to just stand there until she offered some sort of input.

The man approached her, his eyes seeming to search the ground for an answer or perhaps a sign. When he looked up, she saw for the first time that amount of pain he was feeling.

"You think we could give the place a try? Maybe Ronni will get over our leaving the last place." Chad's hands were twisting and squeezing themselves in nervous agitation.

"We won't know until we give it a try." Caroline shot a look over her shoulder at the young lady who was starting to rise up on tiptoes and cock her head as if that might magically allow her to know what was being said.

"Fine," Chad agreed, "but we do this my way. I will go in and give the place a look. You two make camp over the other side of that ridge." He hiked a thumb over his shoulder to indicate where he wanted them to wait.

"That seems fair enough."

Less than an hour later, camp was made and Chad started off towards where the arrow pointed. It took him the better part of two hours, but at last he crested a ridge. Before him was a massive lake. A wall at least twenty feet high ran alongside what was left of a two-lane road.

There were dozens of cabins spaced out as well as a few large buildings. Even from this distance, he could see more people walking around than he'd seen in one place since this whole nightmare began. Even more important, he saw children. There was a park with dozens of children running around. He could see blankets spread out on the grass as people enjoyed the sun and a picnic. It was enough to bring tears to his eyes.

Could it really be this simple? Was their journey finally over?

***

"Jody, you can't do this," Selina insisted. "Not without me."

Jody turned to face the woman. He loved her with all of his heart, of that there could be no denial. Yet, his daughter was in danger and he was about to go out with the sole intention of doing something horrible. He knew from experience that killing another living being was not as simple as many people believed. Killing a zombie was one thing; but killing a person who might be looking up at you and begging for his (or her) life? He would not allow Selina to see him do such a thing; nor would he allow her to be forced to commit it.

"I need you here in case she returns or whoever did this thinks twice about the road they are heading down." Jody put his hands on Selina's arms and looked into her eyes. He could see the same pain in hers that he felt all the way to the core of his soul. "And I have no idea what is going to happen once I walk out this door."

Jody saw no need to lie. Besides, he was certain that all of the hardware he was sporting gave away his intentions. He even had two of his handmade flash-bang grenades dangling from his vest. He also had his crossbow with a high-powered scope that he only used if he was hunting game.

"Do me one favor," Selina whispered, her head against his chest so tight that his heartbeat could be felt by both of them.

"Name it."

"Bring her back."

Jody kissed Selina and walked out the door. He was not to the bottom of the steps when he saw somebody in the shadows of the trees at the corner of his street. The person was outfitted in camo gear and had a wide-brimmed hat that cast a shadow preventing the face from being recognized. For a moment, the two stood facing each other. Neither seemed inclined to move for an uncomfortable amount of time. Jody was making a study of this person. He was looking at the weapons this person had all over their body. They obviously meant business.

At last, the figure raised both hands, laced them behind the head and knelt. That had Jody curious. Certainly it was obvious as to what he, Jody Rafe, had in mind. And if this person was one of the people responsible, it seemed incredibly peculiar that he or she would submit so easily.

Instantly, Jody went on guard. This could, in all likelihood, be a trap. Erring on the side of caution, he brought up his crossbow and advanced. His gaze went everywhere, but continued to flick back to this individual to be sure they were not doing anything devious.

Once he was about ten or fifteen feet away, the figure spoke. "Can I take my hat off? Maybe then you won't be as anxious and accidentally shoot that damn thing."

"Danny?"

"Yeah, and this is really playing hell on my ankles. Can I please get up now?"

"What?" Jody was confused for a moment. "Oh, crap…yes!"

He stepped back and reached down to give Danny a hand up. The man was wobbly at best, but at last he was on his feet.

"I thought that you needed a cane to even get around a little?" Jody stepped back. He was trying his best to sound more concerned than suspicious.

"Yeah. I have been going through some gnarly physical therapy. And honestly, I just got to the point where I could go anyplace without my cane. It hurts wicked bad, but I gotta push myself, ya know?"

"Okay, but that still doesn't really explain how you are here or how you knew what I was about to do."

"Funny thing when you are seeming to be crippled. Folks

forget that you are even around. Can you believe I even have some folks that talk slow and loud like I might be deaf or mentally challenged?" Danny scoffed.

"Yeah...that ain't really stretching things," Jody said with just the hint of a smile on his lips.

"Screw you, Rafe."

"Listen, I appreciate the offer. Seriously, but you look like you can barely handle going to the end of the street, much less scour the freaking community as well as the surrounding areas. No offense." Jody gave a raised eyebrow and glanced down at Danny's feet.

"Good to know you still don't listen to a damn thing I say," Danny said after a moment. "If you paid any attention, I just told you that people tend to ignore me because they think my ruined freakin' ankles got anything to do with my hearing or ability to understand."

"I don't think I follow."

Jody stepped back. He knew that Danny wanted to at least appear to be helpful. And that might do a lot to mend their ruined friendship, but right now, he had much bigger things to deal with and no time for further delays. He could not deny that it felt good to see that a person he had considered to be a dear friend was standing in front of him, offering his help despite the fact that there seemed very little he could actually do.

"Jesus, Rafe!" Danny hissed. "Not only do I know who took your daughter, but I know right where they are."

* * *

Entry Seven—

I don't usually hunt women. Seriously, in this day and age, I figure they have gotten the short end of the stick enough times, that anything they did would pretty much be justified. The zombie apocalypse set back women's rights about a hundred years in some places. And in others, well, they don't have any at all. Every once in a while, I hear tales of some poor gal reaching her breaking point. Some abusive jerk ends up castrated or worse;

and believe me, there are things that are worse.

I could give two squirts about that sort of thing. And honestly (I will probably piss a few people off here), I don't delve in domestic issues. If I started down that road, I would probably lose what is left of my mind.

This woman is an exception. I first heard about her when I was spending the night at this little community by some nameless creek. The stories were such that I thought it was just some tale to keep the kids in check. When I looked around and realized that the kids had all gone to bed and then saw the expectant faces looking at me, I knew otherwise.

Sometimes my reputation precedes me. I never meant for that to happen. But in this new world, news can travel in strange ways. Of course it is often so distorted that you can't tell where the actual story resides in the morass of fabrication.

The woman in question actually begins the story as a victim. The way it is told, she was living alone with some guy in a cabin on a bluff. She got pregnant and gave birth to a son. Unfortunately, she turned out to be like those women you heard about every blue moon in the old days. She was like that lady that put her kids in a van and drove it into a lake, then tried to blame some imaginary minority.

This woman's husband comes home from a day of chopping wood or whatever to discover his nine-month-old son floating face down in the wash basin. The husband goes nuts and beats the woman near to death. Only, after all that, the bastard felt guilty and slit his wrists. The story says that he thought that he had *actually* beaten her to death.

From there, it gets sort of strange. The woman survives and in the process, whether due to the beating or her own mind's inability to process the terrible thing that she has done, she goes crazy. She starts slipping in to other communities. Once she is accepted, it is just a matter of time before she snatches some poor kid and takes off.

Nobody is certain what happens to these children, but they are never seen or heard from again. Unfortunately for the woman, she has some pretty identifiable disfigurement around her left eye. It did not take too long for her to strike enough times so that people started sending word to other settlements. Also, traders and merchant caravans were given the story and the description.

One day, she shows up and somebody freaks. They call her out, saying that they knew what she had done. That is not the best way to deal with crazy. And I am sure that, with hindsight being twenty-twenty, the poor fool would have kept his mouth shut.

The woman did not even blink or bat an eye. She just walked up to the sap and stuck a knife in his belly. Then she walked away as cool as the other side of the pillow. People heard the shouts or screams and came running. By the time they showed up, the woman was gone.

People went out to search, but in this world, if somebody wants to stay hidden, they can damn sure do it. I guess that was just over a week ago. Things were getting back to normal and folks were going about their business. Only, yesterday, some poor mother woke to find her daughter gone.

The girl is just eleven months old. Her mom put her to bed for the night like any other. When the father woke he ducked his head in to check and made the discovery. I showed up to people in an absolute sea of rage. They were all about going out to find her and deal justice. I totally understand.

When I arrived, I was questioned as to if I had seen anything. When I said I had not, but that I would certainly be willing to look, one of the men pulled me aside. He'd heard about me. Said he recognized me from the description some merchant gave. It is hard to believe, but I guess I am getting references.

I told him I was the person in question and then he called a bunch of the citizens together to get the community blessing on me going out to find this person. It was a short discussion.

I ate, got a good night's sleep, and then picked up some gear. The guy at the shop told me it was on the house, but I told him that would not be necessary. If he wanted to hook me up when the job was done, that would be fine, but I just didn't feel right taking stuff for a job that I have not done yet.

I left a few hours before dark. I had no idea which direction to go, but the surrounding landscape actually narrowed my choices. There is some nasty and mountainous terrain to the east. To the south is a massive river. Nobody crosses that without being on one of the barges that ferry people over.

That left me with heading west or north. Coin toss said west.

5

Making Her Geek Proud

She walked down the street, but she could not get a read from anybody as to where there might be something amiss. Of course, she assumed that these people had survived a great deal already. It would likely take something considerable to get them riled up. Still, she had to find out where Denise DeCarlo had run off to after getting the news that Kalisha had been taken to the administrator's office.

"May as well just ask," she muttered, changing her course to intercept a young man walking along by himself and actually whistling.

"Excuse me?" Catie hailed the man, having to step almost directly in front of him to get him to stop.

"Huh?" The young man's head popped up and his eyes were a mix of alarm and confusion for a second. He apparently came to some conclusion and then relaxed visibly.

"Can you tell me where the administrator's office is?"

"Sure." The man turned and pointed to a large white building that had a steeple on top.

"Thanks," Catie said, taking off at a jog.

"But they are in session right now," the man called after her. "You probably don't want to interrupt them."

Catie heard the warning and chose to ignore it. She reached

the stairs and looked up at what had obviously once been a chapel. This set a few more of her warning bells off, but she forced them down. While there were certainly those who had a twisted and convoluted idea of religion, there were others who were just trying to desperately cling to something safe and familiar. It was not fair for her to assume. Still, that did not mean that she did not need to be prepared.

Climbing the stairs, she could hear a rather heated argument taking place inside. Catie took one more deep breath and opened the doors. It was like the interior of any church that she had ever visited for the most part. Even the long wooden pews were still in place. The biggest difference came up in the pulpit. Instead of an altar or podium, there was a large, ornate desk.

A man was seated behind it and standing to his left were two big, rough looking men who had Kalisha between them; each one had a grip on her arm. The girl had obviously been crying. Standing at the bottom of the three tiered steps that ran all the way across the front of the raised dais was Denise, Eldon, and another man Catie did not recognize.

"...as the rules clearly state," the man behind the desk was almost shouting. He stopped when Catie entered. One of the men holding on to Kalisha released her arm and took a step forward.

"Don't stop on my account," Catie said with a shrug. "I was just coming in to observe. Or are the hearings here of a private nature?"

"Who is this woman?" the administrator demanded. "Don't tell me this is the young woman that Kalisha brought to our very gates."

"My name is Catie...Catie Dreon. And I guess I am the person you are talking about. I met her outside of town in some territory supposedly run by a group calling themselves the Beastie Boys. I always thought *Paul's Boutique* was perhaps one of the greatest albums ever made." She paused and allowed herself a smile. "But I doubt you are old enough to remember. Hell, I bet you never had the pleasure of pulling a piece of vinyl from the sleeve and scouring the dust jacket while you gave a record its first spin on your turntable."

"Your presence is not welcome here, Miss Dreon," the man behind the desk said flatly.

"Actually..." Catie took another couple of steps into the large open room, letting the heavy doors shut behind her, "it's *missus.*"

"I don't care," the man scoffed. "You are not a member of the council, you are a stranger at the very least and an intruder in any case. This is not a meeting open to the public."

"The public? Or just those who are immune?" Catie saw Denise close her eyes and press her lips tight in disapproval. She also saw Eldon smile.

"As I was saying, Dean, the new arrival is not only openly hostile, but she is immune," Eldon chirped, putting a few steps between himself and Denise.

"You say that like it is a crime." Catie turned her focus to the man and leveled her harshest glare his direction. He quickly looked away, obviously unable to maintain eye contact.

"I will only ask you this one time, *Missus* Dreon," Dean, the man behind the desk, made it a point to drip sarcasm over the title, "you need to leave immediately. Do so now by choice, or else—"

"Or else what?" Catie challenged. "Because if you say that you will have me forcibly removed, that means you lack the stones to do it yourself. That also means you are nothing but a bully and a coward. You know how I deal with bullies? A swift punch in the nose."

The administrator sat back in his chair for a moment and actually seemed to consider her words. He steepled his fingers and stared at her. If he was waiting for her to blink, Catie had news for the man.

"Eldon?" Dean turned in his chair to the man. "Would you remove this person from these proceedings?"

The man seemed to almost stagger back, but it was quickly apparent that it was from excitement and not anything like fear or hesitation. "Yes, Mr. Administrator."

"Oh please."

Catie suppressed a smile at the barely audible whisper that

came from Denise. She also widened her stance a bit and eyed Eldon as he turned her direction. The man had taken a few steps, but his pace faltered noticeably when she obviously showed no signs of being the least bit concerned.

"You do understand there will be no going back for you once you put so much as a finger on me," Catie warned. "You will get your ass handed to you by a woman in front of these idiots that you are obviously and blindly trying to impress."

Giving the man a better once over now that they were about to square off, a thought came unbidden and Catie let a chuckle escape. She bit her lower lip and shrugged at Eldon's raised eyebrows. She also noticed that he had stopped his advance.

"What's so funny?" the man snarled.

"I just realized who you remind me of." Catie let the laugh carry over in her reply.

"Oh? And who is that?"

"Biff, from *Back to the Future*."

That earned a chuckle from Denise, and the woman quickly threw a hand over her mouth to stifle it when all eyes shot her glares of overwhelming disapproval—all eyes except for those of Kalisha. The girl looked equal parts confused and frightened.

This had the exact effect that Catie had hoped for from the oafish man. He let loose with a bellow and charged her with reckless abandon. Catie had hoped for this result because she was concerned deep down about her ability to bring a man of Eldon's size to heel without some slight advantage offered.

Just as he was lunging, she made an agile sidestep and whipped her foot out to sweep the man at the ankles. The man, already having a full head of steam and unable to slow much less stop, went careening in a graceless belly flop and slide that did not end until he collided heavily with the massive doors. The impact was a mix of frame shuddering reverberation as well as a nasty crack that was punctuated with a yelp.

Diving onto Eldon's back with both knees, Catie reached over and dug her fingers into the man's eyes and yanked his head back. She leaned down to his ear and hissed, "Move and you will need a seeing eye dog for the rest of your short and miserable life."

Catie shot a look over her shoulder to ensure that the goons were still staying put. While they were certainly giving anxious looks to this administrator named Dean, neither man had taken a step closer.

"Please let my man up, Missus Dreon," Dean said as he rose from his chair. "And everybody else please clear the chamber. Take our little juvenile delinquent to her quarters, and Denise, you may return to yours as well." The men actually looked like they might question the order, but any such thoughts vanished when Dean slammed his hand on the desk. "Now!"

Catie rose to her feet and made a point to get well clear of Eldon's striking range. The man pushed himself up and scrambled to his feet in a hurry, one arm shooting out in a near-blind backhanded swipe.

"Eldon!" Dean barked. "I said to clear the room. I did not say for you to attack our new guest."

The man wiped at his face and Catie was happy to see a series of perfect crescent moon-shaped marks that were leaking blood from where her fingers had dug into the tender flesh around the eyes. One side looked like it might even swell shut. When he headed for the door, Catie was even happier to see the man walking with a bit of a limp.

At last the large open room was empty save for Catie and this man named Dean. Not being a fool, Catie kept her mouth shut and chose to let him be the first to speak.

"They tell me that you come from out west."

"News travels fast." Catie moved into the middle pew and sat down.

"Not really," Dean said with a shrug. "It is a small town. Most are these days from what I understand." He stood and came around his desk, sitting on the edge and folding his hands in front of him. "So, what are we to do with you?"

"How about you let me ask all of those who are immune if they would like to leave of their own free will? We could find a new place to live and let you and yours live in peace." Dean opened his mouth, but Catie cut him off as she continued. "But since I doubt you want to let go of all of your indentured servants, I think it will be a shade more complicated than me asking and you just agreeing."

"Indentured servants!" Dean sputtered. He made a few gasps of incredulity, but then he stopped just as suddenly and his lips curved in a huge smile. "So, you are some sort of avenging angel? A do-gooder out to right wrongs and be the voice for the oppressed? That sort of thing?"

"Nothing quite so grand," Catie replied. "In fact, if that creep Eldon hadn't been such a jerk during my interrogation, I might have minded my own business and gone on my way. But then the whole thing about that girl being brought in like a criminal when all she was guilty of was going after her brother, and it got me to thinking."

"I would be careful, Missus Dreon," Dean warned.

"What deal have you made with these Beastie Boys?" Catie had considered how she was going to go about this. She knew that she did not have the patience to tiptoe around things. She was an "every problem looks like a nail" sort of gal.

"I have no—" Dean began to protest.

"Just don't," Catie snapped, cutting the man off. "We can dance around this and play silly games, but, and maybe this is the hormones talking, I simply do not have the desire to play games. Tell me what you have going on."

"And what do you intend to do with any information I might offer?" Dean went back behind his desk and Catie watched his hands. If he went for any sort of weapon, she knew perfectly well that she was screwed.

"It depends."

The man seemed to consider Catie with an appraising eye rather than a defensive one. Catie knew what it felt like to be sized up, and that is exactly what this felt like. At last, he seemed to come to a conclusion.

"You have two choices," Dean spoke as he once again got to his feet. "You can get your gear and leave today. If you return after being escorted to the edge of our territory, you will be considered an invader and I will have you executed."

70

"That sounds fun," Catie sniffed. "You would just execute a woman who is pregnant?"

"Your…condition…is the only reason that you are being given that first choice of leaving. Too many people know about you. At this point, doing something would not be greeted with a positive result. I may be a lot of things, but stupid isn't one of them."

"You mentioned a second choice."

"Something tells me that you are former military." Dean folded his hand on his desk. His voice reminded Catie of a teacher giving a lecture. It was not overly emotional. A guy like this might not be all that difficult to work for…or at least with. "The way that you handled Eldon? That was impressive. If you were to perhaps lead a team of men that I chose to remove the head from the group that calls themselves the Beastie Boys, then we would be in your debt and I would consider asking you to stay on and accept a post as one of our chiefs of security."

"And if I do this, I will have some stipulations of my own."

"Such as?" Dean asked, a bemused smile curling his lips in the start of a grin that was more creepy than pleasant.

"We will deal with that when I return." Catie walked up to the desk and planted her hands on it. She leaned down so that her face was inches from Dean's. "And I want some people of my choosing on the team just in case you plan on having me killed after I complete this mission."

"After?" Dean scoffed. "You make it sound like it is already done. You are quite confident in your abilities."

"Yes, I am."

***

"I just want one person that you trust with our life." Catie sipped on the tea and savored its sweetness. She had not enjoyed honey in an age. And tea? Not only was this delicious, but it had just a hint of citrus in it that made her want to risk scalding her tongue just so she could have a second cup.

"That is a rather short list. But you are asking me to have

this person put their life at risk," Denise replied with a slow shake of her head. "You are asking me to join you, a total stranger, along with a handpicked goon squad that the administrator assigns for a mission that has been attempted twice and resulted in utter failure."

"I wasn't on those other two missions," Catie countered.

"And you make that much of a difference?"

"Yes." Catie glanced over at Kalisha who sat quietly, holding her cup and staring down into it with almost no expression on her face. "I got her released to us, didn't I?"

There was a long silence. Catie was still organizing her thoughts, and she had something up her sleeve that she was not ready to reveal yet. She knew that it was a risky plan at best. It could very well lead to her death as well as some or all of the team. However, over the years, she had dealt with plenty of groups like these Beastie Boys. She also saw something in their actions that led her to believe that she might be able to do something that would assure her safety as well as her unborn child's.

After leaving the little chapel and being escorted back to the dorm, Catie considered her possibilities. She knew very well that she was rolling the dice being out and alone in the world. She had a strong desire to return home and let everybody know that Kevin had been killed. Yet, once she really thought about it, she came to the conclusion that there was simply no need to hurry. She and Kevin had left with the idea of not returning. It was not something they talked about much, but the further away they got, the more it felt like they were closing the book on that chapter of their lives. This was her chance to start fresh.

"I know that you have no reason to trust me, but seriously, do you like the way things are here?" Catie set her cup down and eyed the pot with a tiny wisp of steam curling up from the spout. Denise saw her expression of longing and poured her another cup.

"Not exactly," Denise admitted. "But I know how things are outside of our walls. I have heard the stories of the immune being hunted like animals, treated worse than zombies. And, lest we forget, the undead do still hold their own and are still a good reason to not be outside of the protection that the walls of this town provide."

"So you want to spend whatever is left of your life hiding behind a wall and being treated like a second class citizen at best?" Catie glanced at the wrist guard that Denise was wearing. It identified her as immune to the zombie virus. It may as well be a scarlet "I" considering the fact that it basically identified her as something of which to be afraid, or at least leery. "You happy wearing that thing and having people give you a clear berth when you pass?"

"It is for the protection of others," Denise insisted. Catie could hear the tremor in her voice. The woman was not an idiot; she knew damn good and well that she was marked as an outcast, a pariah.

"If you help me, you will be helping yourself. Wouldn't you like to live a somewhat normal life?" Catie pressed.

"Normal? How can anybody ever conceive the possibility of living a normal life again?"

"We might not be tweeting and Facebooking our lives away, but I can assure you that it is very possible to live a normal life. It is up here." Catie tapped her head with her index finger. "It is a state of mind. You are telling yourself that you are doing this to protect others. Yet you live with people who lord over you. Sure, this is a so-called mixed community. But you are nothing more than servants and grunts that get to do the dirty work. Keep it up and that system will become so entrenched that you guys will be developing your very own caste system. You will all know your place, and the rest of the community will become more and more gluttonous for power and control." Catie felt her anger build and allowed her passion to spill into her voice.

"You want us to take this place from the unknowns?" Kalisha whispered. "You are talking like we can just stomp our feet and change things. That is what Elliot thought. Now he lives out there like a wild animal."

"Elliot?" Catie heard something in the girl's voice that made her perk up. "Who is Elliot?"

"A man that used to live here. Helped Dean and some of the

others get the walls up. He was bit way back when this all began," Denise explained. She glanced at Catie and then over at Kalisha who nodded for her to continue. "He did a lot of the foraging back in the early days since a bite or scratch wouldn't be his death."

"And why did he get the boot?" Catie asked. She noticed Kalisha's expression grow dark; obviously this was a sensitive subject for the girl.

"As the months passed, and then years, the community grew," Denise continued. "Of course there were some that arrived with the scars of attack. We welcomed them like anybody else. Dean and Elliot sort of ran things. They even held an election in case somebody felt like there might be a better person or people to be in charge. Elliot actually received about forty or so more votes than Dean.

"Then this small group arrived. Every single one of them was immune! It was the first time that such a group came to our gates. Dean was pretty excited. It was also when the first of the children born to a pair of immune parents arrived in our community." Denise glanced at Kalisha.

"You were the first one?" Catie asked.

The girl shook her head. "My little brother Caleb..." She began to choke up and waved for Denise to continue.

"Things were good for a while. We had to fight off a few other groups, but most people arriving at our walls were in terrible shape and thankful for a place to call home. Our number continued to swell and we actually had to design a new wall. The immune community stepped forward and basically did the entire construction project. They lost three people building that wall.

"About three weeks after the wall was built, people started getting sick and turning. It was just men, and none of them were on any of the details that went out to forage, so people began to get scared. They were afraid that it might be something in the air." Denise paused and her eyes seemed to find something interesting to look at in her lap.

"Let me guess," Catie finally said. "Some girl was going around and having sex with men, exposing them to whatever it is that makes people become a zombie."

"Her name was Sandy Bennet, and her husband was one of the men working on the wall," Denise said with a sigh. "She was upset. At the trial, she accused the community of taking advantage of her husband and the other immunes. She said that they were being treated unfairly and that nobody had even made a point to hold some sort of memorial service for the men who had died to build the walls. She also claimed that five men she had sex with did not turn, and that if they did not step forward by the next day of the trial, she would give their names."

"So?" Catie said with a shrug. "Who cares? Wouldn't that just bolster the numbers of the immune? I would think that was a good thing. Hell, if I was gonna be infected, I would take a roll in the hay over a hunk of my flesh being ripped from my body any day of the week."

"And that would probably have been the case," Denise agreed, "but after the deaths, it was mandated that any who were immune needed to have some sort of permanent identification. At one point, tattoos were even suggested, but we had children who were immune. Nobody would consent to a child being forced to get a tattoo. That is when the bracers were mentioned. It was also when we were all rounded up. It was temporary according to Dean."

"Tell her what happened to Sandy," Kalisha urged.

Denise paled just a bit, and it was clear that she was recalling something horrible. At last, she sat up straight and fixed Catie with a somber expression.

"She was supposedly being kept in isolation. It was for her own protection according to Dean. Only, the next morning, she was found in a hallway. Her guard was torn apart and at her side. At some point that night, she had died of some unknown cause and then managed to get out of her cell. The hallway was locked from the outside and the poor guy tasked to supposedly keep an eye on her was attacked and turned as well. Of course that confirmed reports that an immune person would still turn upon their death. Still, nobody could explain how she died, much less how she was let out of her cell."

"So the secret of who else she slept with that did not turn was never revealed," Catie finished the predictable ending to the story.

"That was only the start of it. As soon as the council reconvened, it was mandated that all the immune be removed from any supervisory position. They were deemed a risk. Elliot and Dean got into an actual fight in the council chamber, but it was like Dean had been ready for him. A bunch of men jumped in and took Elliot down, tied him up, and then carted him off. A few months passed, and a dozen or so others in the community that were immune just disappeared. That was when the Beastie Boys started making their presence known. That is also when children started coming up missing."

Catie listened to the recounting of the story with mixed feelings. She knew as well as the woman speaking how those things managed to *just* happen. That also helped steel her resolve for the plan that she had brewing in her head.

Of course, a lot of things would need to happen for it to work. There was a better chance that it would fail than succeed. Still, she needed to do this; if not for herself, then for the baby. She wanted Kevin's child to have an honest chance at a good life. That did not include living as a second class citizen.

Catie wanted desperately to honor Kevin's legacy and make him proud of her. She did not necessarily believe that he was "looking down on her" or anything. It was just something that she felt very strongly about.

Catie was a realist. She had been one before Kevin, and she was certainly even more so now. Her entire being was focused on something long term. Yes, there would be risk involved. That was normal in the world she lived in now. She was more certain than ever that she could not do this on her own. She would not be out in the middle of God-knows-where when this baby came. And she would not be living in some walled community where her status of being immune was a liability.

"So then your dad is one of these Beastie Boys?" Catie turned to Kalisha who nodded. "And he took your brother. So why not you? And why are you afraid of them?"

"We aren't sure that my dad is still the one in charge. There was rumor that he died. And they take women, but not girls. Supposedly they are using the women like baby mills. One person said that the women are being kept in cells and made to do nothing except give birth, nurse, and care for the babies," Kalisha said softly. "I can't believe that my dad would do that. He loved my mom. He treated her good. When she died on a run, he was heartbroken."

"There are other stories, most of them awful. These Beastie Boys are a scary bunch," Denise said, reaching across and taking Kalisha's hand, giving it a pat.

"I still don't believe any of it," the girl spat, tears of anger starting to well in her eyes.

Catie considered all that she heard. It was certainly cause for concern. However, that did not change things. She had to at least try.

"You can either be a part of the solution, or you can sit back and let things happen around you," Catie said to Denise with a tone that was perhaps a bit harsher than she intended. "I can't promise you that things will work. But I can guaran-damn-tee that sitting back and letting others decide your fate will not be the least bit satisfying."

"I'm going," Kalisha said. "Whatever you have in mind, I bet it will be better than this. And I want to see for myself if my dad is doing these things. If he is..." Her voice trailed off and the tears that had threatened finally spilled down her cheeks.

"So, what is your plan?" Denise asked.

"Not now. I will fill you in once we are out of here."

"You don't trust me?"

"It's not that," Catie said, although that was not entirely true. The reality was that she wanted to trust this woman, but trust was something earned, not given. "I need to work it out in my head. If I tell you now, it is likely things will change by the time we leave. I have a few more things I need to know before I can be certain of what I am going to do."

"You aren't inspiring a lot of confidence right now," Denise quipped.

77

"Just hang tight," Catie said, getting up and excusing herself.

She walked back to her dorm. Both Denise and Kalisha offered to walk with her, but she refused, saying that she needed some time to think. As she did, she paid close attention to those that she saw wearing the bracers. She needed to lay some groundwork for her full plan to have a chance. That meant talking to a few more citizens. The hard part was deciding which ones. One mistake would end things in a hurry. If her plan was discovered, it was likely that she would end up dead...or worse.

***

"Get your hand offa me!" the man snapped, shoving the two burly guards away and snatching up a small mallet that looked like it could do some wicked damage.

Catie stepped out of the dorm. She had heard what sounded like a scuffle outside and had gone to see partially due to curiosity, but mostly out of boredom. It had been three days since her little deal with Dean Stockton. He claimed the title of the administrator, but Catie saw him more as a dictator. There was a council, but it was handpicked and seemed to consist of nothing more than a few yes men.

Twice she had gone to see him and both times she was turned away. She was beginning to wonder if the man had not been able to round up enough of his men to make the trip. After all, the Beastie Boys were rumored to be a nasty bunch. Over the past few days, Catie had made it a point to go into public places and drop casual inquiries about them to the residents of this community. It was as if she had mentioned honest to goodness boogeymen.

"You need to put that down, Marty," one of the men warned.

"You ain't taking me no place," the man, Marty apparently, said with a snarl. "If the administrator wants to talk to me, he can come down here his own damn self. And if you think that the two of you have what it takes to bring me in..." The man began to laugh, and it wasn't pleasant sounding at all. There was serious menace and derision in that little outburst.

"This doesn't have to be like this," said one of the two men dressed in the black Catie had seen on the roving security that wandered the confines of the community.

In her own wanderings, Catie had discovered something rather curious. There was actually more security on the ground than up on the walls. No surprise, none of them wore the bracers of the immune. It began to remind Catie of a prison camp in many ways. She saw those wearing the bracers make way any time that the roving goons passed.

"All I am saying is that the first one of you that puts hands on me goes to the morgue."

Catie leaned against the doorframe and watched the ordeal with growing interest. She appraised the situation and felt that it was very likely that this Marty would be more than capable of following up on his threat.

He was a massive man. His head was clean shaven and seemed to attach directly to his shoulders with no trace of a neck. He stood at least a foot taller than the tallest of his two antagonists. His arms were easily the size of a normal man's legs and his legs were tree trunks. His torso was tapered from amazingly broad shoulders down to a surprisingly trim waist. In her experience, most men she met with that much size had either a solid but pronounced gut, or were just plain sloppy looking.

"Marty, what seems to be the problem?" another voice called out.

Catie glanced left to the voice and saw a man that was either Marty's twin, or a clone. Catie blinked to be sure that she was not imagining things. She also noticed the two security personnel take a step back.

"Nothing, little brother," Marty grumbled. "At least nothing I can't handle."

Little? Catie thought. There was absolutely nothing little about this man.

"We have been requested to escort Mister Sabonis to the administrator's office," one of the men managed, his voice squeaking and cracking like a pubescent young man.

"Just one of us?" the second behemoth asked with a surprising amount of mirth in his voice. He seemed more amused than anything else. "Now you guys know that we are a package deal. If Marty goes, I go."

"We were only told to bring in Marty," the security guard insisted.

"Tell ya what," Marty's twin said as he stepped up beside his brother, "I will accompany my brother. That way, you guys don't get hurt and my brother doesn't end up in the clink."

"But—" one of the guards began, but his partner silenced him with an elbow.

"That would be fine."

Catie watched the foursome head towards the chapel. That must mean that Dean was at the office. He had all but vanished since their initial meeting. She was sick of waiting. It couldn't hurt to tag along. If nothing else, she could simply camp out across the street and wait for him to leave.

Catie was closing the door to the dorm when another pair of security guards arrived; this pair was making a beeline for her. Perhaps she would not have to wait outside after all.

"Missus Dreon?" one of the pair called out. This one was a woman and sounded like she was a two-pack a day chain smoker.

"Yeah?" Catie stepped back into the alcove of the entrance out of habit. She liked to have her back covered whenever possible. It wasn't that she expected trouble, it was just her custom.

"We have been sent to escort you to the administrator's office." The woman took a few steps ahead of her partner.

"You guys must have won the coin toss," Catie muttered.

"Excuse me?" the woman asked.

"Nothing," Catie replied with a wave of her hand. "Let's go."

She walked the few blocks to the chapel, a sense of excitement building. Could this finally be it? And if so, were those two mountains of manflesh going to be accompanying her? If that was the case, it was almost too perfect.

She entered the chapel and was only a little surprised to discover Denise, Kalisha, and a dozen or so other people she did not recognize all seated in the pews. She did not need to see bracers to know that those seated on the left were part of the so-called unknown. Kalisha, Denise, Marty and his twin were seated on the right.

"Missus Dreon, you leave tonight," Dean announced.

Superstitious Nonsense

"Why did she do it, Jim?" I sat by the fire, staring into it as my stomach churned.

The anger had not receded as the day drew on and we started up into the hills to the east of what had once been La Grande. If anything, it only intensified as we passed the still smoldering ruins of Island City. This was all Suzi's doing. She and her people had come into our little valley and just decided to take it.

I thought all day about what Billy might be able to do against these people, but the more I really sorted things out, the more that I came to realize that we were helpless. This was an army. They took what they wanted because they could. Certainly the people of Platypus Creek were no match.

The more it sunk in, the more hurt, angry, and miserable I became. By the time we stopped for the night, I was desperate for somebody to tell me something good. And if that could not be the case, then at least perhaps I could gain some sort of understanding.

"I got no idea, cupcake," Jim said with a lack of his usual optimism. "What I do know is that that Suzi broad is wackier than a football bat. Nothing good can come from having anything to do with her."

"So you think Billy will have a way to deal with this?" I

tried not to sound like a scared little girl pinning her hopes on some big, strong man to save the day, but damn if that was not exactly how I felt.

"Not likely."

I turned to Jim with my mouth open in disbelief. He had never encountered a situation that he couldn't handle or see a rosy side to—at least that I knew of anyway. Yet, there was no mistaking the sound of...defeat?

I felt my shoulders slump, and I returned my attention to the fire. Meanwhile, our so-called escorts were having a great time toying with Hunter's still-animated head. They were playing a game of chicken where one of them would put his or her hand up to the mouth and yank it away just as the teeth clicked shut.

I watched for a while and eventually found myself getting up and wandering closer. They were so engrossed that they did not even notice once I stood right there in their midst. They were laughing and having a great time oblivious to anything so unimportant like their prisoner wandering around.

"Thalia!" I heard Jim hiss, but I pretended that I was too engrossed in what was going on.

My hand slipped down to my belt. We were not given anything really powerful like a crossbow, but we at least got to carry a belt knife and a machete. I slipped my knife free, trying my best not to draw any attention. I felt more than heard it slide from its sheath in a rasp of metal on leather. I also heard Jim growling my name. Just as the blade came free, one of the goons turned to regard me with a big, stupid grin on his face. I smiled sweetly.

Then I plunged my knife into the eye socket of Hunter's head. It was over just that quick; at least for Hunter. From the look on the faces that turned my direction, it might just be starting for me.

"You stupid little cunt!" one of the men snarled and sent me flying backwards with a hard backhand. I think I landed right in front of where Jim sat.

"Hey!" Jim barked, jumping to his feet, but I couldn't tell much through my blurred vision and ringing ears.

Somebody yelped, and it took me a second to clear my head enough and see that one of the women in our escort was standing over the man who had hit me. She had her fists balled up, and the man was actually on his back with his hands up in surrender.

"What have I told you about that word, Chick?" the woman spat, drawing one fist back for emphasis.

"Sorry, Maddy, it just slipped out," Chick practically pleaded. Something told me that this Maddy could beat his ass, and he knew it.

"Next time it *just slips out*, I am gonna cut off those tiny things you try to pass off as your balls. We clear?" Maddy gave Chick a foot to the ribs for good measure and turned away.

I could already see what was going to happen. Part of me wanted to yell a warning. After all, even though I know she was not actually defending or protecting me, this Maddy had given that Chick guy a little bit of his own medicine. Still, I was also having fantasies about these people all turning on each other in a frenzy and killing one another in a quick but ferocious bloodbath, allowing me and Jim to escape to Platypus Creek and warn everybody.

Chick was coming up to a crouch, but he was not so much getting up as he was obviously getting ready to launch himself at Maddy's back. I did not move for fear that anything I did might actually bring the attention my direction. Sure enough, Chick sprung, launching himself at Maddy's exposed back.

There was a nasty crack and almost a yelp. Only, Chick was out cold before he landed, so he didn't actually get the chance to finish that noise after Maddy's elbow came back hard and smashed him in the jaw.

The rest of the camp was practically frozen in place. I waited, hoping that there would be this moment of silence, and then a massive brawl would erupt. No such luck. There was that moment of quiet; but then everybody started laughing. Well, almost everybody. Jim and I did not join in, and I doubted that Chick would be laughing for quite some time.

I was just getting to my feet when somebody shoved me hard in the back. I turned to see Maddy standing there with three of the men. They did not look at all happy now in contrast to that braying laughter of mere moments ago.

"Why did you do that?" Maddy demanded.

It took me a moment to know what it was that I had supposedly done. One of the men was holding Hunter's head. Apparently that was the thing I had done that had them so peeved.

"He deserved better than that," I said with a shrug.

"*He* was dead!" Maddy snapped. "And part of our instructions were to deliver this to your camp with our message."

"So deliver it." I sounded cool and calm, but inside I was shaking just a little. None of these people were something that I wanted to tangle with in a fight. And while I was confident that they were instructed to bring me to Platypus Creek alive, that did not mean I couldn't show up with a few cuts and bruises like poor Jim.

"You are on the verge of really pissing me off, little girl," Maddy growled.

"Look, folks," Jim came up and put an arm around my shoulder, "I won't tell. Thalia won't tell. And unless that comes up in conversation, who is to know?"

"Suzi will know," one of the men said, his voice holding a hint of awe like he believed that she would appear out of the darkness and punish them on the spot.

"What, does she have some sort of magic powers?" Jim teased. "Is she some sort of zombie apocalypse Randall Flagg?"

I had no idea what Jim was talking about, but it was clear that Maddy and one of the guys beside her did. They looked over their shoulders and then back to Jim. They actually appeared afraid. Personally, I was having a hard time not laughing.

"There is something about her. Nobody can say a word about one thing or another, but she finds out. She always finds out." Maddy looked at the men beside her who were nodding vigorously.

"You guys are being a bit silly," Jim finally said, but I could tell that he was being swept in by whatever the heck had these guys spooked.

"Just go to bed," one of the men finally barked.

They all went back over to their side of the camp, leaving me alone with Jim who had a look on his face like he was seriously concerned about something. I waited for a few minutes before I could not hold it in any longer.

"Who the hell is this Randall guy?"

"Huh?" Jim looked up at me, and it was clear that he had been lost in thought.

"You mentioned some guy named Randall something or other."

"Randall Flagg." Jim put his hands up to warm them in front of the fire. "He was a guy in a book. Don't worry about it."

"You obviously are," I quipped.

"People can convince themselves of anything if they try. That is why there used to be telephone psychics and horoscopes. Something nice and vague can become prophecy if you want it to be. This Suzi is obviously cultivating some sense of mystical power. It's absolute fiction, but the whole zombie thing has folks regressing to a Dark Ages mentality. Pretty soon we will be creating gods and all that nonsense...the sun will cross the sky in a chariot and crap like that."

I had no idea what he was carrying on about. Perhaps we just needed a good night's sleep. I went to my bedroll and climbed in. As my eyes drifted shut, I could see Jim still sitting by the fire. He was mulling over something in his mind.

***

We were actually making pretty good time. Jim was the biggest hold up as he limped along and had to take breaks way more often than our escorts liked. Chick looked like he had been beaten in the mouth with an entire forest of ugly trees. Still, it was easy to see his scowl. That expression had no trouble making its way to his eyes that did not ever seem to drift from me.

A few times, our scouts would return and they would swap out. Sometimes they would tell of a few zombies seen ahead and if they had been taken care of or might still need to be dispatched. I was actually surprised when Chick's turn came. I thought he might be excused, but that was not the case. It felt nice not to have him glaring at me for a while. However, we came to a stop beside a small runoff creek to refresh, and apparently it was also time for him to swap back in, only, there was no sign of him. We waited a while longer, and eventually Maddy made us get up and push on. She had one of the other men run ahead to find out what the deal was.

I glanced at Jim when we were ordered to come to another stop. It was obvious that our escorts were rattled. They kept huddling together in little groups as we walked. They were not talking loud enough for me to hear, but I did not need to hear to know that they were upset. When I glanced over at Jim, he had just the slightest hint of a smile on his face.

I went and sat beside him, took a drink from my canteen and offered him one. He took it, and while he drank, I whispered, "Okay, spill it. What the hell is going on?"

"I don't have any idea what you mean, cupcake."

Jim shrugged and tore off a bite of some of the dried meat and stale travel bread that we'd been given. Two more of our escort spoke briefly with Maddy and then jogged off in the direction that we were headed.

It was not ten minutes when they returned with the one who had left earlier, and I could tell by the looks on their faces that the news was not good. Again there was a conference that consisted of everybody except me and Jim. Finally, and after many instances where they would stop talking and glance our direction, Maddy broke away from the group and came over to stand above me and Jim. I had taken his lead and was currently chewing some unidentifiable meat that had been turned into jerky.

"How far are we from your compound?" Maddy asked.

I am certainly no expert in reading people, but the sweat on her upper lip and the way her eyes seemed to dart everywhere, rest on us for a second, and then look around frantically again, had me pretty confident in my assumption that she was scared out of her mind.

"Still another day and a half." Jim looked up, shading his

eyes as he did so; although the sun was actually a bit behind us, so I had no idea why. "Probably two with my legs being the way they are. I am walking as fast as I can, but you guys did a number on me back in camp."

He was still talking when she simply turned and walked away. Jim looked at me and shrugged. I kept waiting for us to be rousted to our feet and pushed ahead. After all, we still had a few good hours of daylight, and time was a factor. Suzi had given me three weeks. I would not abandon Jackson.

As the sun set behind us, it became clear that we were not moving on any more today. A fire had been built, but I noticed that this one was actually quite large. They even went off the road and cut down a couple of pines that were about eight or nine feet tall. The problem with the fire was that all the sap from the young trees popped and made noise. It wasn't much, but if there were any zombies in the area, they would be coming this way.

We didn't have to wait long for that first moan. I already had my machete in my hand and was deciding that I would likely not be sleeping tonight in any case. Something was strange. I climbed out of my bedroll and glanced at Jim's. He was sleeping just fine. I was going to give him a piece of my mind when this was over. If I didn't still feel so bad for having thought that he might be some sort of spy, I would have woke him right away. However, I could at least hold off until the zombie threat proved to be something worth worrying about.

I positioned myself so that I could intercept anything coming in from the direction we had traveled. So far, the moans were in the direction that we were headed. Maddy had sent two people out with torches as a precaution. They had laid them on the road at about ten and then twenty or so yards out. That would give us plenty of heads-up if this was a mob.

It only sounded like one, maybe two. A few zombies are really no big deal; but it was also clear that these guys were spooked. They obviously wanted to be ready for the worst case scenario. None of us were ready to see our missing scout come shambling into view.

Chick was a mess. His belly had been ripped open, and a zombie had taken a pretty big bite out of his face. It was almost unrecognizable. In fact, the only reason I knew it was Chick was the clothes he was wearing. However, there was one more disturbing thing about the Chick zombie. He had an arrow jutting from the back of each meaty thigh. A shot like that would make it hard to walk, much less run. This indicated that somebody had brought Chick down so that the zombies could get him. Of course, if the crossbow bolts jutting from his legs did not give it away. The ball gag in his mouth certainly did the trick.

"What the…" I heard one of the men gasp as we got a good look at Chick—what was left of him at any rate.

He and another zombie stumbled to the first torch, seemed to regard it for a minute, and then headed for the second. Once they passed that one and approached our camp, I figured that his buddies would take them down. Instead, they spread out a bit, took down the stranger, and then just observed him as he would go for first one of them, and then another.

I started to get up, but Jim grabbed my arm and pulled me down. "You don't learn very well," he breathed.

I turned to see Jim standing there, but my eyes darted to his bed. There was a Jim-shaped lump in it. I looked up at him and he pulled me back while easing down beside his bedroll.

"Okay, Biff, take him down," Maddy finally barked.

A large man that looked like a shaved gorilla with a blond crewcut stomped forward and drove a large knife into Chick's head. The corpse toppled and then his friends, or whatever these people were, moved in and gathered around the body. They started pointing and mumbling to each other.

Meanwhile, Jim was taking pine branches from his bed roll and just sort of feeding them into the fire or tossing them into the shadows. I watched him and then turned back to our escorts. They were engaged in their own thing and did not seem to be paying us any attention. I guess that was a good thing for Jim. He had all evidence of his little ruse disposed of and they had not been any the wiser.

That night, Suzi's people split themselves in half and kept

watch. Apparently they were not content with just one person keeping lookout. I wanted morning to hurry up and get here.

It didn't.

Morning eventually came with a harsh toe to my side. I rolled over on the defensive to see Maddy walking away. She did not even glance back as she went to her gear and shouldered her pack. She did say that things would be different from here on when we traveled.

I still wanted to talk to Jim about last night. I would have asked him then, but the sentries were walking the perimeter of our camp which had been condensed significantly. Maddy wanted us all in close for pretty obvious reasons. I was still amazed that they did not suspect us of this attack.

Jim and I started shouldering our gear, but one of the other women came over to me. "You and me, kid." She stood with her hands on her hips and an expectant look on her face.

Did she mean we were going to fight? I glanced at Jim who currently wore no expression at all as he looked from me to the she-giant.

"Umm..." I started, but then the last of the saliva dried up in my mouth and no more words would come out.

"We have first scout patrol. Give your pack to one of the guys, keep just your canteen, your knife, and your machete."

I am pretty sure my look of relief gave me up, but for added measure, I let a huge sigh escape my lips. "Thank God," I whispered.

The woman gave me a strange look and then walked over to her own gear. I noticed that she was strapping on some extra protection in the form of shin guards and even a helmet with a flip down visor. None of that for me, though. I had jeans and a heavy shirt with a leather jacket and gloves.

I was given a tin cup of lukewarm and watered down oatmeal and then we were told to get started and that Maddy and the rest of the group would be heading out in about an hour at best. With that, the big woman gave me a little shove and we were on the road.

I remember the first time I had walked this pass on the way

to Island City. I recall how amazed and overwhelmed I was with seeing the world. Now, as sad as it seemed, I just wanted to be home. I wanted to see Melissa and Stevie, Billy, and Dr. Zahn. Hell I would even be happy to see Kayla Brockhouse.

"Name's Sylvia," the woman muttered as we climbed over a section of the road that had buckled.

"Thalia," I replied.

A grunt of some sort was her only response to that. We had not gone on another ten minutes when we came across what had obviously been where Chick was ambushed. Sylvia motioned for me to stop as she made an inspection of the area. I looked around and tried to figure out what might have happened by what I saw.

The only thing that I was certain of was that Chick had taken down three zombies. The area where that little scuffle took place was a dark stain on the asphalt. One of the zombies had both arms ripped off. I was admittedly impressed. Eventually, Sylvia either had enough information or decided to give up and motioned for us to resume.

I wanted to talk to this woman. I wanted to ask her how she could feel good about living the way Suzi ran things. The only problem with that was the fact that this woman scared the bee-jeezus out of me.

"Hold up!" she whispered all of a sudden.

I had been walking along minding my own business. I had not really known why I was chosen to join on this little venture, but I quickly found out.

Sylvia moved over by me and I assumed that it was so we could have each other's backs if another ambush came.

Nope.

Her arm whipped out and coiled around my neck so fast, that I barely had time to blink, much less make any attempt to get away. She pulled my body against hers and then turned to the left. I could feel her hunch down to use as much of my body for cover as she could. Sadly for her, it wasn't much.

I heard a sound and then felt Sylvia's arm sort of tighten for just a second and then go completely slack. Unfortunately for me, it didn't exactly go slack in time to keep her from dragging me off my feet. I rolled over as quickly as I could and found myself looking into her dead eyes. Oh…and there was a knife sticking out of one eye socket. I guess she should have pulled down that visor.

I pushed away and was trying to get to my feet while drawing my machete. My eyes went to the crossbow, but it had actually slipped from Sylvia's shoulder and skittered a few feet away. I was stuck out in the middle of the wide open highway with the nearest cover much too far for me to have even half of a chance of making it.

"Thalia Hobart!" a voice called.

I wanted to cry. Never in my life had hearing Paula Yin's voice sounded so good. When she stepped out from behind a derelict and rusted out old car, I could not help it. I did cry. The tears started and I wondered for a few seconds if maybe they might not ever stop. At this point, I might have had the same reaction if it had been Kayla. Probably not…but maybe.

Several more figures emerged from the woods on both sides of the highway, but my vision was too blurry for me to make out faces. However, voices were no problem.

"Thalia!" a familiar voice boomed. A second later, I was scooped up and spun around in a huge circle.

"Billy!" I squealed, although I seriously doubt anybody could make out my words between my throat being a pinhole and Billy squeezing the little air I did manage to get into my lungs right back out in a whoosh.

"You look like warmed over crap, kiddo," Billy said as he put me down.

I started babbling incoherently as I tried to tell him about everything that had happened to us in the span of one or two actual breaths. He held up his hands and told me to slow down. It took a lot of control, but at last I was able to tell him, Paula, and the others gathered around a good outline of my story. I know I left a lot out, but I was pretty sure that I had given them all of the important bits.

"So Jim will be coming this way soon?" Billy asked.

"He should be with the rest of our escorts. The thing is, they were pretty spooked by whatever happened to Chick. They might pull up again if Sylvia doesn't check in. I have no idea what their system is, but it would seem likely that they will not just keep moving. As it was, our scout rotation seemed to be every few hours," I offered.

"I think Jim has them pegged for about half the norm," Billy said.

"What? How do you know that?" I gasped.

"He slipped out of camp the first night and got a message to us. He has a network of runners at communities all over. They sent a guy on horseback. We rode most of the way here and then left our horses at one of the trading posts a ways up the road."

I was floored. My thoughts of how I had been suspicious of him started to creep up on me and I stuffed them. I really should have known better; Jim was one of the greatest and most won-derful men I knew. How could I have ever thought him capable of being a mole? I knew now that I would have to come clean with him some day, otherwise my guilt would eat me alive.

"I owe that mop head a freaking bucket of beer," Paula groused, snapping me back to the situation.

"A bucket of beer for what?" I asked.

"I told him that you would have known that he slipped out. He said that you were clueless and had bought into him being injured just like your escorts," Paula grumbled.

"We can worry about that later," Billy said, sounding all business. "Give me the rundown on this group. I want numbers, weapons, and how they travel. We probably have about ten minutes to get in place, so be quick."

"Didn't Jim tell you?" I asked.

"Yes, but it always helps to use an old carpenter's trick…measure twice, cut once. I just want to be as sure as pos-sible."

I gave them the report, was handed Sylvia's crossbow, and then joined Paula where she would be waiting as we set up this ambush. I was just getting into my spot when a thought hit me hard.

"What about Jackson?" I turned to Paula.

"One thing at a time," the woman said as she brought her binoculars to her eyes.

"But that place is huge, and he is being kept in a cage in dang near the center of camp. It ain't like we are gonna be able to just slip in and save him," I insisted.

"And I said one thing at a time," Paula snapped. Nice to know some things never change.

I stayed quiet for a minute, but then I had another thought. "Have you ever heard or read about a guy named Randall Flagg?"

Paula looked at me with those dark eyes of hers and I wanted to crawl under a rock. "Of course I have. He is a character in an old Stephen King book. Some sort of amalgam of the devil and the boogeyman. He had powers, but he could look like a normal guy. He used the typical animals like crows to spy on the good guys. Why do you ask?"

"Could somebody like that exist?" I pressed, ignoring the question.

"No. That is just fiction."

"Didn't they used to say that about zombies?"

Paula was quiet for a minute, and then she turned on her side to face me. "Why are you asking about this stuff?"

"The leader of that army down in the valley? Her people say that she knows things, and I think they are convinced that she was behind the death of their friend. They were really spooked."

"Yeah, you can thank Jim for that as well. He fed that crap to you knowing that they were listening. It was like telling ghosts stories when you are camping. Now every snapping twig is the crazed killer come for his victims," Paula said with a smile. "That guy is frightening the way his mind works. Sounds like he got them scared out of their pants."

"So then there is no way that Suzi has some sort of powers or magic working for her?" I asked, needing to be reassured.

"It is all a bunch of superstitious nonsense," Paula said. "No!" she exclaimed when I continued to look at her with obvious doubt all over my face.

I turned back to the road. I was torn between still holding on to some sense of doubt and feeling like a complete moron, and accepting Paula's answer.

I was still going over it in my head when I saw something. Coming up the road was the leading element of my escort. I could make out Maddy as she led the way. She was joined by four others. Next came Jim, his limp as well as his being about half the size of the huge man who walked beside him with a crossbow in his hands easy to distinguish. Last were the remaining five members of the group.

This was about to become a slaughter. I shoved thoughts of Jackson out of my head. They had rescued me, we were about to rescue Jim. They would obviously have something in mind for Jackson. Just because I could not think of something did not mean that these more experienced people like Billy, Paula, and Jim did not have a plan already brewing.

"Now!" Paula whispered.

7

Vignettes LXIII

Juan sat on the log watching Della and Denita. Apparently, Gerald had been very thorough in his training. And while Juan was a bit annoyed by how some stranger could tell his girls that their dad might go "live with their mom" or some such nonsense, he couldn't really fault the guy. It was not the world he grew up in.

Juan returned his attention to his daughters. Della was standing in the open field. She was singing "Itsy Bitsy Spider" at the top of her lungs while the deader staggered her direction.

This particular zombie looked like the sort of man that had lived most of his life in the Alaskan Wilderness. His beard hung down almost to his belt and was a macabre nest of all sorts of bugs and might have given home to a nest of rodents at some point. His end looked like perhaps it had come at some of the wolves. One arm was shredded and torn up. The bones of the forearm had been snapped at some point between the elbow and wrist. However, there were some other nasty rips and tears on his legs as well that just did not look like they came from a human zombie.

Juan finally spotted Denita; she was slipping up behind the deader, moving at least quiet enough that neither he nor the walker could hear her approach. At last, she was close enough and came in with a brutal swing of her club. The barrel of it caught the zombie right behind the knees. Then, like sharks in a frenzy, both girls were on the monster, swinging hard and fast until the head busted open.

"I win!" Della crowed.

That was another peculiar aspect to this little event. The girls had turned it into a contest. Whoever struck the blow that broke open the skull was declared the winner.

"Nice work, girls," Juan called from his comfortable spot sitting on the log. "So how many of these deaders have you two killed now?"

"Thirty-seven if we get to count those yucky wolves."

That had been something that Juan would like to bring up with Gerald when he got back. Killing the human versions was one thing, and the wolves were not that much more agile, but they often travelled in small packs as well as being a tiny bit faster. He was not entirely sure that he was okay with his girls being put in that much danger.

"Daddy," Della said, both girls now suddenly stopping in their tracks and looking at him with odd expressions etched on their faces.

"You girls ready for lunch?" Juan asked.

"Don't move," Denita whispered.

In an instant, the two girls split up, each moving out wide of his location. They were looking at something behind him. Juan craned his neck and spotted the problem right away. It was almost prophetic. Heading his direction in their strange swaggering gait were five deader wolves.

"Girls, you need to get back to the cabin," Juan warned.

A lone walker was one thing, but a small pack of wolves? That was an entirely different story. He doubted his own ability to withstand such an attack. He also knew that he would not be able to escape using the crutches. While deader wolves were not much more coordinated than their human counterparts, they could still move at a pace equal to a slow jog or fast walk. That was a speed that Juan was not able to reach at this time. They would drag him down long before he reached the safety of the cabin.

Suddenly, he was very thankful that Gerald seemed to have made it a point to teach some more advanced survival skills to his girls. They were about to become orphans, and it looked like he would be reuniting with Mackenzie sooner rather than later.

The girls did not seem to be taking his demand that they go back to the cabin with any seriousness at all. They were both crouched and had moved past him. They were on either side of the pack and almost even with them at this point.

"This isn't some game, girls. Now do what I told you and get your butts back to that cabin!" Juan snapped, putting his "serious dad" voice in effect for good measure.

"Keep talking, Papi," Della whispered barely loud enough for him to hear. "That will keep them focused on you."

"Dammit, I said this isn't some sort of game. Those are wolves, and there are five of them. Now get back to the cabin."

It was as if his girls had suddenly gone stone cold deaf. They did not even glance his direction. The two tiny figures continued to creep along. At this point, they had gotten past the deader wolves and were now changing course to come up from behind. Meanwhile, the wolves were not making any attempts to approach faster than their stalking creep. It freaked Juan out to watch what was almost a drunken parody of these once beautiful animals as they crept closer.

There had been many discussions about how deaders seemed to hold on to certain instincts. That had become part of the theory about why the children acted so different. Most children were wary of strangers after a certain age. If some sort of vestigial instinct remained, then that was as good of a reason as any. Personally, Juan's stance was that all zombies were bad and needed to be taken down.

"Us or them," had been his mantra for quite some time. Of course, he applied that to the living, the undead, child zombie, wolf, or just plain deader.

"You girls are in big trouble when we get home," Juan warned as he drew his machete.

That acted like a switch. Just as with the child zombie that

99

would ignore or even shy away from a person, the moment that weapon was drawn, the game changed and they reverted to their primary function: kill the living.

"Papi!" Denita scolded. "You did it too soon!"

Juan bit back a comment that would only be fitting if he were to use it directed at an adult. Besides, he had bigger problems; the first wolf came within range and Juan brought his machete down on the top of its flat head.

At that exact moment, both his girls let out blood-curdling shrieks.

**

Vix acted on instinct and rolled to her left just in time to avoid the huge mining pick that came down and plunged into the ground where her head had been only a moment before. Having never changed her values when it came to being out in the wasteland that was now all that remained of her beloved England, Vix was wearing her boots as well as her weapon in her bed roll.

With one smooth move, she drew the machete as she scooted and rolled one more time to come out of her bedroll that she always left unzipped for just such emergencies. She was on her belly and had to shift to the side in order to swing her weapon. She did not get much behind it, but it was enough for the heavy blade to bite into a foolishly unprotected shin.

Her efforts were rewarded with a yelp of pain. In another few heartbeats, she was up in a crouched position. Part of her was now thankful for the fire; however, she was not sure that hadn't been what brought these raiders in the first place. Able to see shadowy shapes, she spied two figures hunched down over somebody who was struggling and still well tangled in their bedroll. The muffled cry gave it away as Chaaya.

Vix saw a dark form coming at her from the left and ducked just in time. The body slammed into her, but she had managed to set her feet and absorb the collision. She was further rewarded by the person folding over her back. Standing, Vix sent the person flipping over and onto the ground with a loud "oof" as the air was forced from his or her lungs.

Not waiting for the person to recover, Vix stepped over and brought her weapon down hard. She knew from experience how jarring a shot to the skull could be for a person's hands, but she still winced at the stinging sensation. Her next move brought her to the man on the ground holding his shin and wailing. She silenced him with another swing, this one cutting into the much softer tissue of the throat.

Rushing over to Chaaya's attackers, Vix caught the first one off guard and drove the belt knife she'd drawn along the way into the small of the back were the kidneys should be located. She'd opted for the smaller, easier to wield weapon now that she was not simply trying to hack her way free. The person crumbled, unable to even yelp as the pain was so completely devastating.

She saw Chaaya holding the wrist of her attacker, a large knife inches from her face. Wasting no time to allow the person to register the loss of his accomplice, Vix plunged her dagger into the side of the man's neck and then gave an added kick to send the body sprawling.

She was just leaning down to give Chaaya a hand up when a strangled whimper came from the darkness. Vix ended up giving the Indian woman an unceremonious yank to her feet before dashing to the sounds of pain coming from just beyond the light of the fire.

It was Marjorie.

The woman was on her side, the shadows making her little more than a dark blob. Even once Vix was kneeling at her side, she could barely make out any details. Between the sudden transition from the campfire to the darkness, and the lack of any moon or even starlight to see by, she was basically blind.

"My side," the woman gasped. Vix leaned over and ran her hand along the woman until she reached the warm wetness of blood. Her hand stopped when it came to the hilt of the weapon that was jammed between Marjorie's ribs.

"Just be still," Vix shifted into her nursing mode and spoke in soft comforting tones to the woman. She eased Marjorie's head into her lap and stroked her brow as Chaaya arrived.

"They did in poor Gordon," she whispered. "Nasty business that. Looks like he was hit in the chest by a pick-axe."

Vix shuddered. Luck of the draw was the only thing that had prevented her fate from being identical.

"How's Marjorie?"

"She's gonna be fine," Vix whispered, knowing it to be a blatant lie. The woman was fading fast. She simply saw no point in letting Marjorie's last seconds be ones of dread.

It was no more than another five or ten minutes before she felt the woman give a slight tremor, a wheeze, and then one final exhale. Vix eased from under Marjorie's head and climbed to her feet.

"I thought…" Chaaya's voice faded as Vix stepped past her and went straight to the campfire.

"We are leaving this place right now."

Vix began kicking dirt onto the fire. Part of her considered leaving it in case another band of miscreants decided to come look for their friends, but she decided against it. That fire would give them a specific location to start from if there was a search.

After gathering up a few of the more choice weapons used by their attackers, Vix started off. Chaaya did not say a word, but simply fell in beside her as they pushed into some tall over-growth that was probably once a farmer's field.

"Are we going back?" Chaaya asked.

"Nope," Vix grunted as she pulled herself up and over a stone wall that was just a shade taller than waist high. "Wherever these blokes came from, it is close by. I want to get someplace where I can look around for any signs of them."

"Okay, first, how do you know that they came from some-place close? And second, what do you plan to do once you find them? There are only two of us."

"They weren't even carrying water. They had to come from someplace nearby. And I will figure out that next bit once I see what we are dealing with."

That seemed to satisfy Chaaya. At last, Vix found what

she'd been searching for. She knew that there had been a power line tower in the area. If she could climb it, she might be able to find where her attackers had come from. And as for her plan…as always, she did not actually have one. They always got blown to hell anyway.

***

"You have to be checked out by the doc, and you will need to fill out a survey about what skills you possess. Also, until you have completed your three month trial, you have to stay in the temp shack. Good news on that is that we haven't had a resident in temp for over five months, so it will be all yours for now," Daryl Sheppard said as he walked along the wide path, pointing out a large building with a huge grassy area in front.

"You still get many folks coming in?" Chad asked.

He was interested in the answer, but at the moment, he was more interested in a single-file line of a dozen children being walked along the banks of the lake by a lanky man with a guitar on his back. He hadn't seen that many children of the living variety in one place since Dustin's compound. Even then, he didn't recall anything like this. None of them could be older than six or seven. That meant every single one had been born post-apocalypse.

"Not so much these days. Last influx came just over a year ago. Some folks from the Lake Tahoe area. Some warlord wanna-be invaded them and basically took all the women, executed the men. A dozen or so managed to escape," Daryl replied. "Hard to believe that people are the biggest threat these days."

Chad nodded, an uncomfortable laugh escaping his lips. "Yeah, we've seen enough of that ourselves."

"Smart idea, by the way," the man said with a shake of the head. "Can't ever be too sure anymore."

Chad chewed on the inside of his cheek a bit as he tried to figure out the best way to bring up his next and largest reason for apprehension. He looked around at what would amount to a paradise as far as Ronni was concerned. The fact that they were this close, but still so far, was plunging daggers of anxiety into his heart.

"I guess I got one more question." Chad stopped and waited for Daryl to face him. "What is this place's stance on people who show immunity?"

"That's the million dollar question, ain't it?" Daryl laughed. "We had a rough experience with that sort of thing back in the early days. Thing is, we learned how to deal with it. Even have a simple blood test that tells if you will show immunity."

Chad's expression must have changed drastically because the man held up his hands. His smile was still there, and it looked genuine all the way to his eyes. Still, Chad could not help it.

"No, we don't shoot people up with tainted blood or anything like that. We are lucky to have honest to goodness doctors here. They worked like crazy for the first few years. We lost some folks bringing in things that they would require to run tests. Even had a bit of a rift over what was more of a priority, the solar grid or the little devices that the doctors needed. Came to blows at a few of the council meetings."

"Wait." Chad held up his hands to stop the man. "Solar grid? I didn't see any solar grid."

"We keep it on the far side of the community. Way back in the day, we rationalized that we would probably get more people coming north from California than we would coming south from Oregon and Washington. We figured that would be the first place that bad guys would want to hit."

"Wow, you guys thought of everything."

"Trust me, this is the result of years of trial and error...mostly error." Again Daryl let loose with a good-natured laugh. "Anyways, we have a blood test that is part of your "welcome to Green Springs" package."

"I guess I will go get the ladies," Chad finally said after another long look around.

"We can send an escort if you like," Daryl offered.

"No thanks," Chad replied with a shake of his head.

He was escorted to what was apparently only one of six entry gates to the community. He shook hands with Daryl as well as the guards who all seemed more than happy to allow him inside when he first arrived. That had actually been his first question. Daryl had pointed to a dozen men and women up on the catwalks that ran the entire length of the walls that kept this place safe. Each of them held a crossbow cradled in their arms.

"We have different protocols based on the number of refugees that show up at our gate. Plus, it is quite likely that you passed at least a dozen of our perimeter sentries. If even one of them had considered you a threat, they would have signaled back to the gates and a welcoming party would have been here instead of just me. Hell, if you would have been a woman, then Sheila or Annette would have been the person to greet you. We even have a few of the younger folks trained in the off chance that a kid arrives at our gates."

As Chad walked back to Caroline and Ronni, he could not help but be impressed. Every step saw his nervous excitement grow. By the time he reached the highway and could see the area where the ladies were supposed to be camped, he was a bundle of nerves.

It was all too simple. Too convenient. How was it that they had gone this long and found nothing even remotely resembling Green Springs? As he crossed the highway, a new feeling replaced his excitement.

Fear.

Surely Caroline and Ronni would have seen him cross the interstate. Yet, he was almost all the way up the hill and not only did he not see any sign of them, but Caroline would have made her presence known and come to greet him and ask what he'd found.

Suddenly, the feeling that he should have never left them behind hit him with the force of a fist to the gut. How could he have been so careless?

***

"What!" Jody actually staggered backwards a step. He was

not sure if he was relieved, or even more suspicious.

"I overheard a couple of them talking about it last night in the tavern. Didn't recognize either of them. I guess I thought that it was just a lot of big talk from a couple of guys who had too much to drink." Jody's expression had obviously changed to reflect his thoughts. Danny threw up his hands. "I swear, pal, I never once gave it a moment of credence."

"So why the sudden change?" Jody spat, his distrust showing clearly as he took a step back, his hand absently drifting over one of his belt knives. "Seems awful strange that you are here all suited up out of the blue if you didn't take these bastards seriously."

"Because I told him to meet me here," a voice called from behind.

Jody spun in a flash of movement that had his knife drawn and in hand before he completed the hundred and eighty degree spin. His hand shot out quick and he had this newest arrival by the throat. With one swift sweep of his foot, he knocked the new arrival's legs out from under him and was straddling the man's chest before the person could do anything to defend himself.

"Jody, no!" Danny barked.

"Stay the fuck back!" Jody growled. The he turned his attention back to the man on the ground with a razor sharp blade to the throat, just a hint of blood already trickling from where the skin had been nicked. "As for you..."

"Jody, I am here to help," Tracy Sasser said in a hoarse whisper. His eyes were wide with fear and a single bead of sweat was already beginning to trickle down the man's temple.

"Is that right?" Jody said, his lips curling up in an ugly snarl. He allowed just a slight hint of an increase in pressure as his hand flexed on the grip of the bone handled hunting knife.

"Yes," Tracy managed, although it was a strangled sound as his ability to swallow was now becoming more uncomfortable with each passing second.

"He was working in the bar last night," Danny called. "He heard everything after I left. He came to my house this morning and told me that those guys had not been kidding. He said they snatched little Alana from the back yard this morning."

"And just how would you know that?" Jody pressed just a bit harder. It was now a simple matter of sliding his hand to the right and the man's throat would be slashed, his jugular sending a geyser of blood across the sidewalk.

"Because I live behind you and over to the left one house," Tracy squeaked. "I heard Selina's cry."

Jody stared into the man's eyes once more. He saw fear, uncertainty...and honesty? If the eyes were supposedly the window to the soul, these were wide open.

"Why didn't you come to me sooner?" Jody eased the blade away revealing a long thin line of blood that was seeping from the three or four inch cut.

"Because I am afraid this is bigger than anything I can handle. And I needed somebody who could convince you that I wasn't part of the plan. You don't know me from Adam. Danny has been staying across the street from me since his rehab. I knew you guys were buddies once." Tracy climbed slowly to his feet, brushing himself off as he did.

Jody gave the man a once over and realized that he was obviously not a soldier. And if he was, then he was a supply type and not a front line sort. Nobody ever looked more out of place with his weapons than Tracy Sasser.

That made Jody recall how they met. The two of them had helped lower Danny when he'd been in that cage after the women had hobbled him. Tracy had gotten sick at the sight of Danny's injuries. He had demonstrated obvious distaste for what George and Margarita had inflicted upon Jan Sieber, the woman they were supposedly going to question about the tower deaths.

"I'm coming as well."

Speaking of Jan, Jody thought as he looked to see the woman come up from behind Danny. He was only a little concerned that she had her own crossbow loaded and pointed in his general direction.

"Okay...and how did *you* know?" Jody sighed, sliding his knife into its place on his belt.

"Tracy and I have been roomies for a while," Jan said with a shrug.

"Now let's get rolling," Danny spoke, clapping his hands together once for emphasis.

"Yeah..." Jody let that word drag out a bit. His eyes drifted down to Danny's feet and then snapped back up as soon as he realized what he was doing.

"Oh no you don't, Rafe," Danny protested, turning and starting up the road. His limp would have been comical any other time but this.

"Sorry, Danny," Jody apologized as he trotted to get ahead of his friend. "I would love to have you at my side for this, but you know as well as I do that you are a liability."

"Kiss my ass."

"He's right," Tracy added. Jan nodded her agreement as she patted the man on the shoulder and walked past him. Jody quickly realized that they obviously knew exactly where they were headed.

"You could do me a solid and go sit with Selina. Partially so she has somebody to talk to, partially because I need somebody to watch her and the baby. I could not think of anybody better." Jody squeezed his friend's arm and then jogged after Tracy and Jan.

"As I understand it, you know where they took my girl?" Jody asked as soon as he caught up.

"Yep," Jan answered. "They took her to Pitts' place."

***

Entry Nineteen—

It has rained for three days straight. I am wet and cold and miserable. If I feel like this, then either that woman has already killed the child, she is long gone, or I simply went the wrong direction when I tossed my coin.

I admit, it is not the most scientific method to use on a search for a missing person, but I am not nearly skilled enough to sniff a footprint or see a crease on a leaf. Finding a person who does not want to be found is damn near impossible these days. This is a big chunk of land, and you can be a hundred yards from another person and not have even the slightest clue.

As I sit under this rocky overhang where about forty percent of my body can stay out of the soaking downpour, I realized that I am probably not as smart as I like to believe. Take the guy who recognized me back at the settlement. I figured it might be because I am a pretty big dude. Not for a moment did it cross my mind that the huge tomahawk I wear on my hip might actually give me away.

While handheld weapons are simply a part of everybody's outfit these days, not many people sport a yard long 'hawk with an ornately hand carved handle. That is probably the sort of thing that stands out in a person's mind.

I think I will double back in the morning. There is a trade route not far. I might be able to hear something from a passing merchant or settler.

Entry Twenty—

I was just waking up from almost no sleep, when I heard the sound of a baby cry. The thing is, back in the early days, that sound probably got a lot of people killed. I think we have all heard that noise at least once and been scared into a brown streak when we happened upon the undead source.

The thing is, all these years later, you can actually tell the difference without hardly even trying. This was an actual baby crying. I had no doubt.

I didn't even finish putting my gear into my pack. I just yanked my tomahawk free and took off. I would not say that I am much of a runner. I am like a bear crashing through the woods, only, not quite as graceful.

I was damn near killed when I reached an embankment. The ground was soaked and I made the rookie nature boy mistake of grabbing a small sapling to hold my weight as I started down. The sapling came out by the roots—something that might have just as easily happened if the ground hadn't been saturated considering it was so small and I am so…not.

I ended up falling head over heels down the embankment

and ended up in a trench about twenty feet long and a few inches deep that was full of muddy water. Of course, when I stood up, it was damn near empty. I had become the human version of SpongeBob Dirtypants. What my clothing did not soak up, I must have swallowed or snorted up my nose.

By the time I quit hacking and throwing up mud, the only sound I heard was that of my own labored breathing. I was now cold, completely soaked...and pissed. I try my best never to let my emotions get the best of me when I am out on these runs. The woman better pray that I don't find her in the next day or two.

Of course I can't even say for certain that it was her and the missing child. In my mind, I am at least eighty percent sure; but that does not cut it. Nor does it make me any warmer or drier.

Entry twenty-one—

I spent most of today walking in a growing circle outwards from where I found the camp this morning. I will give the woman credit, she knows what she is doing out here. She had a nice Dakota hole dug which is why I never saw a fire.

The only mistake, if it truly was one, was that she did not make any effort to hide the fact that a camp had been here. Sure, there is a chance that the place was not even her old camp, but I go off my gut. My gut says it was her.

Besides, there are not a lot of women just roaming the countryside with babies these days. Zombies aside, the wilderness is thick with outlaws and bad guys. Of course I am being general, but that is a simple fact.

No, not every single person out in the world is an evil bastard waiting to victimize others, but those numbers are much higher now percentage-wise than they were back before zombies wiped out the infrastructure. It is a fact.

And for those who might say that perhaps I am just jaded considering the types of filth that I deal with on a regular basis, I would like to point out that we as a species have always had that disposition. And when allowed to run free and unchecked by any sort of law or authority, we are downright evil. The old history books are full of horrors that are hard to imagine.

That was something that Americans really put on blinders to back in the day. The horrible things happening to the oppressed were just bits and blurbs on a newscast. We could ignore them because they were so far away. We only really took offense or became outraged when a single person would commit a horrific act and get caught. Then we acted all surprised that a person could be so base and terrible.

I maintain that it has always been there. Don't believe me? Find a book about the Holocaust or even some of the ethnic cleansing that took places in Yugoslavia, the Middle East, and parts of Africa.

Geek Wife on the Edge

Catie moved down the side street. She might be a few months pregnant, but she was still surprisingly light on her feet and capable of stealth. Still, as happy as she was with her own ability, that did not hold a candle to how surprised she was at Melvin's ability to be just as quiet.

Melvin was Marty's "little" brother. Catie had not been all that surprised to discover that the two were, in fact, twins. Melvin had been born second; thus the whole thing about him being the little brother.

Catie raised a hand. They were at an intersection. The residential neighborhood they were currently moving through was supposedly the location of the Beastie Boys' main hideout. They had spotted a pair of men in hooded sweatshirts walking down the middle of the street about ten minutes ago. They had stayed just about a block behind them, yet, somehow, the two had managed to disappear after rounding a corner. At no time had they given any indication that they knew they were being followed.

Melvin tapped Catie on the shoulder and pointed to the right. Catie's gaze followed the direction the man indicated. Sure enough, the two men were on the roof of a building across the street. By the looks of it, the building had been a school. The signage had long since fallen or been ripped down, but most schools were easy to identify.

Catie spotted the second team just a block over. The man leading that group was obviously not paying attention. Of course that was not a big surprise. He had a real burr under his butt about the fact that Dean had made it clear that Catie was in charge of this mission.

Clarence Carson was the second in command for the security teams in the community of Montague Village. He was a stout man in his own right. Not the size of the Wilson twins, Marty and Melvin, but not a small man by any sense of the imagination. He had long blond hair and a baby face that, despite the man's age, looked like it might seldom have the need for a razor. His blue eyes were hard and cruel, and Catie did not think the man capable of smiling.

Catie stifled a chuckle when the man stopped suddenly and staggered backwards. Marty gave a wave after he made a point of trying to offer the man a hand up. He did not seem the least bit bothered or offended when Clarence slapped the offered hand away.

"How do you want to do this?" Melvin whispered.

Catie considered things a moment before answering. "You two," she pointed to a pair of men she had not bothered to learn the names of, "go scout the perimeter. Do it fast, but do it quietly. Take notice of any type of roving patrols or anybody that you might see stationed on the roof. Once you do a full circuit, one of you report back here and the other report to the other team. Let them know they will be staying back in reserve if we decide to venture in."

The two men nodded and disappeared into the darkness. Catie gave everybody the signal to stand down, but she grabbed Melvin by the sleeve and took him out of hearing range. After making certain that nobody would be able to listen in, she filled the man in on her plan. He remained silent and did not interrupt with any questions. Once she finished, she waited. If she made a mistake, then this was going to be over before it began. She hoped to God that she was not wrong in her assumptions about the twins.

"You need Marty to be in on this," the big man finally rumbled.

Catie hid her sigh of relief and said, "Yes, but I drew you on my team, so I told you first. I will leave it to you to let him know. I don't imagine you guys have some sort of creepy twin telepathy?"

Melvin laughed, covering his mouth with one hand. "You're funny. You know that crap just exists in the movies, right?"

"It was worth a shot."

"Anybody else in on this?"

"Not officially," Catie said with a shake of her head. "We do have two others who I am pretty sure are on board."

"The older lady and the little girl?" Melvin's expression darkened. "You aren't giving us much to work with here. And if this don't work, then we are screwed nine ways to Sunday."

"I know, but I am willing to take a chance. The question is whether you and your brother are, and if so, how likely do you think it will be for others to follow suit?"

"If me and Marty are in, all we need to do is say the word. You ain't the first one to think of this. Just seems funny that you are the first to act. You been in Montague...what? A week?"

"Something like that," Catie said with a shrug.

"I'll go pull Marty aside and fill him in. I think it is best we do that before you put phase one of your little scheme into action."

Catie nodded and the man vanished into the shadows. She could not help but be impressed. *A man that size should not be able to disappear so readily*, she thought.

She waited for him to return. He did so only a moment ahead of the patrol, nodding in affirmation that his brother was apparently on board.

"Nobody on the roof and no sign of any type of roving patrol," the man reported.

"They are either very confident, or very stupid," Catie muttered. She was not sure which she preferred. "Okay, bring everybody in," Catie said after appearing to consider the situation for a moment.

The other team was signaled over and they retreated around the corner from the school just to be certain that they would not be detected. Catie scanned the faces and hoped that this next part of her plan went smoothly.

"This is where it gets dicey, ladies and gentlemen." She let her gaze drift around to the faces staring back at her. Not surprising, Clarence was visibly scowling at her. "I need a few volunteers to join me. The plan is for me and those who step forward to go inside. They could be anywhere, so we will be conducting a room-by-room search."

"And how does that assure that you find the leader?" Clarence challenged. "You just gonna kill everybody you encounter and hope you eventually find the right man?"

"Nope, but applying the right pressure to whoever we do find will likely yield results," Catie answered with a smile and a wink that made Clarence bristle. "Since this will likely be the most dangerous part of the operation, I don't want to force anybody. I will only take volunteers." Before anybody could speak or step forward, Catie raised a finger. "Except for you, Clarence. You are coming."

The man pressed his lips tight, but he stayed silent. Both Marty and Melvin stepped forward, along with Kalisha and a young man not much older than his late teens. Catie fought the desire to tell the young man he could not be part of the team. Yet, she could not raise any possible suspicion now that the wheels were in motion. She shot a glance at Denise, but the woman did not budge. That was a little upsetting. While she had not divulged her plan to the woman, Denise did know that Catie had something in mind. Also, she would be the lone immune with these other unknowns. It would make things complicated, but again, she could not risk things at this point.

"Okay, you all fall back to that little house." Catie pointed. "It is directly across the street and will provide a good view. If you see anything suspicious, deal with it. If we are not out before sunrise, head back to Montague."

There were assorted nods and sounds of confirmation. With that, Catie and her five person team slipped away into the darkness. They reached the front door of the school. Melvin gave it a tug and it opened with no problem. Once again, Catie was unsure what to think.

The hallway was a four-way intersection. Looking left and right, Catie decided to continue straight ahead when there was not a single glow that might indicate somebody was inside one of the rooms. That much was a least a little reassuring.

The next intersection yielded more of the same. They were now out of the range of any sort of ambient light and Catie popped one of the glow sticks. It seemed almost as bright as a flare compared to the relative darkness of a moment before. They only had one more intersection and then they would be forced to choose a direction. They reached it, and Catie peered around the corner.

Eureka, she thought. To the right, five doorways in a row had a soft glow coming from the tall, skinny windows. Stuffing the glow stick in her pocket, Catie stepped back and relayed the findings. She told the team that she would creep to the first window and look in to see what they might be facing. Nobody objected.

Catie only had to hide her smile until she rounded the corner and started down the corridor. Before too long, she was at the first doorway. She crouched down and peeked inside. Her blood went cold and she suddenly felt like a fool.

The room was empty!

She spun in time to see her team coming around the corner with hands in the air and at least twenty people fanned out around them. She had been so confident. Now she felt like an idiot.

"How about you come on over and join your friends," a man growled. It was not a request.

Catie laced her fingers behind her head and walked back up the hallway. They were marched back the way they had come in and taken back to the previous intersection and to the right. They stopped at a set of double doors and then were escorted inside.

It was the gymnasium. There were no windows, but the set of doors across the way was open. They passed a dozen or so fairly large cubicles that had men and women in them. Most were asleep, but a few were up reading or playing a board game around a card table.

They went out the other double doors to a covered area that looked like it had once been the playground. A handful of tents were here. The fence that kept this area secure was covered with heavy, dark tarp. A man was standing at the entrance of what looked like it had once been a large military tent. As soon as he saw them, he waved for Catie and her team to be escorted over and then ducked inside.

Catie was not certain, but she thought that she heard Kalisha gasp. She started to look around, but the man behind her gave Catie an unceremonious shove in the back and demanded that she keep her eyes forward and continue walking. They reached the large tent and two of their escorts ducked inside. A moment later, they emerged and motioned for everybody to enter.

"Daddy!" Kalisha breathed.

A slender, athletic looking man with dark skin stood waiting with his hands clasped in front of him. His black hair was a wild afro that bobbed just slightly when he moved. A young boy sat on the desk to the right, his head tilted to the side in curiosity as these newcomers entered. There was no doubt as to whose son he was, as well as who his sister might be. As soon as he spied Kalisha, the boy jumped from the desk and started for the girl.

"Kalisha!" the boy squealed.

"Caleb!" the man barked, and the boy skidded to a halt. He edged in front of the confused looking young lad and approached Catie's group. "You have any idea what we do with trespassers? And is that Clarence Carson?"

Catie stepped forward. The two men who had been acting as her escort grabbed her and yanked her backwards, but she spun and swept the feet out from one and brought an elbow into the gut of the other. The sounds of blades being drawn came from everywhere, but the man that Catie had to assume to be Elliot brought everything to a halt.

"Nobody move! My daughter is with these people." The man walked over to Catie and stopped before actually coming

118

within striking range. "Nice moves. You want to tell me what brings you here in the middle of the night with my daughter?"

"Clear the room and we can talk," Catie said, doing her best to sound as cool and collected as her captor.

"Not likely. You just took down two of my guys. I don't think I want to be alone with you. You have something to say, do it. Otherwise…" He gave a nod and there was a strangled cry. Catie spun on instinct, instantly regretting that she had just given her back to this man.

The young boy who had volunteered to join them on the mission was holding his throat, but that wasn't stopping the dark wave of crimson that trickled through his fingers. The man to his right winked at her as he slid his knife back into it place on his belt.

Catie spun back to Elliot who had no readable expression on his face. The man folded his arms across his chest and continued to stare at her, obviously waiting.

"Okay," Catie sighed. She looked over at Marty and Melvin. Both men gave the slightest of nods. She hated playing her cards all at once, but her hand had been forced. She looked back to Elliot. "I came here to make a deal with you. I can help you take back Montague Village."

"You bitch!" Clarence snarled. His curse ended in a wheeze and fit of coughing as he was obviously struck in the gut.

Elliot smiled and went back to his son. He stood beside the boy and put an arm around his shoulder. "Why would you want to do something like that?"

"Because, I think it is crappy that Dean and his group of cronies are treating people who are immune like crap. When you think about it, we are the best shot that humanity has of making it. If anybody should be treated like second class citizens, it is the people who are not immune to this."

Catie could not believe the words coming out of her mouth. At one time, they would have been unthinkable. Yet, time and again she had run into people who thought that those who were immune should be killed. Granted, sometimes they had done things that might have warranted such treatment.

The reality was that she had reached a point in her life where she needed to choose a side. That had been something that Kevin never wanted to be forced into doing. He had some small hope that maybe people could come together and try to eradicate the undead. Catie had always felt that time had passed. Now it was time to make the best of what was left.

"How do you propose we do this?" Elliot asked. "And what makes you think that I would even want to do such a thing?"

"You want to live like this forever?"

The man looked around and then back to Catie. "What is wrong with how we live?"

"Tents? An abandoned school? Are you really asking that question?"

"Okay, you have my attention."

Catie looked around once more and then back to Elliot. "Not like this. Me and you alone."

The man seemed to consider the offer. Finally, he nodded. "Ladies and gentlemen, if you will excuse us. Caleb, take your sister to your tent. Everybody else, I want the rest of the prisoners taken to the holding cells." Once the room was empty, Elliot went over and sat down. He motioned for Catie to join him.

"You have ten minutes. If I think you are bullshitting me, all your friends die. That includes the ones just outside."

"You knew?" Catie asked, only partially astonished.

"We brought you here. And if you think this is my actual compound, then maybe you aren't as clever as I thought you to be. This is simply one of our observation posts. We keep it manned so that we can keep tabs on Montague Village and two other nearby settlements."

Catie had to clench her teeth to keep her mouth from dropping open. Not only had she basically been led here, but if this man was not bluffing—and at this very moment, she had no reason to believe that he was—then this was not even his actual camp.

Catie explained to Elliot her plan. She talked quick and kept worrying when it did not seem like the man was going to ask her any questions. At last she finished. Elliot sat back, his fingers steepled under his chin as he thought.

"Terry!" he called. A man stuck his head inside the tent.

"Yeah, boss?"

"Execute the prisoners."

"What?" Catie yelped.

"Just kidding." Elliot shot a wink at Catie. "Give them the injection. Then, go out and bring in the rest of the intruders. Take them to the cells."

"Injection?" Catie asked.

"We have a serum that we have refined over the years." Elliot actually laughed like he was truly amused. "Hard to believe that we just used actual zombie blood in the early days. Hell, that crap has more contamination and infectious crap than you can believe. It probably resulted in a few people that might have been immune actually getting sick enough and dying. And of course we already know that even if you are immune, if you have been infected, you will turn when you die no matter what."

"Wait," Catie gasped, holding her hands up. "Are you saying that you inject people with something that turns them or proves they are immune?"

"How else will we be certain? Don't worry, if a person is actually immune, then it is perfectly safe."

"I think you are missing the point."

"What point is that?" Elliot seemed to be honestly perplexed.

"You are turning people into zombies. I think that explains the problem in one sentence," Catie snapped.

"Wait." Elliot held up his hands, a smirk falling into place so quickly that it seemed like that might be more natural than anything else. "You are on board for going in and being part of a coup to overthrow Dean and his band of idiots where we might slit throats, hack people up, or fill 'em with a few crossbow bolts. Yet, and let me see if I am just missing something here, you draw the line at dosing them with something that will kill them or prove that they are immune?"

"Turning a person into a zombie is an agonizing and slow process. That is torture. Why would you think anything about that is okay?"

"You do know that there are people in that compound that are immune, right? And some of them know damn good and well that is the case. Sandy was going to reveal the names, but somebody killed her before she could talk. That points to some people high up in the command structure. I would be willing to bet that one of them is the illustrious leader, Dean Stockton."

Elliot still had that same nasty sneer on his face, but somehow, he had become even uglier. What Catie saw was a man obsessed with revenge; consumed by anger. He was toxic. That was never a good thing for somebody in a position of power. If she had learned just one thing in her years, it was that anything to an extreme was bad.

"So, let me see if I have this straight. You want to go in, inject the entire community—men, women, and children—you want to shoot them up with this serum that you have and then see who is left standing?"

"Let me respond with answering your question with my own. You are okay with going in and killing people outright?"

Catie ran her hands through her hair. Her mind was whirling with all sorts of things. At the center of it was the death of Kevin. He'd died at the hands of a group that was bent on wiping out people who showed immunity. He'd died caught up in somebody else's fight. He had died a horrible and violent death.

A few weeks later, she stumbles into this situation. She still had not really taken any time to deal with her loss. Could all of this be weeds that have sprouted in her garden of misery and pain? And was Elliot right? What made his way any worse than hers? She wanted to go in with a 'Trojan Horse' plan and launch an assault on the people of Montague Village. She was using her anger at seeing the immune relegated to some lower class than others as fuel to her fire.

Somewhere along the way she had become irrational. Was she ready to become the villain? Because, when you stripped it down to its core, that would be exactly how she would be perceived by most sane and rational people. If she was on the outside looking down on these actions, she would be waiting for the good guys to save the day. Wasn't that always how things ended in the movies?

Catie began to laugh. It was just a giggle at first, but it grew into something more. Pretty soon, she could not stop. Tears rolled down her cheeks and her vision was blurred. She noticed Elliot stand up, she thought he came to her and put his hands on her arms, but she pulled away. At some point, she ended up on the floor. Through it all, she could not stop laughing. Her mind spun and tried to anchor itself to anything, put the current was too swift and everything she reached for would slip away before she could actually get a grasp.

Her emotions were coming fast and furious. Happiness, sorrow, and rage. It was the rage that came on greatest and began to crush everything else. It smashed her happiness like some massive monster. Her mind flashed on an image of Godzilla stomping through some Japanese city. That only pushed her faster down the stream of madness.

Madness.

Catie knew that was where she was headed. She knew that to continue on this path would be her undoing. She would cease to be Catie. She would become something else. Something dark and evil. She would become Erin!

Was this how that poor little girl became the leader of an army that sought to destroy something simply because it was different? Catie could hardly breathe now as she fought herself. Part of her did want to let go and embrace whatever might come if she allowed the madness to assume control. Yet, part of her knew that to be wrong on every level.

Catie felt hands on her. She heard voices, but she could not understand them. She felt something stick her arm, and then she felt the world begin to slip away. She was sliding into darkness. She welcomed it. Perhaps she would find answers there.

9

Dancing on the Head of a Pin

I have heard the phrase, "like shooting fish in a barrel" before. I just never really gave it much thought. For one, who would keep fish in a barrel in the first place? At least now I am pretty certain that I know what they are trying to allude to with an analogy like that.

We cut the escorts down so fast that none of them had the chance to do more than bleed and die. However, I think the biggest surprise to those who had been tasked to escort me and Jim came when Jim yanked his machete free from its sheath and actually sprinted up behind Maddy.

You would think that his first instinct would be to free himself once and for all and run for cover. Apparently he is just as cool as I have always believed him to be. He slammed the pommel of his weapon into her temple and dropped her in her tracks. That meant that we had a prisoner.

The rest were afforded no such mercy. The killing was swift and violent. I was beginning to see the people that I lived my life with, grew up around, in an entirely new light. Inside the walls of Platypus Creek, everybody knows each other. We all smiled and shared good times. The select few that were chosen to venture well beyond our little area have known the world as it really is and not how those inside the walls believe (or wish) it so.

The truth is harsh and horrible. The world is chaos, bloodshed, and death. I think that, over the years, those who decided to stay inside and farm or make clothes, or whatever…they have all lost sight of—or, more likely suppressed the memories of—the brutal world we live in.

It has not taken me long to realize that we must be prepared to do whatever we can to survive. But much more than that, we must be prepared to do things that make us into something else. To combat those who wish to destroy our way of life or harm those we love, we must be able to commit acts that are unspeakable.

It seems an eternity ago when I took that first human life. I recall the warnings from Jim and Jackson. And now I think I might understand why they tried to keep me from killing that man. As sick as it seems, once you have crossed that bridge, you will be able to continue to do so much easier. Not because you enjoy it (at least that is not the case for me), but rather because a little bit more of your goodness and compassion dies each time.

We came out from where we had hidden to lay the ambush and I saw almost the same expressions on every single face. Acceptance. And as we walked to Jim and gathered around the unconscious body of Maddy, I felt another little piece of my soul wither, dry up, and die.

"Tie her up," Billy ordered.

Paula went to work on that job and I decided that I needed to talk to Billy away from the others. I wanted him to know that the leader of that army in the valley knew his name. That seemed oddly important.

"Whatever it is, hurry it up, Thalia," Billy said once I managed to pull him away from the group.

"They know your name. That lady? Suzi? She knew who you were," I blurted, not knowing any other way.

Billy seemed to think it over for a long time; way longer than I would have expected considering he was the one saying we had to hurry and get moving back to Platypus Creek. He rubbed his stubbled head and cocked it one way and then the other like a dog hearing a strange sound.

"I wonder if she knew Winter...or if she knew Jon?" he mumbled.

Of course I was familiar with those names. They were part of the history of our community. One stood for all that was bad, and the other for heroism and good. Sunshine had never moved on after Jon. She rarely went a day without mentioning something about that man. I did not really remember him. There were flashes of the man they spoke of, but most of my memories centered on Steve and Emily, the girl who had become my sister in many ways.

"Well, I guess I will never know," Billy mumbled.

"What do you mean?"

"Huh?" He looked at me and his eyes focused like he had forgotten that I was there. "Oh, nothing. Don't give it another thought, Thalia."

"But don't you think that they might have a spy in our community? Maybe somebody has been living with us the whole time and reporting back to that horrible woman."

"I don't see that as very likely," Billy said with a tired smile. "More likely, some random person that I crossed paths with at some point. I ran with Jon and Jake and Jesus, quite a bit in the early days. And we didn't necessarily take down all of Winter's people."

"But how would she know that you are in charge?" I pressed.

"Lucky guess? Hell, I don't know. And it is likely that I never will."

With that, Billy gave me a pat on the head and just walked away. He did not seem to know, and more important, he sure didn't seem to care. He and Jim got Maddy up after making sure that she was tied up nice and tight. They carried her off the road and into the woods after telling Paula to round us up, get everybody fed, and prepare to move out.

The two returned less than twenty minutes later. Alone.

I really wanted to know what they found out, so I ignored Paula's demands that I move up with some guy named Morris and take point for the team, and instead walked over to the two men who were still basically whispering back and forth so intently that they did not even notice me until I was right up on them.

"...and I say it is the only choice," Billy hissed.

"Hey there, Thalia," Jim said much too loudly.

He might be really cool under pressure and excellent in a fight, but he is lousy when it comes to being truly phony. For one, he never calls me by my name unless he knows I have caught him at something or there is a serious problem. The thing was, I had no idea what I'd just caught him doing wrong.

"What did you find out?" I demanded, shaking off Paula's hand as she tried to pull me back.

"Not a damn thing," Billy said, his face grim and tight with agitation.

"Where is she?" I asked. I'm not stupid, I had a good idea. I just wanted to see if these two would at least give me some semblance of a straight answer, or if they were going to continue to treat me like a child.

"We couldn't risk leaving her behind, we don't have the time to bring her along, and we didn't think she deserved going down to the next passing zombie." Jim looked me in the eye as he spoke. It did not escape me that Billy was very obviously displeased by Jim's apparent honesty.

"She didn't have any useful information at all?" I pressed. "Not even how they know about Billy?"

I saw a look flicker on Jim's face for a second that let me know that he was perhaps not aware that Suzi knew about Billy; or at the least how she knew his name and that he was our leader. Billy flushed just a bit for some reason.

"We didn't get to that part. It isn't mission critical," Billy finally said after he glared at me and then rolled his eyes at Jim as if to indicate I might be a little bit crazy.

"How do you not ask something like that?" I insisted. I glanced over and saw looks on both Jim and Paula's face that let me know I was on the right path in my questioning. It seemed as if they might be curious as well.

"Look, I was Jon's shadow for a while. He wanted to mold

me into a Marine or something. Kept telling me that I had a lot of potential. He also let that tidbit of information slip way back before we knew that Winter and his men were bad guys. It is highly doubtful that every single one of Winters' men died when that compound fell after he and Jake and I went there and they poisoned the water supply or whatever. The number of living people these days makes it likely that you will cross paths with somebody that knew you or knew of you if you were in any way active in those early days. Our group, for those of you who were not there in the beginning..." he glanced at Jim and Paula before continuing as if to make some sort of point, "...was very active in these parts. We also dealt with the military. We were hooked up with a man named Randall Smith of the CDC. He was the head honcho at the first place we thought we would call home."

He continued to ramble on for whatever reason. It just sounded to me a bunch of "blah, blah, blah" stuff. However, when he mentioned Randall Smith, it made me once again re-member my sister of the apocalypse: Emily. I could still see her laughing as we played in the snow, and then that creeper got her. They kept me away from her after that except for one time when Steve let me see her. Then she was gone.

I heard Dr. Zahn and Sunshine say once that she had turned and that Steve had not been able to kill her. I thought that had to be wrong. He would not want her to walk the world as one of those things for the rest of forever. However, I'd also heard a story from Billy one night when he was drunk. In that story, he insisted that he saw her in La Grande with a bunch of other zombie children...and cats. That was when I decided that the story was just Billy being drunk. The thing about the cats was too weird.

"Thalia!" Paula snapped.

"What?" I shot back a little more aggressively than I proba-bly should.

"You and Morris get moving. We need to get back to Platy-pus Creek as soon as possible. We are marching straight through."

I had to fight back the urge to stomp my feet as I stormed to where the man I assumed to be Morris was waiting. He looked like a real creep. He had stringy hair that looked like it hadn't been washed in a month. His mouth looked weird like he was kissing somebody, and his left eye had a patch over it. Once I got closer, I felt just a little bit bad.

His mouth looked that way because he did not have any teeth in front. I could tell by looking that he had suffered something rather violent to end up that way. I seemed to recall that Morris was one of the people who were out on field operations a lot. In fact, he was gone almost as much as Jim. He often by-passed the offered rest period of two weeks after a run and signed up to leave with the next group. I seem to recall something about how he had been searching for his wife since he arrived at our community on a stretcher with a group that we took in almost five years ago.

We started out after Paula gave us instructions. Even though Morris and I were a team, they wanted us to separate by about a quarter mile. I guess our little ambush had everybody on a state of hyper alert. It stood to reason that, with all the activity in the valley, some of the groups in the area might be a little nervous. With Morris and I separated, we would not likely both end up captured or killed.

Comforting thought, that.

My day went by in a blur. I was doing my best to be alert, and early on, I was pretty focused. My problem came towards the last half of my shift on patrol. I kept finding my mind wandering. At last, I reached the marker that Paula told me to stop at and wait for the rest of the team.

We played leap frog like this for the rest of the day. As darkness fell, it was once more my turn to be out on point. I was given the landmark and told that, unlike earlier, Morris and I would stay close. I walked along for a ways before Morris finally broke the silence.

"You really had folks worried back home," he started.

"I'm sure they were upset about the others. Jim and Jackson are much more important, and I imagine that losing them would hurt the community more than just my being gone," I said with a shrug.

"Yeah, but Jim and Jackson didn't have their mom in the town square chewing poor Billy a new one in front of God and everybody."

"Melissa came down to the square?" I was honestly blown away.

"Came down? More like exploded into. She was pissed that Billy sent you out there on a mission that was a sham to begin with. I guess word got out that it was some personal issue between Billy and one of the science geeks."

That is the thing about a small community like ours; everybody knows everybody else's business. Keeping any kind of secret is next to impossible.

"And once the doc got that guy to talk, well, I guess that put everybody on edge." Morris reached down, picked up a rock and threw it at a shadow. Nothing moved and we kept walking. That was a common way to flush out any zombies that might be lurking in the shadows. They react to whatever noise is the most recent.

"Wait? What?" I blurted, probably a little louder than I should considering the fact that we were supposed to be scouting for any possible trouble. Not likely that we would sneak up on anybody as I was making all this noise.

"Yeah, I guess the guy was one of the scouts from that army. He gave up numbers, all sorts of stuff. Said that they had no quarrel with us, and that they actually wanted to ask us to join them. Supposedly, he said that little college settlement near Island City was really the bad guys. If you can believe him, they were the ones manufacturing some sort of weaponized version of the zombie virus. It supposedly even takes down the immune if you can take his word for anything. And I guess, according to those who were present for some or all of the doc's questioning, he was beyond being able to lie. She did a real number on him."

I took this in and mulled it over the rest of my time out. Morris tried to talk to me some more, but I was not much for conversation. If all of this was true, then why would Billy lead a team out to ambush our escorts? Why not let them show up, bring them in and see what they had to say? Was there more to what they discovered in the interrogation that had not been leaked?

We reached our marker and awaited the group. The rest of the night, I walked sort of off to myself. Jim tried to come chat with me once, but I told him I wasn't in the mood to talk.

One of my favorite things to do to pass time is to read. I love stories that take me away from everything. We don't have a lot of books, and I have probably read all the ones that we do have at least a dozen times each. The best part about books (or any story for that matter) is that things might seem bleak and fuzzy in the beginning, but they always clear up by the time you reach the end. I have found that life is nothing like that in any way, shape, or form. More often than not, you don't get any answers; just more questions. I was hoping that this was not going to be one of those times where I was left wondering.

***

When we reached the first picket of sentries, I was actually surprised to discover Kayla walking the ridge. I guess she earned her place after that last run. If seeing her out on roving patrol was a surprise, it did not hold a candle to what happened the moment she spotted us.

"Thalia!" the girl squealed loud enough to bring any zombie for five miles heading our direction. If that wasn't odd enough, she bounded down the hill and grabbed me in a very uncomfortable hug.

"Hey, Kayla," I said once she pulled back to reveal that she had honest-to-goodness tears rolling down her cheeks.

"I thought that we would never see you again," she gushed.

"Surprise!" I said meekly, throwing my hands up for emphasis.

We moved on and eventually arrived at the gates. That was where I discovered my next shock. The place was a beehive of activity. People were loading carts, horses, mules, and anything that could carry anything with as much stuff as possible.

"Umm…" I turned to Paula, but she just moved past me like I wasn't even there. When I spun to Billy, he was simply gone!

I looked over to Jim and he made the mistake of meeting my gaze. I stormed over to him, a terrible feeling in my gut.

"What is going on?" I demanded.

"Listen, cupcake, I hate to—" he began, but was interrupted.

"Thalia!" I turned to see Melissa and Stevie running for me.

Stevie was actually falling behind as Melissa came with a speed I did not know she possessed. She hit me full force, her arms throwing themselves around me and sweeping me into the biggest hug I can ever recall receiving from the woman. A second later, Stevie caught up and it was now a Thalia sandwich.

I struggled with this encounter. Yes, I was happy to see them both; thrilled to be perfectly honest. But I had something else on my mind. Apparently it would have to wait, because coming for us on a beeline, as people cleared a path to avoid being run over, was Dr. Zahn.

"Young lady, you are a sight for sore eyes," the doctor said with more emotion than I think I had ever seen from her in my entire life (except anger, I'd seen the doc pissed plenty of times over the years).

"And I am glad to see all of you," I finally said once I was able to get free of Melissa's grip. "What is going on?"

"We're moving!" Stevie blurted.

I caught the scowl on Dr. Zahn's face. That made no sense to me. Not that any of this did. Why would everybody agree to just pack and leave? This was our home. We had been here for most of my life. We had a good thing here.

"What about Jackson?" I asked, my voice a bit choked up as the realization of a very unpleasant possibility hit me in the gut.

"Excuse me?" Dr. Zahn seemed genuinely perplexed.

I wriggled free of all the arms trying to wrap around me. Suddenly they felt suffocating. I pulled away and faced Melissa, Stevie, and Dr. Zahn.

"What are we going to do about Jackson? He is prisoner back at that woman's camp," I said very slowly, making a point to try and watch everybody's face at once for some sense of a reaction.

"I have no idea what you are talking about," Dr. Zahn finally said.

I saw her look past my shoulder. I turned to see Jim, Billy, and Paula heading for the cabin. They were ducking out of this madness and heading for the community's council chambers. I took off after them at a sprint.

I reached the big porch and took a deep breath before I entered. I did not want to come across like a child. I wanted to be taken seriously. I would ask direct questions and expect direct answers.

When I walked into the open chamber, I was met by three heads that turned to face me all at once. Of the three, one of them looked as guilty as Stevie that one time when he got caught with an entire loaf of fresh pumpkin bread that Melissa had just baked.

"What are we doing about Jackson?" I asked as I came up the aisle.

Billy was seated on the edge of the little stage, his feet actually touching the floor where my own would be a good foot off the ground. Paula was standing beside him, and Jim had spun one of the chairs around backwards and had straddled it.

"Thalia," Billy began, but I shook my head.

"Don't you dare say what I think you are gonna say!"

"He knew this going into the mission," Paula whispered. Only, it wasn't a whisper of sadness or anything like that; instead, she seemed to almost be warning me off like I was out of line.

"Every single time you leave the walls, you run that risk," Billy added, only minus the veiled warning or threat I thought I was hearing from Paula.

"So we leave him to die?" I exploded. "What if I was still there?"

"Then it would be the same," Paula said flatly, her voice now as emotionless as I'd ever heard it. "We have to think of the community. One person does not merit risking several lives."

I turned to Jim. He was only able to hold my glare for a second or two before he looked at the floor. "It's the truth, cupcake," he said sadly. "Any one of us would knowingly give our lives for the better and greater good of the rest. Jackson would say the same to you if it were me left behind and he somehow managed to end up free from that place."

"But there has to be something—" I started, only, the tears had sent a signal to my throat and closed it off, strangling my words.

"You saw how many of them there are," Jim said sadly. "We don't stand a chance if we try and fight them."

"But they wanted us on their side!"

"That is one person's word under duress. He could be lying. We do not have the luxury of trusting him," Billy said, his lips pressed tight in a grim expression of finality.

I looked from one to the other and saw it in their eyes. The choice had been made. Paula had obviously lied to me back at the ambush to shut me up. She knew already that Platypus Creek was packing and preparing to leave.

"Maybe if you hadn't killed the escorts, then maybe we could have spoken to Suzi and come to terms," I insisted.

"After what she did to that guy Hunter, do you really think that true for even a moment?" Jim asked, his head finally coming up as he now found the strength or courage to meet my gaze.

I stared back at him. A part of my brain was telling me that he was exactly right. Not to mention, how could I think for a moment that we could ever be friends with a person like that and not spend the rest of our lives sleeping with one eye open?

Still, my brain was in no mood to think rationally. I was angry, hurt, and confused. I was tired of being lied to by everybody. Was that just the way of the world once you became an adult? Lie, lie, lie, and lie some more?

I wanted to scream. I wanted to yell and throw a fit. More importantly, I wanted to have things back the way they were before I went off on that stupid field run.

I turned and left. I almost thought that one of them might call me back or come after me, but none of them did. I stood outside and looked at people jogging one way or another. And while there was certainly a lot of urgency, the one thing I didn't see was panic.

"Are you going to be okay?" a voice said from my left.

I turned to see Cynthia Bird coming up the path. Sunshine was beside her and both women looked like they had been up for about a week straight without any sleep.

"How can anybody ever say yes to that question?" I said, allowing my tears to finally escape my eyes.

"I'm just glad that you made it back," Sunshine said, closing the distance and putting an arm around me.

"Yeah, Jim and I are the lucky ones, right?"

"I'd heard that Mister Sagar made it back as well. Not Jackson, though?" Cynthia joined us.

"He is being sacrificed for some imaginary greater good." I made no effort to hide my anger and bitterness.

"That is the way of things now," Cynthia said, and I saw a sadness cross her face that made me pause. "Did I ever tell you how I lost my husband?"

I shook my head.

"We had been on the road for a while. We'd recently lost Xander's mom and dad. It was just the three of us on our own and we were pretty beat up. Glenn, my husband, he was probably in the best shape between he and I and so he did almost all of the hunting and foraging as we headed north towards a settlement that we'd heard of…this one as it would turn out.

"To make a long story short, we got to this river. Glenn had to cross it with a rope so that we could get to the other side with the baby. We'd been outrunning this group of raiders for almost a week and felt that getting across that river would be our only chance as they were gaining ground at a scary clip. The thing is, Glenn got this whole thing hooked up and then, once we were across, he cut the rope. He said that he would lead the people chasing us in another direction for a while so that Xander and I could get a good distance ahead. He promised that he would catch up to us eventually, but he made me promise to keep going until I reached the settlement we had heard was a safe place. I never saw him again."

I sat there for a minute and tried to see how this matched up to what we were doing with Jackson. It wasn't that I was stupid, but it sounded to me like Cynthia's husband had made an actual choice. We were making Jackson's choice for him.

"I know it's tough, Thalia," Sunshine said, her arm around my shoulders as she started to lead me back to my home. "But you have to trust that this is the right choice. Jackson would probably say those very words if he were standing right here with us."

I let her lead me away. I was tired. Everything was blurring together into one big lump. I was having a very difficult time sorting out one part of this mess from the other. The loss of Island City; Hunter being turned into a zombie by Suzi; Jim pretending to be gimpy and then supposedly sneaking out of the camp and sending for help.

And through it all, my mind returned to Jackson. What terrible fate would we be consigning him to by just abandoning him like this?

Somehow, I found myself walking through the door to the apartment I shared with Stevie and Melissa. They both welcomed me home again with almost as much excitement as they had when I'd first walked through the gates. There were crates stacked by the door. I saw that my stuff had somehow been packed as if they fully expected me to return.

I tried to smile as Melissa sat us down to dinner. Only, I couldn't taste a thing. I forced myself to be pleasant as Stevie made it a point to try and catch me up on every single thing that had happened in my absence.

When dinner was at its merciful end, I excused myself and went in to bed. I waved a hand to acknowledge that I understood we would be leaving with the first caravan tomorrow. I heard Stevie ask if I was okay and Melissa's attempt to give him some sort of soothing answer stating that I was fine, but just tired.

I wasn't fine.

I lay down; certain that I would fall into a fitful sleep plagued with nightmares about Jackson being turned into a zombie. That was only partly true. I did fall asleep eventually. But when my eyes opened, it was still dark and I did not recall one single nightmare. I felt numb.

When I got up and walked into the living room, I already knew what I was going to do. I grabbed a piece of paper and jotted a note. It was simple and to the point. It read: I can't leave Jackson like this. I am sorry.

I slipped into my field gear and walked out into the darkness.

10

Vignettes LXIV

Juan jerked his weapon free, his eyes frantically seeking his daughters who had suddenly vanished from sight. A handful of seconds later, he had his answer. Both girls sprang up from seemingly out of nowhere. Each had her knobbed, baseball bat-like club in her hands.

Della and Denita rushed in, each taking down one of the deader wolves as the confused creatures turned to face this new stimulus. Juan could only watch in amazement. It had been sort of impressive to see his little seven-year-old girls take down a small pack of these horrors.

"Bad dog!" Denita scolded as she dodged a gore-crusted maw that was just a heartbeat too slow to snap shut on its intended target of the girl's ankle. It was rewarded with a smashing blow to the back of the head.

Before he realized it, the little battle was over and his daughters turned with proud smiles plastered in their faces. Each was grinning so wide that Juan almost thought the tops of their heads would fall off if a sudden breeze were to whip up right about now.

"You learned all of this from Gerald?" he asked once he was able to speak without sounding like he was absolutely furious.

"Yes, Papi," the girls crowed in unison.

"Gerald said he was making us lean, mean fightin' machines," Denita added, her hands covering her mouth as she started to giggle.

Juan had to admit that he was extremely impressed. What he'd just witnessed showed more skills than he'd observed in grown men; much less a pair of seven-year-old girls. His only hang-up came in the fact that it felt like the man had taught them the skills without teaching them anything remotely resembling caution. It was like teaching a child to shoot a gun, but then skipping the part about how they are holding a dangerous weapon and should not ever think of it as a toy.

What he'd just seen from his daughters was a modern day version of a game; at least that is how they acted. He needed to put this right, but he wanted to do it in a way that would not have them reluctant to use their newly discovered talent. His mind easily went to a scenario where his scolding would leave them just standing there as a deader strolled up and took a bite out of one or both of his daughters.

"Okay, I want you two to listen to me," Juan said patting a spot to either side of where he sat, indicating with a nod that the girls come sit beside him. "I want to tell you both how proud I am of each of you. You did very well. However, I want to make it clear that this is not a game."

"But Gerald said—" Denita began.

"I don't care..." Juan snapped, then he reigned himself in and started over in a much calmer tone. "I don't care what Gerald said. He isn't your papi. I am telling you that this is serious stuff. You should be proud of what you can do, but the moment that you don't take this serious, that is the moment that one of those deaders takes a bite out of you."

The two girls sat silent for as moment. Each of them kept looking at the other. Juan had that vibe like they were doing one of those creepy twin things from the movies where they were communicating telepathically or something. At last, Della broke her sister's gaze and looked up at Juan with her large dark eyes.

"Can I tell you one thing that Gerald said, Papi?" the girl asked innocently.

With a sigh, Juan nodded his head in agreement. He noticed Della shoot a worried look at Denita before she spoke.

"Gerald said that Denita didn't need to be ascared of the deaders. That it was just like a game of tag. She didn't want to play at first, but when he showed her how easy it was to win, she started to play."

"And he said I am very good at it," Denita whispered.

Juan was struck speechless. Apparently Gerald had learned a great deal about the girls while he'd been out of commission. He wanted to say something to refute the man's claims, but then he saw how the man had turned Denita's reluctance and closed off personality into something he could work with.

"You are very good at it, *hija*," Juan said softly, a smile on his face. "I was very proud of you both. But I want you to make me a promise."

The girls both scooted close, their heads tilted up at him expectantly. In that instant, Juan saw every single detail of Mackenzie's beauty in their little faces. He recalled how he had been ready to give up that day when his horse had fallen and he thought that the end was near. He made a quick vow to himself to do everything in his power to live a long life and be there for his girls.

"I want you to promise that, if we are ever fighting deaders and I tell you to run, that you will do what I say."

"We promise."

***

Vix shimmied up to the first cross beam and then began the arduous climb up the power line tower. She was still climbing as the first crease of light began to show on the horizon to the east. From the looks of things, the clouds were breaking up and the day might actually yield some sunshine.

When she finally reached a spot where she felt she could see just about any place that their attackers might have come from, Vix halted. She had been keeping her eyes on every single hand hold as she climbed. It would be just her luck that she would grab some rusted piece of metal and fall to her doom; or worse, become seriously injured and left to die a slow and miserable death.

"You really need to find a rosier outlook on life, missy," she muttered to herself as she began to scan the landscape.

She discovered not one, but a pair of places, where the gray tendrils of smoke wafted up indicating that some sort of fire was burning. After making a point to locate a few solid landmarks that would lead her in and help to find both locations, Vix climbed back down. Despite her earlier self-talk about becoming a bit more optimistic, she still kept her eyes on what she was doing all the way to the ground.

"Well?" Chaaya asked, her voice habitually returning to that whisper a person used when they were scared of being discovered.

"Two possibilities," Vix announced.

She described everything in detail just in case they were separated for any unforeseen reason. They could either head west towards High Halstow, or they could turn east. Since they knew with a fair amount of certainty what they would find heading west, they opted for the signs of life to the east.

It had looked much closer from up high. But once you added in hiking up and down every hill and dale, along with maintaining a high degree of caution in order to minimize their chances of being discovered if anybody might be out looking, it took them most of the morning to finally reach a spot where the smells of burning wood and roasting meat carried on the breeze.

"Okay, here is how we do this." Vix turned to Chaaya, bringing their journey to a momentary halt. "You are going to stay out of sight and keep your eyes and ears open. I'm going in alone."

"But that never works out well," Chaaya insisted.

"You're right, but if we both go in, then there will be nobody to go back home and warn the others that there are some very hostile people out here. Also, you will need to tell them everything that Marjorie told us before this fuck-all of a mission began."

"Fuck-all?" Chaaya stifled a snort of laughter.

"You have a better term?"

The woman seemed to consider things for a moment. Vix had to admit, if she were the sort to find women attractive, Chaaya would be right up in her top ten. Lips pursed and brow furrowed as she thought, the woman was an absolute beauty.

"I suppose not."

"Good," Vix said with a sigh as she gave her machete a pat. "And now I guess there is nothing left to do but the doing."

"Are you seriously attempting to try out a new catch phrase or something? Because you are completely awful at it if I may be permitted to say."

After making a very deliberate and uncouth hand gesture and sticking out her tongue, Vix spun on her heel and started up the road. She covered less than a half of a mile—struggling mightily not to look over her shoulder just in case she was being watched—when a voice from her left called out, "Stop where you are."

Vix did as she was asked. As an added attempt to appear un-threatening, she put her hands in the air and then laced her fingers together and put them behind her head. A moment later, she heard somebody emerge from the heavy, dense grass to her left and right.

"Let's get down on our knees, shall we?" a voice asked with far too much joviality.

"Great, another bloody Irishman," Vix snorted just loud enough to be heard.

"I think we can call the entire Catholics versus Protestants thing behind us now, don't you, love?"

A man stepped in front of Vix and she had to restrain her desire to actually laugh out loud. If she was being generous, she would guess the man to be perhaps a hand or so higher than a meter. His red hair was curly and jutting from under a small cap. He wore a waist coat that was belted and held secure with a large brass buckle. As far as she was concerned, all he lacked was a little pipe and some clogs.

"Name's Paddy." The tiny man made a grand bow.

"Of course it is," Vix said with a straight face that was threatening to crumble into hysterics.

"And this is my friend, Seamus O' Hara."

The laugh that started to escape died on Vix's lips as a mountain of a man that was as large as this Paddy was small stepped in front of her. He had the same hair, but his face was a mess of scars and his grinning mouth showed three remaining teeth at best. Dangling from the behemoth's belt were three zombie heads; each one still had eyes darting back and forth. Their mouths were sewn shut with what looked like a piece of leather cord.

"So, what brings a flower like yourself all the way out here by your lonesome?" Paddy asked.

Vix considered her options. It took her a moment, but she decided to take an approach that most would probably shun out of hand in a situation like this: Vix told the truth.

***

Chad felt his heart trying to escape his chest. The last time he'd been so overwhelmed with real fear had been months ago when he'd returned to find Ronni and Caroline to let them know that the Green Springs community might actually have real potential as a place for them to live.

It was probably just a simple case of seeing a possible dream-come-true dangled before him and basically being prepared for something of greater or equal negative value having to take place. The women had been just on the other side of the ridge and were actually sitting on a massive boulder, having a heart-to-heart talk about how Ronni needed to try and understand that her dad would do anything to keep her safe and that the people they'd left behind seemed to harbor a real hatred for the immune.

Green Springs had lived up to his hopes and brought out a deep happiness in his daughter that Chad had not seen in a long time. They had been accepted into the community with open arms. Chad had quickly earned his place as a member of the hunting detail. That had been his first step in earning a chance to join security.

It was a measured process, and before long, Chad had been accepted by a team that handled mobile patrols. He was still not yet able to apply for mounted patrols, but he found that he enjoyed being out on foot every other day.

At least that had been the case until today. He'd left for his sector just before sunrise after kissing his daughter on the forehead as she sat bent over her manual that she needed to complete to become a teacher in the grade school classes. Caroline was already at the bakery where she would no doubt be treating the house to some special pastry; one of her favorite perks of the job.

It was just an hour or so into his patrol. He'd been tasked to the Barron Creek area on the west side of what the map said was Old Siskiyou Highway. It was little more than a two-lane road that was more weeds and grass coming up through the cracks than anything else.

He was following one of the many game trails when he heard something. He knew the sound of a crier when he heard it. After so many years, it had become much easier to tell the difference between a real crying baby and the zombie sound. They were remarkably similar, but a crier could only make short bursts of the noise. If you waited, they would fade and then follow up with a moan, or even silence. Anybody who had any time with a real crying baby could tell you that they seldom quieted that quickly.

This one had only lasted a few seconds, and Chad went to investigate. If it were one or just a few, he was given a green light to take them down. Large groups numbering over twenty were required to be reported if they were heading in the general direction of Green Springs, otherwise, it was best to simply let them go on their way.

This group numbered in the hundreds. Not the largest he'd seen, but worthy of letting the people back at Green Springs know. Because there were so many, and they were on a direct track towards the walls, he was authorized to fire his flare gun.

That would bring the mounted patrol in to handle things.

Since he wanted to join this group, Chad decided to stay close. There was a rocky outcropping over the creek that he could climb up on that would allow him a pretty good view of the area. He had just reached it when he spied the ten person horse patrol approaching from the south. They were coming up a shallow ravine and would hit this herd from almost directly behind the main body.

The riders apparently spotted the trailing elements and went into a wide formation; this put three riders up on each side of the gulley and four riding abreast down the middle. Chad was so intent on trying to watch the big picture that it took him a few seconds before he realized that one of the riders' horses had started to veer away from the group. It was one of the three riding along the right side of the gulley as he faced them.

When the rider slid sideways and then fell from the back of the horse, disappearing in the grass that was tall enough to brush the bellies of the horses, that was when Chad realized that there was a problem. In a flash, everything went bad. From both sides, arrows flew and the ten riders were being taken down before any of them had a chance to draw his or her flare gun and signal that there was trouble.

Chad jumped to his feet and pulled his own. He jammed the parachute flare into the gun and aimed skyward. A sudden pain came from his leg. He looked down to see a wooden shaft jutting from his thigh.

"Ah-ah-ah," a voice from behind him warned.

Chad spun to see three hooded figures at the base of little boulder. One of them had the drawstring of his bow pulled back, arrow aimed at him. Another was pulling another arrow from a quiver and the third had a wicked axe held across his or her chest. The metal caught the sun and gleamed brightly, sending a beam of light into Chad's eyes.

His mind made a snap decision. Judging by how the riders had been treated, he did not expect that he would be allowed to live under any condition. These people were here with a deadly purpose. He had no idea if they were part of an invasion, or just a nasty group of raiders. He was not anxious to find out. Chad took his chances and flung himself backwards and into the creek below. As he fell, he prayed that, if he did strike one of the rocks jutting from the water, it killed him quickly.

***

Jody dropped down low in the grass. The place that Pitts called home was a farm in between the two settlements. It was actually a stopping place for some as they made their way back and forth. Pitts was no fool and recognized the need for a rest area of sorts. He had a small staff on hand who kept the farm going and manned grills and the like during the warmer months.

Jody was still blown away by this revelation. Pitts had been one of his most vocal and strongest supporters during that whole trial. He had even been the one to come over to Jody's house one night and say that the only reasonable outcome had to be exile.

"Are you completely sure?" Jody whispered to Jan.

She nodded. "I was just as surprised when I heard where they were going to take her. I thought that fellow was on our side."

"So did I," Jody said, not hiding his disappointment.

"You guys want me to just stay here?" Tracy asked.

Jody turned to face the man. He did not want to hurt Tracy's feelings, but he had already seen enough to know that the man was out of his element in a situation such as this. Tracy was not a fighter. It was not a bad thing, it was just not a good one at the moment.

"If they get out and run, you need to be here to see which way they go. If Jan and I do not make it out, you are to go back to Danny. He will know what to do."

"I can believe that," Jan muttered.

Without another word, Jody started for the house. There was no sign of any of the workers out doing anything in the massive garden. Jody had been out here a few days ago and arrived just after sunrise. Even at that early hour, the garden had been a bee-hive of activity.

"Something is wrong here." Jody stopped.

He brought up his field glasses and scanned the house. It was actually quite modest considering. And there was an area with luxury RVs lined up for the summer staff to use as quarters. This was one of those things that had become like a rite of passage. Kids waited until they were old enough and then signed up to work out here. It was no secret that the man took excellent care of them. It had surprised Jody at first, but one night, Pitts had confided in him that he'd always wanted a family. When he made sergeant, he saw the men under his command as his children. It was nice, but had never filled the hole. Now, he had a fresh batch of faces every spring and summer.

"You mean how there is nobody working?"

Just as Jan spoke, a figure emerged from between a pair of the RVs. He was holding a long sword in one hand and a pistol-sized crossbow in the other. The light was not the greatest, and shadows played hell, but he swore he saw movement in the front window of one of the RVs.

He watched a little longer and counted five men patrolling the area of the vehicles. He also spotted one man on the second floor balcony that jutted from the right side of the house.

"We may be dealing with a seriously lopsided situation," Jody whispered. "But I have an idea."

He laid out his plan to Jan who nodded. After one final check of their gear, both separated and went their opposite directions. Jan was headed for the right side of the house and Jody was moving around to the rear of the RV area.

He was able to drop down into an irrigation ditch at one point and pick up his pace considerably. At last he came to the spot where he was almost dead center of the eleven RVs that were side by side. He peered up over the edge of the trench and saw one man leaning with his back up against the side of one of the vehicles. He was taking a piss!

Jody knew this was a perfect opportunity and moved to the left a little in order to be at the man's back. He came in fast and quiet. Just as the man was stuffing himself back into his pants, Jody sprung; clamping one hand over the guy's mouth, Jody drove his blade into the kidney. The man went stiff and then slumped to the ground.

As quick as possible, Jody rolled the man under the nearest RV and then crawled under himself. He scanned until he located the other four sets of legs. He judged where each one was and picked out the one farthest from the rest. He knew it would be tricky from here on out, and realistically, he only gave himself a fifty-fifty chance at success.

The next sentry walked past and Jody rolled out quietly from under the RV. He was just about to attack when the person suddenly spun to face him! It was a young woman, maybe early twenties at best. On sheer reflex, Jody thrust his blade forward. It plunged into the woman's throat. She coughed and gagged on her own blood. It was not loud, but it was apparently enough. He heard somebody call out. A second later, footsteps were coming on the run.

Jody had just enough time to drop, roll, and drag the body under the RV when a set of legs came into view. He held his breath until they passed. As soon as they did, Jody looked around and then came out the other side. He was just rising to his feet when a voice made him freeze.

"Hands in the air, Mister Rafe," a man said with unveiled menace. "Any move other than that and I plug you right here, right now."

Jody did as he was told. He laced his fingers behind his head and waited for whoever this was to approach. For the life of him, he could not place the voice.

"On your knees, you know the drill."

Jody did as he was told. There was a distinct jangle that he recognized as handcuffs being pulled out. He was considering the likelihood that he could drop and kick his feet out when his captor approached. He knew that he was dead either way. Why not go out fighting?

He spied the shadow of his captor and prepared to give it his best effort when the person behind him made a strange grunt. There was a brief second where Jody was deciding whether to turn around, but before he could act, a body landed hard beside him. The person's head was turned at an awkward angle; glazed eyes stared at him with the blankness of death.

"You Jody Rafe?" another unfamiliar voice asked.

***

Entry Twenty-nine—
My back is killing me. I spent all day today helping a small settlement with the repairs on their main gate. A herd of a few thousand undead hit them and the sheer weight of them eventually folded down the wall as well as the gate itself blowing wide open.

On the plus side, they saw my girl. She was using the name "Mary" when she arrived. I guess she managed to move beyond the area where her reputation is well known. I was almost as surprised to discover that I am almost to Old Seattle. According to these people, I could reach it as early as the day after tomorrow.

That got me to wondering if perhaps Seattle might be her target. Lots of old buildings are still standing. Sure, they are not up to code any longer, but who cares about that sort of thing these days? Also, there are at least forty settlements in and around that area. The zombies that once roamed the streets have all moved on and left behind plenty of places for people to shore up and settle. The old city sat in between the Cascades and the Olympics. There is plenty of water and an abundance of islands that are supposed to be populated with fairly large communities by the modern standard.

She would have basically an endless supply of children in a place like this. It is no secret that the clans in this region are a warlike bunch. The area has established trade, but everybody seems to have taken sides in one dispute or another.

Supposedly it goes back to some old dust up between some of the soldiers at Fort Lewis and some of the sailors at Bangor. Toss in some Marines for good measure and you have a built in rivalry. As settlements were established, those divisions became part of the landscape.

She might be able to operate for quite a while before the word crossed the battle lines. Likely, these groups would blame each other. She would become secondary.

I know I am giving her a lot of credit. However, one thing that I have learned over the years is that crazy does not always equate to being stupid. She might know exactly what she is doing. It is equally likely that she is selling the children, using them as barter, or any number of possibilities.

I have to find her soon and put her down.

Entry Thirty—
I was so damn close that I could taste it.

She was in this very settlement just yesterday. She left this morning. On the sad side, while her description brought instant recognition, nobody recalled seeing a child. I also think that the only reason she was not still here or had this place in an uproar is because the youngest child is almost two. Apparently there has been a span of infertility here.

It is funny how folks start believing in things like curses and other nonsense so easily. They have been holding fertility rituals every day for almost five months according to one young man. (Basically orgies if you want to call things as you see them.)

Judging by what I saw, there might be something wrong with the gene pool. This place reminded me too much of that little spot that Burt Reynolds and his gang stopped at before they went off on that damn fool canoe trip. I swear, if I would have walked past a kid on the porch with a banjo, I would not have been in the tiniest bit surprised.

Fortunately, they did not live up to all of the stereotypes that movie created. Nobody was the least bit mean, and not once was I asked to squeal like a pig.

I only stayed long enough to get some supplies and then I was back out in the woods. I saw one of the first zombies that I have seen in a week. It was just one, and the thing almost had me feeling sorry for it. It was caught in some think vines and had fallen down into a stream. It could not quite lift its head out from the water, and I swear that it looked like it was actually blown up a bit like a water balloon. It was at the bottom of a very steep hill or I might have gone over and ended the poor thing's misery.

My camp for tonight is up on top of a big green water tower that could have been mistaken for one of the alien invaders from *War of the Worlds*. I can see fires of various sizes burning in every direction. Even more impressive, I can see that many of the skyscrapers of the old Seattle skyline have become home to probably more people than I have seen in all my travels. It is like the stars have come down from the sky.

Things could get really difficult or I could strike gold. I will be spreading the word about "Mary" to each community that I stop in. That way, even if I do not actually catch her, these people can be aware that a very nasty wolf is hiding in sheep's clothing.

Tonight, I will get some rest. I have this feeling that it is about to get crazy. And while it could just be nerves or whatever, I always make it a point to trust what I feel. I think we got too far away from that before. We relied on people to tell us how we should feel instead of looking inside ourselves and making that decision.

11

The Geek's Wife Awakens

Catie's eyes fluttered open. She looked around and was amazed to discover that she was in a clean white room with a bed, water pitcher, basin, and a window that looked outside and allowed all of the sunlight to pour in. However, she was more surprised at what she did not discover. There were no bars on her window. She was not chained or manacled, and the door to her room was wide open, revealing an equally clean hallway.

At that moment, a woman wearing what looked like a short-sleeved white uniform walked past. She had a clipboard in hand and was busy scrawling something. Catie tried to sit up and call out, but the attempt left her dizzy and she only managed a moan. That was apparently sufficient. A moment later, the woman was beside her bed, leaning down with a peaceful smile on her face.

"Catie Dreon, nice of you to join us," the woman took Catie's arm and made a check of her pulse and then attached a cuff and took her blood pressure. She shook a thermometer and stuck it in Catie's mouth; all with amazing proficiency and a sense of ease that made Catie lie back and allow all of this to happen without protest.

Catie looked the woman up and down. She was of middle age with short brown hair, muddy brown eyes, a few creases on her face where wrinkles were just beginning to take hold, and a gentle smile. Her hands were soft and warm, no signs of callous. It was when she looked down at the woman's hands that she saw the long healed scar of a bite on the forearm.

"So, how are we feeling?" the woman asked.

Catie was still staring at the woman's scar. She had to tear her eyes away to meet this stranger's gaze.

"Huh?" Catie asked, still not entirely sure what to think.

"I asked how we are feeling," the woman repeated without the slightest trace of annoyance. If anything, she smiled even brighter.

"Who the hell are you?" Catie asked, making a point of easing up very slowly into a sitting position.

"I am the floor nurse. My name is Bonny Tate. I was bitten over four years ago and got run out of my home because I was considered a danger to others. I was taken in by a group of Elliot's men about six days later when they found me trapped on the roof of an apartment complex that I had spent the night in and woke to find surrounded by about a hundred walkers." The nurse sat down in the chair beside Catie's bed as she recounted her tale. "I studied to be a nurse and now I am the day shift floor supervisor here. I like long walks in the park and sunsets." Bonny winked. "Your turn."

Catie eyed the woman. She was having a difficult time with the situation. Worse, she could only remember bits and pieces of the meeting with Elliot. She did know that, at some point, she had gone a bit (for lack of a better term) cuckoo.

"My name is Catie. Catie Dreon. I came here from out west with my husband. We were checking to see if any of his family managed to survive. After that, we got a little caught up in a nasty bunch of crap and he was brutally killed. I was looking for a safe place to have my child when I fell into all of this." Catie threw her arms out to gesture at the room.

"Well, Catie, I have some very good news for you. Since you are visibly showing signs of being pregnant, we already gave you a full checkup and both you and the baby seem fine. There was a bit of concern over the sedative that was used when you had your…" Bonny's voice trailed off for a second and her smile faltered, but she recovered fast enough that Catie would have probably missed it if she had not been staring right at the woman, "...episode. The good news is that it did not seem to cause any problems that we could see. Both hearts are beating just fine."

Catie eyed the woman even closer now. She was being pleasant, and even downright kind. That was simply not at all what she expected. Granted, she did not really know what she did expect; all she knew for sure was that it was not this. It was too...*Stepford.*

"What's the game?" Catie finally asked. "If I get up and try to leave the room, what happens?"

"Well," Bonny pushed her chair back and stood, "you will certainly draw attention. Those hospital gowns don't cover much in back, so everybody will get a good look at your butt."

"That's not what I mean," Catie growled.

"If you would like your clothes, I will get them for you and you are certainly free to go. Elliot did wish to be made aware when you recovered, so I will send somebody to let him know. Beyond that, there is nothing holding you here."

Catie made a face. She was having a hard time believing any of this. Another woman came to the door and stuck her head inside while Catie was still trying to figure out what exactly to say or do next.

"Should I bring a tray?" the woman asked.

Bonny turned to Catie with a raised eyebrow. "Are you hungry? Breakfast was just served. It would be nothing to grab you something to eat before you go."

Catie wanted to refuse, but her stomach had other plans and answered for her with a gurgle. She nodded, feeling betrayed by her own hunger. When the tray arrived a moment later, she wolfed it down and discovered that she could have probably taken on another of equal portion.

"I will have somebody bring you a sack lunch before you head over to meet with Elliot," Bonny said as she left the room once Catie's clothes were delivered.

155

Despite everything, Catie was still surprised when she discovered that her clothing was freshly washed and a rip on one of the legs of her jeans had been stitched up. She was not exactly sure how to take things, and her confusion was actually increasing. After all, these were the bad guys. She recalled that much of the dilemma that she had struggled with as she spiraled into some sort of mental breakdown.

Once she was dressed, she stepped out of the room and into the hallway. The first room that she passed contained a woman. She was holding a newborn up and nursing. An instant sense of caution hit. She remembered hearing that women in the Beastie Boy compound were being used as baby factories. She had taken three steps past the room when she stopped in her tracks.

Spinning on her heel, Catie walked back to the room. Each step, she waited to hear somebody demand that she stop; nothing of the sort happened, and she ducked inside the room. The woman looked up at her and her face was instantly that of confusion.

"You aren't one of the nurses," the woman said, her voice a bit shaky.

"No, my name is Catie." She took one more step inside and then stopped when she saw obvious concern crease the mother's brow as she clutched her child just a little tighter. "And I am not here to cause any trouble, I just haven't seen a baby in a while. I am expecting my own before long." She pulled her heavy jacket open and ran a hand on her own belly for emphasis.

The woman relaxed visibly. She eased her baby back up to allow the infant to resume nursing. "He was born last night. His name is Jonathan."

Catie smiled and made a tentative motion forward. When the mother nodded, she came up beside the bed and looked down at the mother and child. From her position, she could see the horrible scarring around the collar bone, but her eyes were more interested in the baby. The child was beautiful. He looked pink and absolutely perfect.

"He's gorgeous," Catie breathed. She reached a tentative hand and brushed aside a lock of fine, curly blond hair. "Congratulations."

Catie turned and left. She did not see anybody try to stop her or even shoot her a questioning look. She took the stairs and was surprised to discover that she was on the sixth floor of a building. She hadn't taken the time to even look out her window and had not realized she was that high up.

She received another surprise on the bottom floor; the stairs were gone. There was a series of rungs bolted to the wall. Also, there was some sort of ramp mounted on the wall that could easily be removed. That had to be for anybody unable to use the metal rungs.

The entire bottom floor was cleaned out. The windows were gone, but there were huge steel shutters that could be drawn and a massive grate that looked like a king-sized jail cell door that could be pulled shut.

When she walked outside, the warmth of the sun was verging on actually being hot. She turned to get a better look at the building that she exited and was astounded to see that it was well over a dozen stories high. Turning her attention back to this compound, Catie saw only a few people moving, and all with a very deliberate purpose. This was in stark contrast to the multitude of wandering citizens of Montague Village. Another thing that she noticed was that, while there were not many actual people on the street, every single one of them wore a weapon.

Then she realized something else about her surroundings. This was very likely what had once been downtown Chattanooga. None of the buildings had any real discernable markings, but there was no mistaking the feel of the place as having once been a city center. Also, and there was a chance that they might just not be in sight at the moment, but she did not see anything like a fence. The entire area looked open.

Catie unfolded the piece of paper that Bonny had given her when she handed over her clothing. It was a hand drawn map as to where she needed to go to find Elliot. She reached a building that had no visible entrance. It was shorter and a bit squat by comparison to many of the others, and it sat across the street from what had once been a large, open parking lot. There was a massive overhang that jutted from this structure, and the entire front of it was sealed off with the same sort of heavy steel grating. It sort of looked like they had cut the sides off of train cars and then bolted them to the front of the building.

"You Catie Dreon?" a voice called from above.

Catie craned her neck and had to shield her eyes to see the woman up on the roof of the building. "Yeah," she hollered.

A rope ladder was tossed over. She was about to protest. Climbing a rope ladder was no easy task. If it just hung in space, it would wiggle and move all over the place. She was concerned about her condition, but she was also not entirely confident that she had shrugged off all of the effects of having been sedated. To fall from any height to the concrete below would be painful if not fatal.

"Clip the bottom into those eye bolts," the woman called down as if she could read Catie's thoughts.

Catie saw the bolts jutting from the concrete. Sure enough, the bottom of the rope ladder had heavy clasps. She did as instructed and climbed up to the roof.

"Elliot is inside, not hard to find, he will be in the pit." Catie's face must have given her away. The woman chuckled and actually flushed a bit. "The reading pit. It is like some sort of ode to the Seventies. Bean bag chairs and crap all piled around with books everywhere."

"Books?" Catie almost spat the word.

"Oh, this place used to be the library. It is still mostly intact. Not a lot of people made runs on libraries when the zombies started wiping out civilization. Strange, I still remember being at a store. Folks were grabbing food and all that stuff, but I actually saw some idiots hauling big screen televisions and video games. Can you believe it? This place? Not even a single smear of blood on the floor. So not only did it never get looted, but nobody tried to hide here. Sort of shows you how screwed up priorities were back in the day, doesn't it?"

Catie could not help but laugh. She walked to the metal door that allowed her to enter, casting a glance over her shoulder at the woman just before she ducked inside. Here was another woman; granted, she was probably nearing or at the end of her child bearing years, but her presence did not fall in line with the stories she'd been fed.

Catie was only halfway down the stairs when she heard a familiar voice calling her name. She looked down to see Kalisha running for the corkscrew stairs that she was currently descending. She also spied Caleb. The boy was sitting in an area that had to be the "pit" of reference. Elliot was sprawled on a massive, brown bean bag chair, book in hand.

Catie did not hide her smile. She hurried down and met Kalisha who had sprinted to reach the second floor where the stairs deposited Catie amidst rows of tall bookshelves.

"Can you believe this place?" the little girl said, throwing her arms up and spinning around to indicate the massive open library.

"It is certainly something," Catie admitted.

She disentangled herself from the second hug and then followed to the stairs and down to where Elliot waited. As she did, Catie's eyes were scanning the room for any signs of trouble. She did not see anything extraordinary. There were men and women wandering the rows of books, some thumbing through one title or another, but nobody seemed to be paying her even the slightest bit of attention.

Catie walked up to Elliot and stood, her eyes still habitually scanning everywhere. Despite the good vibrations emanating from just about everybody and in every situation, she could not help but be cautious.

"Please, Catie, have a seat." Elliot gestured for any of the bean bag chairs scattered about. A few were occupied, but there were at least twenty that were not.

Catie lowered herself into one of the squishy chairs and had to wriggle and squirm until she was in some semblance of a seated position where she could see Elliot. The man did not make any attempt to hide the bemused smile on his face. Caleb was actually giggling and Kalisha had her hands over her mouth and was looking at something that had suddenly caught her interest over her left shoulder.

"How are you feeling?" the man finally asked after shushing his son.

"It depends," Catie answered the rather broad question with a slight shrug of her shoulders.

"You had a few of us worried," the man admitted.

"Yeah, well, I am gonna chalk that up to hormones. I figure I got a built in excuse for at least another six or so months. After that, I will blame post-partum." Catie shifted around. Despite the calm attitude of this man, there were still some problems that she needed to deal with. For one, this man had mentioned injecting people to see if they would die and turn into a zombie, or prove that they were immune.

"I think a couple of people would like to see you for themselves. Maybe after that we can resume our discussion regarding Montague Village." Elliot raised a hand and an instant later a door opened and a pair of massive men were escorted into view from behind a series of giant book shelves.

"Catie!" Melvin and Marty rumbled in unison.

She was still trying to make it to her feet when the twin giants scooped her up like a discarded rag doll and literally handed her back and forth for each to hug. She managed to eventually push free and step back.

"You trying to squeeze this baby outta me?" she quipped, giving both men a genuine smile and patting each on one of his massive forearms.

Catie looked around, her eyes expecting to see at least one more face appear. She looked over to Kalisha who suddenly could not meet her gaze. She glanced at Marty and Melvin, but neither said a word.

"Miss DeCarlo is in the holding cells," Elliot finally spoke. Catie spun to him, her mouth open to say something harsh, but he held up a hand and continued. "The woman is not as receptive to things as your friends here. In fact, she tried to kill one of my men just this morning. He came with breakfast and she was hunched over in the corner of her cell seeming to cry. He went inside, asking her if she was okay, and the woman attacked."

Catie had to wonder if maybe she would not have done the same thing at one time. As it was, she wasn't sure that she was on board with Elliot or his plan. That brought up her first question.

"Did you already inject all of the team I arrived with?" Catie glanced over at Marty and Melvin, but the two remained stone-faced.

"Yes, I have," Elliot answered. He made it seem as if it were no big deal.

Catie felt something inside of her twist just a bit. She felt as if she were once again standing on the precipice to madness. This was no doubt a razor's edge. If she tipped even slightly in one direction, then the choice was made, final, and irreversible.

"And what are the results?" she asked. Despite the hint of nausea that churned in her gut, she was equally curious.

"Actually, above average. Two of your men are not showing any signs. It is very early still, but we usually at least see the tracers in the eyes within the first hour or so even if they don't turn right away." Catie started to say something, but Elliot silenced her once again with his hand and continued. "The ones who have already shown the signs were given the option of a very quick and painless lethal cocktail."

"You folks sure love your needles," Catie said, the bitterness clear in her voice.

Elliot seemed to suddenly be aware that his son and daughter were still present. He asked his daughter to please take Caleb over to the children's section. Once they were gone, he returned his attention to Catie.

"Actually, I was serious when I said cocktail. It is a drink. It induces a state of high and the body just shuts down. The person dies in their sleep. It is as painless as can be."

Catie opened her mouth three or four times before speaking. "I guess that makes it all better."

"We do not get any happiness in taking a human life," Elliot said, his own tone just a shade cold. "However, we are doing what we can to preserve our own chance at survival. You have seen for yourself the way some people react."

Catie could admit that, but she was still not entirely happy with things. Then another thought came. "What about Clarence?" she blurted.

"Oh, he is not immune. He also refused our offer of mercy." A cloud crossed Elliot's features.

"He wants to see you," Marty finally spoke. "He said he wants you to look him in the eye and be the one to put him down."

Catie swallowed hard. Yet, for some reason, she was not entirely surprised by the man's request. "Fine, let's go." She rose to her feet.

"Just like that?" Elliot asked, sounding just a bit surprised.

"It is a reasonable request. One that I see no reason to deny. Do *you* have a problem with it?" Catie eyed Elliot, her expression one of open challenge.

"Nope." However, there was something in his expression that she did not trust or care for in the slightest. It was like he was keeping a secret.

Spinning on her heel, Catie started for where the actual doors exiting this place were located. She got all the way to them and then remembered that they were secured from the outside. She walked back to see Elliot smiling at her.

"Shut up," she snapped as she headed up the stairs and made her way to the roof.

***

She reached a corner where there had obviously once been a park with a series of empty flagpoles still standing. Also, there was some sort of granite slab in front with the letters "TVA" on it. The building itself was almost stair step shaped. That was where she was told to go if she wanted to see Clarence.

She reached the building and was now used to the fact that all of the bottom floors of the buildings in this area had been not only gutted, but also had either massive sides of steel, or, as in the case here, huge grates of what could have perhaps been the front faces of a large animal cage. The bars were almost an inch in diameter and certainly able to withstand any zombie attack. She took a few seconds to admire the way that these facings were mounted. Even the largest herd would fail in any attempt to get inside. They would not be able to exert enough force to bend or bust open these protective measures, and since they were all larger than the space they covered, and the bottom few inches were sunk into concrete that was now years old, they were not going anywhere. And, on some odd chance that those measures did fail, the bottom floors were totally stripped clean. Nothing but support pillars were in place. Also, the bottom floor of stairs was gone.

Catie was once again greeted by a roof sentry. This one was actually at the first stair step. He directed her to a single story outcropping that stuck out from the left side of the building as she faced it. There was a cargo net in place. This one was already hooked to ground clamps. A few quick questions let her know that many of the buildings had their access gear already lowered and secure. They were taken up each night, but the need was not seen during the day. When Catie asked about the buildings that were handled differently, she was told that anyplace where the children might be were not kept open to prevent a child from wandering off. Nobody under the age of sixteen was allowed out alone and unescorted.

Catie made a quip about how she bet that fathers of the old world who had daughters would have loved those sorts of constraints. The guard, barely out of his teens himself only shrugged.

She entered the building and went to the fifth floor as instructed. A pair of guards greeted her at the entrance to a long hallway with cell doors all down the left hand wall. One of the guards looked like he was barely past puberty. His face was still fighting a losing war with acne. The other was not much older, but he was a fresh-faced poster boy type. His skin was flawless, his cheeks rosy, and his eyelashes just long and dark enough to make women simultaneously jealous, and just a shade weak in the knees.

She told them who she was there to see. One of them escorted her through and then fell in behind.

"Do I really need an escort?" she asked the young man.

"Sorry, those are the rules. Also," he pointed to the floor, "you have to stay on this side of the yellow line."

Catie sighed and started down the hall. She was told Clarence would be in the ninth cell. When she reached it, she had to fight the feeling of sickness that swept her up and threatened to turn her breakfast out onto the dingy tiled floor.

Clarence was definitely infected. She could see it in his eyes. The tracers were black and ugly, making his already unpleasant face into something even more terrible. However, it was also the smell. She had picked up the first hints of it while she was still a few doors down. Since she was passing one empty room after another, she was certain that the sole source of the stench was the one man.

Looking in, she saw Clarence seated on a cot. He had a mask that looked like some sort of respirator over his face. It appeared to be cinched tight enough for the straps to practically dig into the skin. The cell was actually quite large considering. The cot was up against the rear wall and still had almost its entire length again left in open width. There were an assortment of dark clumps on the wall that she had no trouble identifying as fecal waste. There was a puddle of urine in front of the cell that, due to the slight tilt of the floor, had run back into the cell to join a much larger puddle.

There was another smear that did not match the others. It was still a bit runny and had almost reached the floor from its ugly splatter design on the wall to her right. The smear that was still dripping down the wall was likely the morning's breakfast by the looks. The man was stripped completely naked and his hands were cuffed behind his back.

"Is this the condition you keep your prisoners?" Catie turned to the guard. "And are those cuffs and that mask really necessary?"

"Yes, ma'am...I mean, no ma'am," the pleasant sounding young man said. "This man has a habit of throwing his waste bucket at us. So we have removed the bucket and will have to send in somebody to take care of the cell when he expires. Also, he's a spitter."

"Expires!" Clarence barked harshly. "C'mon, you snot-nosed little punk. Call it what it is. I'm gonna die, then I will turn into one of those walking bags of rot."

"We already made that clear, sir. As soon as you pass, we will spike you. You will never open your eyes." To his credit, the young man did not seem the least bit bothered by Clarence's outburst.

"Yeah?" Clarence challenged. "Well, I am gonna try extra hard to come back quick in hopes that I will get to take a bite out of one of you sorry pieces of shit."

"To what purpose?" Catie could not help herself as she stepped up to the very edge of the yellow line.

"These freaks might not turn, but I bet they feel pain, and last I heard, having a piece of yourself ripped away is pretty damn painful. Hell, I'll eat you before I die if I get the chance." Clarence rose to his feet and walked to the bars. He did not seem the least bit bothered by being naked.

"Is this really how you want to spend the last moments of your life, Clarence?" Catie asked with a tired sigh.

"Says the bitch that will be responsible for the murder of how many innocent women and children?" Clarence challenged. Catie's mouth made an 'O' of surprise and the man laughed long and hard. When he stopped, he fixed her with his glare, made all the more sinister from over the top of that mask. "Oh yeah, old Elliot told us how things were gonna go down, and how you are gonna help them. I hope you burn in Hell!"

"If I do, I am certain that we will cross paths at some point," Catie replied. "Look, I did not come here for this. Elliot told me that you won't let them give you the cocktail. He said that you would only let me put you down."

"Then he wasted your time. He didn't tell you everything. I said that you could execute me. I told him that if you had the guts to spike me while you looked me in the eye, then that was the only way I would allow it."

"Why?" Catie asked, not hiding even the slightest bit of how incredulous she was over this demand. "What purpose does it serve?"

"If you do it, then you will have my blood on your hands forever. If you don't then you confirm to me that you are the weak coward I believe you to be."

Catie dropped her gaze. There was a moment of silence. She felt the hand of the guard on her arm.

"C'mon, ma'am," he whispered. "You don't need to put up with this from the likes of him." She heard Clarence start to laugh; bitter, nasty, and full of hate.

"No." Catie jerked her arm away. Her head popped back up and now it was her turn to fix Clarence with her own glare. "You gambled and lost, hot shot." She turned to the guard. Her eyes scanned him until she found what she was looking for. She pointed to the fisherman's spike at the young man's belt. "Give me that."

"Umm—" the young man began, but Catie cut him off.

"I take it you were not given instructions as to what to do if I actually agreed to end this person?"

"No, ma'am."

"Well that ain't my problem." Catie craned her neck past the guard standing before her. "You down there, get your ass up here."

The second guard at the end of the hallway looked at her with absolute confusion. The one beside her started to say something, but Catie spun on him.

"You two can either do what I say and see to my security, or you might just be next. I think you are about to discover that doubting or underestimating me is a tragic, if not fatal, mistake."

12

Unlikely Pair

I moved quietly along the wall. I could hear the normal sounds of the night as well as the occasional conversations as I hugged the shadows. Having been the curious sort when I was younger, I had learned a few places where one could slip out of the compound if they wanted to do so without being caught.

Getting out was not much of a problem and it was not long before I was jogging through the woods. The adrenaline kept me going for those first hours, but once it seeped away, I realized that I had been on the go for quite a while in the past several days. My body needed rest.

A little after sunrise I spied a fire watch tower and veered that direction. I had to shimmy up one of the support legs until I reached what remained of the ladder. That was fairly common for these old towers. Most travelers who passed through these parts sort of viewed the towers as an oasis; a nice place to be able to rest and relax. Many were kept stocked by surrounding communities since we all sort of relied on them and a person never knew what condition they might be in when they arrived. This one had some dried meats, travel bread, and water.

I ate light and then laid down on one of the cots. When I awoke, imagine my surprise when I saw the sleep blurred silhouette of somebody else in the tower with me!

"How could you do this!" a familiar voice snapped.

I scrubbed at my eyes and felt confused more than anything to find Kayla Brockhouse sitting there warming her hands at a fire that I had forgone to minimize the chance of giving myself away. She was in full field gear with her crossbow on her lap like she thought I might try to attack her or something.

"Go back home, Kayla," I snarled as I stood up and grabbed my stuff that was miraculously still hanging on the hooks where I'd left it all before going to sleep.

"Not without you," she insisted.

I decided that I would just ignore her. If she did anything stupid like try to stop me physically, I would take her down. Paula had taught me an excellent sleeper hold that would put her away in just a few seconds. She would wake with a nasty head-ache and I would be long gone before she could return to Platypus Creek and give me up.

"How can you be this selfish?" Kayla moved in front of me as I started for the door. "I don't get it. Everybody thinks that you are just so special. One of the first children of the settlement and the daughter of the founder, Steve Hobart, big deal. And just because you wanted to grow up to be like Billy and Paula in-stead of have a family, that makes you the town pet."

I was hearing this tirade and could not believe that Kayla ac-tually sounded jealous…of me! She was the pretty one with long hair and big boobs with hips and curves that made boys turn around and walk backwards until they ran into something. I had the body more like that of a boy my age than a girl. If anybody had something to be jealous about, it was me in regards to her. However, right now, I simply did not have the time.

"I am leaving, Kayla. You are going to get out of my way or I will move you by force." My eyes flicked to the crossbow in her hands, but I barely gave it a second thought. She wouldn't shoot me, of that much I was certain. Mostly.

"Then why did you come back in the first place?"

"You wouldn't understand."

"Because I am just stupid Kayla. Never quite good enough for you."

I heard the tears and did not need to turn around to know that she was crying. I imagine that I could have just walked out the door and been done with this scene, but I am not entirely heartless.

"It's not like that, Kayla." I turned. Sure enough, she had tears streaming down her cheeks. "I am going after Jackson. I have no idea how I am going to do this, or if I am going to end up dead. But I can't just leave him behind."

There was a moment of silence, and I thought that maybe Kayla understood. I thought that she would stand down. Heck, she might even return to Platypus Creek and not give me away.

I was only partially correct.

"I am coming with you." She slung her crossbow over her shoulder and crossed her arms in some signal of finality on the subject. I was going to make it a point in my life to never make that gesture ever again.

"I don't think that is a good idea," I said slowly. Think? No, I was certain. "You should just go back home. This is going to be an ugly situation and I would hate it if I got you hurt...or worse."

"You think I can't handle myself. You and everybody else it seems. I am not just some dumb girl, ya know!"

I thought it over. I could do something drastic like take her out and then be on my way, or...an idea formed, and I actually felt just a little bit naughty. It was devious and cruel, but it might be the best choice.

"Okay."

"You don't understand—" Kayla stared at me with the next words apparently stuck in her throat. "Really?"

Her face bloomed like a flower, becoming annoyingly pretty as she smiled and her eyes actually seemed to sparkle. Yuck! Then she leaped at me and hugged me.

"Don't make me change my mind," I grumbled, extracting myself from her embrace.

"You won't regret this, I promise," she squealed as we headed out the door."

Too late, I thought. *But* you *certainly will before I'm through.*

We headed out into the wilderness together. I set a pretty hard pace and felt that it would not take long for the complaints to begin. As the sun slid across the sky and eventually ended up directly overhead, I had to actually back my pace down a bit because it was wearing me out.

Kayla soldiered on, every time I shot a look her direction, she would flash me a smile or a thumbs-up, even if she did have sweat dripping into her eyes. Obviously she was made of sturdier stuff than I gave her credit.

When it came time to stop under a cluster of trees and nibble on a bit of our travel rations and sip some tepid water, she was quiet and did not even bitch when I ended the break and resumed the journey. Honestly, I wanted to take a while longer, but I did not want to give her the satisfaction of seeing that I was feeling the effects of being on the move these past couple of days with minimal rest.

We reached the now familiar bus that acted as a major landmark, and I saw Kayla's pace slow. I was about to say something when she suddenly sped up, grabbed my hand and led me to the side of the road. We had just climbed over the old guardrail when I finally heard the clopping of horses that she obviously had already detected.

I slid into the scrub brush, willing the gravel that was skittering down with us to come to a merciful and silent stop. I heard voices now and they did not sound happy…or familiar. I glanced at Kayla and saw that she was at least as scared as me. Her jaw was clenched so tight that you could almost hear her teeth breaking.

"…don't care what you thought you saw, Zeke. Ain't nobody on the road. Damn sure ain't no two kids," a man said with a lazy slur and drawl.

I was still looking at Kayla and saw her mouth the word "kids" with her nose wrinkled and eyebrows furrowed. I could think of worse insults.

"Yeah?" I had to guess that was the unseen Zeke now talking. "Well one of them *kids* had titties out to here!"

If the kids comment had struck Kayla wrong, that last one had absolutely pissed her off. She reached over her shoulder to pull her crossbow around. I grabbed her arm and gave a curt shake of my head.

"Looked like one of 'em was a young boy, though. That oughtta suit you fine, Merle," Zeke hooted.

I had not even realized that I'd grabbed for my own crossbow until Kayla's hand clutched my wrist. Now it was her turn to shake her head at me.

The voices grew faint and the topic of conversation turned to some woman named Marybeth who could apparently "suck the chrome off a trailer hitch" for whatever good that might do. I noticed Kayla blush, so I had to imagine they were hinting at something dirty.

Once they were gone and then we waited a while longer, I finally crept up the little embankment and glanced in the direction the men had been heading. I caught sight of them just as they rounded a distant bend in the road.

We stood up and dusted ourselves off and resumed our trip. At last we came across a small pack of zombies. I almost welcomed the break in what had been a long and uneventful day. Yes, I knew it was foolish to invite trouble, but a few zombies would allow me to get out some of my frustration. Also, I could see how well Kayla could handle herself.

The head count came to seven. No problem. I could take that many by myself. I darted in and stuck the first one in the head and then jumped back. Kayla was just moving in on her first target and I was admittedly impressed with the way she came in and stuck the thing in the eye without hesitation or appearing even a little bit awkward.

In no time, she had gone through the small group all on her own. I had stepped back and simply watched. To me, that was actually another plus in her book. She had focused on the task that needed to be done instead of worrying about where I might be at the moment.

"You didn't think it might be easier if we both took them down?" she asked with just that slightest hint of annoyance creeping into her voice that reminded me of the old Kayla.

"You want an honest answer?"

"I don't think so." Kayla wiped off her blade and gave it a quick inspection for any nicks before putting it away. "You wanted to make sure that I would not need you to babysit me. I get it."

And then she walked off, continuing on in the direction we'd been going. I stood there like an idiot for a moment before I realized that she was not going to stop or wait for me. She was irked. I guess she had a good reason. I was being a bit of a bitch and could admit as much. It was time to accept her help graciously and treat her like she was my partner on this little mission.

***

We had spotted the camp while we were still in the foothills. It was massive and only seemed larger now that I'd been back to Platypus Creek and seen how tiny we were in comparison. Kayla, to her credit, had not even suggested that perhaps we abandon this foolish quest that was certainly doomed to fail. Instead, she had simply shrugged her shoulders and followed me down to the creek that would bring us to the walls of Island City.

We had entered through a grate that allowed the creek to flow through. When we came out of the creek bed, we got a bit of a scare as a lone zombie had just apparently been sitting up against a tree. It had stringy hair and was so old that it looked like just another nearly rotten corpse that was slowly decaying away into oblivion. Also, the grass was tall enough that we basically walked right past the thing unaware until it reached out and grabbed Kayla by the leg. She let loose with a shriek that echoed in my ears like an alarm bell. It was hard for me to be mad at her since it had scared the hell out of me as well. Plus, I noticed just the slightest dark stain in the crotch of her pants, so I figured that she had suffered enough. She also managed to impress me once more by spiking that pathetic thing right on the top of its head.

When we reached the first street, that was when Kayla got

her first look at one of the massive piles of corpses. Also, now that I was looking again, I was very cognizant that there were no children. Suzi had made a point of asking me about that when we'd first met.

"They destroyed this place," Kayla said, her voice muffled from the rag she held over her nose and mouth.

It had been a while, and the flies were thick on the mounds of corpses. Some had been burnt, but even those had not been tended well, and so there were plenty of bodies that did not get devoured by the flames and were providing a disgusting layer of putrefying flesh under the charred skeletal remains. Various rodents and skittering creatures were burrowing amidst the carnage, some trotting away boldly with one prize or another.

One rat in particular actually stopped and faced me. It was holding a huge gray piece of something that I did not want to even try and identify in its mouth. Apparently it had not been around people enough to fear them. Considering its size, I imagined it to be the rat bully of the neighborhood. That might explain why it dropped its prize and made a sort of ratty growl at me before reaching back down, picking up its offal reward and trotting away with its long tail dragging in the dust.

"We need to be on our guard," I whispered.

"Why? It looks like they took down most if not all the zombies. Although why they would bother is beyond me."

"Unless they plan on inhabiting the city," I offered.

Kayla seemed to consider it. "If that was the case, why not move in yet?"

"You know…" I started as I climbed up onto the porch of one of the homes and then used a tree to reach the overhang so that I could see the area better. "I think you have a good point. Why hasn't Suzi moved her people in? They are living in tents on the plains when they could be sleeping under roofs and on actual beds."

"Maybe they keep losing their scouts and they are scared," a voice said from some neat hedges that made a natural fence between this house and the one next door.

"Cricket?" I asked.

I saw Kayla bring her crossbow up to her shoulder and turn in the direction of the voice. Good for her, but I recognized the old man's rasp in an instant.

"Girly? What in tarnation are you doing here?"

Sure enough, Cricket emerged, but he was not alone. Four more people came out; each of them was dressed in camo gear including hats that had nets over the faces. As an added effect, some had branches and such jutting from their clothes. Each had a scoped crossbow in hand. Kayla might get off one shot, but she would not likely survive to see if the bolt even struck her intended target.

"It's okay, Kayla," I called down. "Lower your weapon."

"Them first."

"She's a spunky one," a young woman said with a laugh that was not teasing or mean. If anything, she actually sounded impressed.

"Weapons down, kids," Cricket said to his companions. "These ain't from that army out there."

There was not the slightest argument or hesitation. All four crossbows dropped almost as one. A couple of the new arrivals even went so far as to remove their Panama hats so that we could see their faces. I was only a little surprised to discover that both were women. They didn't look much older than Kayla or me.

"Well they ain't locals," one of the girls said, the same one who had commented on Kayla's spunk from the sound of her voice.

"No, Nat, these here gals is from up the hill," Cricket said.

Nat was a stocky girl with curly brown hair. She had brown eyes that were bright and crinkled around the edges from her seemingly perpetual smile. She had a crooked nose that looked more cute than anything else and had a generous sprinkle of freckles for added measure. She could give Kayla a run for her money in the cleavage department for sure. That much was apparent even with all the heavy clothing. It was further accentuated by an unfairly skinny waist and equally curvy hips.

The other girl who had removed her hat had dark brown skin and thick, full lips. Her hair was worn in several braids that had been coiled and tied into a knot that would impress Medusa as it looked like she had a nest of snakes on top of her head.

"What brings you back here, Girly?" Cricket asked as the rest of his little band sauntered over to the porch of the house I'd been using to scout the area.

I was not quite ready to trust this man. It wasn't that I thought he might be one of the bad guys so to speak, but I was still just a bit leery.

"We came down to see if that army had moved on yet," I lied. I saw Kayla shoot me a quizzical look, but she quickly wiped all expression from her face and pretended to search for something in her pack.

"I don't see that as likely," Cricket said. He climbed up on the porch and took a seat, patting the spot beside him as an indication that I should join him.

"Been a lot of strange things since I saw you last. You ain't been the only ones skulking around Island City. Been a group of real suspicious types the past few days coming and poking around. They only come into the place when it is dark."

"Were they from that camp?" I asked.

"Nope, we got eyes on that camp. They have not been back inside the walls for quite a while. Kept losing too many foot patrols for some mysterious reason." That last statement was greeted by a few titters from his group.

There was a long silence that began to become more than a little uncomfortable. The other two members of Cricket's little band had removed their head gear. Both were men. One of them looked to be about Melissa's age, maybe close to forty. He had a nasty scar on his face, but it did not look like a bite. It was more like a burn. The skin of his right cheek was all lumpy and puckered. He had dark brown hair that was turning gray, and his eyes could not seem to find any one place to settle. We made eye contact once and he almost looked embarrassed by it.

The other guy was perhaps in his twenties. He was Hispanic and I could see the hint of a tattoo peeking above the neckline of his jacket. His black hair was buzzed down to just stubble, and he had an oddly well-trimmed beard. I say oddly because they all looked like they were living in the wilderness where things like shaving or trimming a beard to such precision takes time and a few minutes in front of a mirror. He smiled when we made eye contact and now it was my turn to blush just a little as I realized that I had been staring. He was perhaps the most attractive man I think I have ever seen in my life.

"We should be going," I blurted, catching just the hint of a smile on the man's face as I took one more look before forcing my eyes to tear away from him.

"Rodrigo!" Cricket snapped. "Quit it!"

"Quit what?" the young man asked in confusion.

"Put your damn hat back on, you're getting the young lady all twitterpated." Cricket winked at me and made me blush so hard that I felt like my ears might catch on fire if this continued.

"Thalia? Are you okay?" I heard Kayla ask over the rushing of blood echoing in my ears and my thudding heart that had somehow moved up to my throat instead of staying in my chest where it belonged.

"F-f-fine," I managed. I hopped from the porch and turned to face Cricket. "I would love to stay for a while, but I have to get going. I need to make some observations and then report back."

"Oh my!" Cricket laughed. "Girly, you are perhaps the worst liar I have ever seen in my life. If I ever get the old gang back together for our regular poker night, I absolutely must invite you."

"I don't know what you are talking about." Even I heard how fast I was talking. The lie was leaping from my tongue and waving its arms for everybody to see.

"Please tell me you and this other young lady are not out here by yourselves?" Cricket jumped down beside me and leaned down to where he could look me in the eyes.

I wanted to tell him that the rest of my group was around someplace, but I knew that he would see through me. While I did not have to actually tell him everything, I felt that maybe I could share part of my reason for being here.

"A couple of us got captured by those people." I hiked a

thumb over my shoulder to indicate the sprawling camp. "We got away, but there is concern that she might try to hunt us down and attack. I was just trying to check and see if they showed any signs of coming after us."

"You escaped from that place?" Nat asked, sounding impressed.

"I had help," I said, deciding that I was still being truthful enough that I would not give myself away.

Cricket seemed to consider my words for a moment. At last, he clapped his hands together and stood up. "Okay, kids, we should move along. It is obvious that this girl don't want our help. Trust is a thing earned more than given. She don't want us meddling in her business."

I looked around and saw shrugs, but nothing much more than that as the four fell in and began to follow Cricket away. I looked at Kayla for any clue as to what she felt and got nothing but a raised eyebrow.

"Wait!" I called.

Cricket turned around and motioned for the others to stop. He said something to Rodrigo and then broke away from them to return to where I was still trying to figure out exactly what I was doing.

For better or worse, I took a gamble and told most of the story to the old man. I left out little things like how I had actually run away to do this and that it would be very probable that somebody might come looking for me since it would not be a mystery as to where I had run off.

Cricket was silent for several seconds. I looked over at Kayla and saw that she was not entirely pleased with my revealing all that I had to these strangers. Then I scanned the faces of Cricket's little team who had strolled up during my account. They appeared to be interested in what the old man might say and kept glancing back and forth between me and him.

"I guess we know what we will be doing today, kids," Cricket finally said, rubbing his hands together for emphasis. "We will need to be extra careful. That group over yonder is nothing to take lightly. We already seen how they done our people. And I still ain't heard good reasons one way or the other to make me believe them folks is here for any reason but to take what ain't theirs. This Suzi woman is feeding you a yarn, pure and simple. She rolled into this valley and destroyed everything that she saw fit to mow down. The smaller communities were not her target. She wants Island City. We got walls and farms and proper houses. Hell, even gots a power grid once somebody that knows how to fix it can come in and take care of the damage."

"So what do you suggest?" Kayla asked. "You seem to be all fired up to do something, let's hear your plan."

Cricket smiled and gave Kayla a wink. "You are a spunky one, I'll give ya that much." He turned back to me. "You say that terrible noise we heard was something they did to lure the zombie mob away?"

"Yep, they had noisemakers. A bunch of them went out on horses and actually changed the path the zombies were taking. Led them south, back down the valley and away from La Grande," I explained.

"Well then, seems to me like we need to bring them back, only, we gotta do it in such a way that they won't be able to just send out a few people on horseback. If we plan this right, we can split that herd into smaller groups. Once we do that, we bring those groups in from different sides. If they use the noisemakers, it will only serve to lure in some or all of the other groups."

It sounded like a good idea. The only problem that I saw with it was how we would manage such a feat. We would have to get close to that herd for one thing, and that was not something I was all that excited to do. Then there was the whole thing about trying to split the herd into smaller groups and bring them along until they were positioned just so.

Cricket had already come back to the porch and tossed his knapsack on it so he could rummage through it. Eventually he produced a very worn and tattered looking map. He unfolded it and spread it for us to see. It was hand drawn, but I could tell that great pains had been taken to ensure that it was not only detailed, but very accurate.

He showed us where everything was in relation to our current position. He traced a path with his finger in the direction that the zombie herd had been taken. The land to the southeast had all been farms way back in the old days.

"Seems likely that they will move along the La Grande-Baker Highway. Zombies ain't much in the way of brains, but they are a lot like electricity and follow the path of least resistance," Cricket explained. "If we can break them up into smaller groups, we can actually come in from the north and the south. The hard part will be keeping that group moving up from the south from getting too far away. This will rely on timing, and without any form of communication, that will be tricky at best."

"Bicycle." Rodrigo stepped up and I felt my heart do a flip in my chest as he placed a hand on my shoulder to make room and squeeze in. "If one of us travels with each team and has a bicycle ready, we can give updates."

"Something moving like that is bound to draw attention," Cricket warned. "It ain't like runnin' in the shadows or the tall grass. Whoever does that will have to be using the roads. How do we know that Suzi woman ain't got patrols out there?"

"They have horses," I finally managed to say once I found a drop of saliva in my mouth.

"Horses are easy to spot, plus, they make noise. A good bicycle is pretty quiet," Rodrigo insisted.

"So I take it you are one of the volunteers," Cricket said, and then turned to the others. "Who else thinks they can do this?"

There was a moment of silence, and I saw Nat start to open her mouth, but Kayla blurted, "I'll do it."

Now it was my turn to give dirty looks. She and I needed to stay together. We still did not know how we could rescue Jackson. And if we were going to bring in a herd of zombies, then getting him out was even more important. It would be like I was putting the gun to his head and pulling the trigger.

"Well then we best get a move on. The more we talk, the further away them walkers get." Cricket turned to me. "You and I will pick teams. You go first."

Pick teams? I thought. This wasn't some sort of game. My friend's life was at stake. Still, if he was willing to help, and since I did not have a better plan, I guess I would have to make do with what I had at my disposal.

Also, beggars can't be choosers. I was not so foolish as to believe that I was going to somehow pull off a miracle. In fact, if I gave it too much thought, I began to wonder about my sanity. This plan had lots of flaws, but it was simple at its very core; and one of the things that I had learned in my relatively few years on this earth was that simplicity was often best. Too many times, things were botched because we made them much more difficult than necessary.

"Nat?" I finally said once Cricket gave me a nudge.

Once we had finished, it was also decided that the odd person out, the other girl who went by the name of Nadine, would post up on top of the old Island City Elementary School. A forty foot tower had been built on top of the building that gave at least some sort of vantage point. Nadine was told to slip into one of the houses and find some sheets. If it looked like any serious activity was taking place in the encampment, she was to hang the sheets from the tower. Again, it wasn't a perfect system, but it would have to do.

We all headed out once a pair of bicycles in good working order was found. Kayla would stick with me and Rodrigo with Cricket once we had to go our separate ways.

By the end of the day, I was beginning to wonder if we would ever find the zombies. It was obvious that they had come this way as the ground was littered with things best not looked at too closely. Also, there were the occasional creepers that could not keep pace. Those were easy to spike as we traveled all that day and then the next.

At last, on the third day, we could see the tail end of the herd. Fortunately, it looked like we had caught a bit of a break. A small town had acted almost as a natural jetty for the zombies. They had sort of scattered a bit and diffused. I did notice that a few structures had large mobs of the undead gathered around them, and I had to wonder if we might actually be saving some strangers as we went about our business.

It was not easy to get the zombies' attention. With so many of them moaning and crying, they were really quite loud. We banged on the hoods of cars using the pommels of our machetes, but that only generated a limited interest from those closest. It wasn't until Rodrigo appeared with a huge sledge hammer that we finally managed to start pulling a good number away. It was far from the majority of the herd, though; and as we moved away leading the chunk that had been enticed, I noticed two locations in particular where the mobs of the undead had not been drawn away. There had to be somebody or a group inside. I would try to make it a point to come back here if we managed to pull this off.

And free Jackson.

And survive.

It took the better part of the next four days to get half the distance covered. At this rate, I did not think that we would ever get back to the La Grande area. Cricket sent Rodrigo ahead on his own after the second day just to get a visual on Suzi's people and ensure that they were still encamped in the open valley.

I had to wonder why she had yet to occupy Island City. It made no sense to remain out in the open. The second time that Rodrigo was sent was also the day that our groups separated. That proved to be quite a chore and my herd ended up being the smaller of the two by almost half. It was still a very large group numbering in the thousands, but the group following Cricket back along the La Grande-Baker Highway stretched on for at least a mile and were shoulder to shoulder across all four lanes and then some as they trudged along.

The early days had been a simple matter of all of us moving ahead far enough so that we could make camp and get some rest. One person was tasked to stay with the herd and keep them coming, and we rotated out of that position regularly. Once we got closer to the valley, we knew that sleep was going to be a luxury that we could not afford as we needed to try and keep the herds on track after the split.

Cricket had the unenviable task of looping them back

around and actually leading his bunch in a massive circle before re-directing them back towards the encampment. As the sun set, on this, the sixth day, I knew that tomorrow would see things happen fast and furious.

I was excited as well as scared. It had already been agreed that once we knew the herd was moving towards the encampment and riders were sent out to whichever one of our groups came within sight of their patrols to employ the noisemakers, I would be going off on my own to see if there was any way that I would be able to save Jackson.

Oddly enough, it was Kayla who pulled me aside. We had moved ahead far enough that I would be able to catch a final nap before embarking on my mission. Nat was currently down the road a ways and leading the zombies along by banging on a huge garbage can lid with a rather nifty looking spiked club she usually carried on her hip.

"Thalia, don't do anything foolish. Jackson would not want you to die trying to save him. It would sort of defeat the purpose. If you can do this, great, but if not, you need to be smart enough to run. Just promise me that you will keep that option open."

I was actually a little choked up.

"I promise," I finally answered.

I had no idea if I was being honest, and I don't know if she believed me, but it would have to do. Things were about to get crazy.

13

Vignettes LXV

The next several days, Juan continued to test out his leg. The swelling was almost gone, leaving only some nasty discoloration behind. The girls liked to tease him and say he had a deader leg because of the ugly greens, blacks, and purples.

While there were moments when he would feel the pull of sorrow at the loss of Mackenzie, it would usually end up being a short-lived dip as his daughters filled his heart with a happiness that he had not realized until now that he had taken for granted.

One morning, Juan woke to absolute silence. While that was not all too uncommon, there was also something else niggling at the back of his mind. He sat up in bed, his eyes going over to where Denita and Della slept.

Empty.

"Girls?" he called, pulling on his boots.

There was no answer, and Juan reached over for his crutches. Making his way to the door, he opened it to discover a slight drizzle beginning. The sky was overcast, and a breeze made the chill morning air seem that much colder.

Juan stepped out onto the porch and looked around. He didn't see anything. Listening, he heard nothing except the sound of raindrops hitting on the corrugated metal roof of the smokehouse.

183

Juan called again, still not alarmed. After all, it wasn't the first time that he'd woken up to discover that the girls were already up and about. They'd become very good at keeping themselves busy. Juan had decided to steal a page from Gerald's book and shown them the game of "who can pick the most weeds from Gerald's garden" one afternoon. Oddly enough, it hadn't caught on. Still, the girls were receptive to the idea that it would be nice to keep things taken care of for the man in his absence and had made it a point to pick weeds despite its lack of a fun factor.

By the time he'd made a complete circuit of the cabin's grounds, occasionally calling out Della and Denita's name, Juan was beginning to grow concerned. The one rule that he had stressed repeatedly was the one about not going out of sight of the cabin unless he was with them.

While the girls were both smart, that did not give them all the necessary tools to deal with an unforgiving Alaskan wilderness that still sported bears, wolves (living and undead), as well as zombies. A shudder rippled through Juan as a few other ideas still ingrained in his mind from the days of the old world made an appearance. The main problem with those thoughts resided in the simple fact that, if anything, people had gotten worse.

After two more circuits around the cabin, and a third where he hugged the tree line, Juan was overwhelmed with dread. He'd gotten lazy. He'd let himself believe that the girls would be fine and that they would not get into any trouble.

"They're freaking seven years old, you idiot!" he cursed himself. "Of course they are going to disobey…get into trouble."

Juan looked skyward. "Is this how it goes, God? I find happiness with Mackenzie, so you take her away. I come to the realization that I still have my girls to live for, so you take them from me too? Are you trying to tell me something?"

Juan raged and swore. He said things to God that would have made his mother cry. He alternated between challenging any deity that would listen, to begging for their help. He was still kneeling in the mud when the snap of a stick made his head pop up. He looked in the direction that he was certain the sound had come and hoped for a very specific outcome. He wanted his daughters to come through that brush...alive. He knew it was important that he specify. At this exact moment, he doubted his ability to do anything but accept a horrible fate if the zombified versions of Della and Denita emerged.

As luck would have it, it was not his daughters in any form. A rabbit made a meek series of hops until it was out in the clear. Juan looked at the animal, its nose twitching and eyes trying to scan everything at once for any sign of a predator. After a moment, a second rabbit joined the first and the two made a hopping scamper for the lush green shoots of Gerald's garden.

Juan sighed and dropped his chin to his chest. A moment later, there was a louder commotion from the woods. Juan barely had time to register that the rabbits had taken off in response to the new and sudden noise. Another tremendous crash came, and the dense woods seemed to rip open and give birth to a moose!

The creature was easily a foot taller than Juan if Juan had been standing. From his knees, the animal looked even more massive. It snorted once and pawed at the ground with a mighty hoof before its head swung so that it could look over its shoulder.

Juan knew what fear looked like in an animal. He'd seen it before when he managed to bring down a deer but the pathetic thing had been wounded but still alive, unable to flee, and thus, helpless as he stood over it with his knife. He remembered hesitating to finish the job. Keith had been on hand and had to nudge him, reminding him that he was only making the poor thing suffer.

After Juan had slit the deer's throat, he'd gone about the normal routine of field stripping it and bringing it back to camp. However, he'd never been able to take a bite of the meat from that kill. Something about it had seemed too personal.

His eyes scanned the moose for any sign of injury. He didn't see anything. That was a relief as well as a bit unsettling. A few seconds later, the huge beast took off in an awkward but deliberate run. Thankfully, it was running at an angle away from him, because Juan doubted his ability to get out of the way in time had things been different.

Then his troubles grew exponentially. There was that single moment of silence that made the hairs on the back of his neck stand up. And then, there was a crash as the woods right by where the moose had emerged a moment ago just seemed to fold down flat.

"Holy crap," Juan breathed.

***

"So you are saying that some group of crazies is outfitting the stench bags with noisemakers and then somehow herding them to someplace where they just march into the water and come up on the shores of your little island paradise?" Paddy sat on a log with his feet dangling in the air.

When he had in fact pulled out a small corn cob pipe and lit it up, Vix had reached her limit. "Oh, come on!" she exclaimed. "You can't really be doing this. Is this on purpose? Are you toying with me?"

"What on earth could you be meanin' there, lassie?" Paddy's lips curled up in an impish smile, his eyes glittering with mirth and mischief.

Using her arms in a head-to-toe gesture; she had indicated the man's garb and striking resemblance to every cartoon leprechaun she'd ever seen. "You look like you just fell out of a child's box of cereal."

"You wouldn't be meanin' the frosted oat variety with sweet surprises, now would you?"

"Alright, cut that out!"

There was a moment of silence, and Vix felt the giant introduced as Seamus take a step closer. She felt her mouth go dry. She was about to die because she'd offended an Irishman who refused to accept that he was dressed like a caricature.

"You have to let her off the hook now, Paddy," a deep voice that sounded like gravel being crushed spoke from behind her.

"Okay. When you are right, you are right. But I believe that I have now paid my losing bet and we are square." Paddy still had the Irish lilt, but he ripped the hat off and glared at the thing before tossing it into the tall grass. "Now, back to this very interesting tale you have shared about some sort of zombie apocalypse version of *The Pied Piper*. You say that they are attaching noise makers to some of the beasts and then somehow luring them to the ends of England where they are willingly walking into the sea, only to come ashore at your little island settlement?"

Vix nodded.

"I would be willing to bet that it is Dolph and his gang of criminals," Seamus muttered and then spat as if he'd just tasted something foul.

"Dolph has been making quite a name for himself the past few years," Paddy said when Vix simply looked from one man to the other with a blank expression. "He and his band of miscreants came across the channel from France as best anybody can tell. Apparently he has organized some sort of make-believe Nazi thing and has been making a point of finishing what that idiot Hitler failed to do. He has been leading what his broadcasts claim as the New Blitzkrieg in his quest to conquer Great Britain."

"Wait!" Vix held up a hand. "Did you say broadcasts?"

"Oh yes, he has managed to power up a transmitter and everything. He has his army—or whatever they call themselves—slip in close to populated settlements and mount these horrendous PA systems. The poor bastards wake to Ride of the Valkyries, and then they get the German, French, and finally the English translation of his rousing speech, most of which he very blatantly stole from the original German lunatic, Adolph Hitler."

Vix was at a loss for words. She looked from one man to the other. Each simply stared back at her and smiled.

"This is another joke. Which one of you lost the bet that has you saying this?" she finally asked, breaking her silence after what felt like forever.

"Sadly, this is not one of our little wagers," Paddy replied.

"And is nobody doing anything to stop this guy?"

"I think your little tale of zombies with noise makers actually answers the very question we have been asking for quite some time. You see, nobody has survived to tell the tale of how he has conquered everything in his path. There were rumors of course, but who wants to believe that somebody would mobilize an army of the undead?"

"We have to tell Mike," Seamus said, rising to his feet. "Would you be kind enough to join us and let our commander know everything that you have shared with us?"

"Do I really have a choice?" Vix asked.

"Actually," Paddy hopped off the log and scrubbed his hands together to clean them off, "you are more than free to go. We are not the sort to take people prisoner. However, I do believe that it would be a benefit to us, your people, as well as any other settlements that might yet remain if we were to perhaps do something to put a stop to this lunatic once and for all."

Vix had to admit, going it alone was not likely to yield her much results. Also, now that she knew more about the possible enemy, she was more than certain that she would need all the help she could find. Besides, the people of New England had grown soft in her opinion. They had become too reliant on their island as the primary source of their protection. They were ripe for the picking for somebody like this Dolph person.

"I'll come with you," Vix finally agreed.

"That would be splendid," Paddy said with a clap of his hands. "And would your hidden friend like to join us? Or do you plan to leave her behind?"

As if that were a cue, three more men emerged from the tall grass. Each of them wore a variety of blades and held some rather exquisite looking bows in their hand. Also emerging with a gag tied around her mouth was Chaaya.

***

Luck was certainly with Chad. He hit the water and stopped just shy of the river bed, the force of his body impacting with the churning surface almost knocking the wind from him. A second later, he brushed past the giant rock that he had missed by inches. As he emerged, he coughed and sputtered, his body still dealing with the shock of the icy waters, but his lungs needing to be free of liquid overriding everything at the moment.

Chad spun, his neck craning up to the ledge that he'd just thrown himself from a few seconds ago. Two people on horseback arrived just as he went around a small bend in the stream. Once he was out of sight, he made for the shore. It was a bit more difficult than he expected, and by the time he was able to stand up and walk, he was panting like he'd just finished a mile long sprint.

Taking a quick personal inventory, Chad was not surprised that the only weapon he still possessed was a belt knife. He was going to have to proceed with extreme caution. He knew that there were a large number of zombies to be wary of; but those did not hold a candle to these mysterious people that had come from out of nowhere.

Moving into the tall ferns and dense undergrowth of a forest allowed to reclaim the land unhindered, Chad made it a point to stay quiet. He moved in small bursts. The moment he even thought that he heard something, he froze and held his breath.

He had been on the move in what he was almost certain had to be the general direction of home, Chad eventually reached the old interstate. He had to work his way down a little slash between two sheer and rocky slopes to actually reach the edge of where the road carved its way north and south. At this very moment, the interstate seemed a thousand miles wide. There would be absolutely no cover.

Peeking up from his location, Chad could not see any signs of the horsemen. He also did not see any of the undead. Actually, at the moment, he would welcome a zombie...hell, even a herd would be okay. Zombies were just not that scary any longer. They were easy to distract and seldom a cause of death these days.

Deciding that he did not want to just stay here until he was discovered, Chad finally rose to a crouch. Despite the fact that it would probably be an exercise in futility, he unsnapped the little leather strap and pulled his knife from its sheath.

Taking one more look in both directions, Chad steadied his breath and mentally gave himself a 'Ready...set...go!' command. Taking off at a sprint, Chad was at the concrete divider in short order. He threw a leg over and landed awkwardly as he made the mistake of looking back over his shoulder instead of where he put his feet.

Landing hard, Chad felt his chin bounce off the pavement. The pain and warmth were instant and he had no doubt that he'd busted himself open. Scrambling to his feet, he fully expected to see his hunters emerge and turn towards him in pursuit.

Nothing.

Chad took off again. This time, it was like that 'running in sand' nightmare where you ran as fast as you could and made no progress. And then he was on the other side and diving down into the dense and welcome growth of the tall grass. He stayed in a crouch until he reached the woods. Once he felt safe enough, he slowed to a walk. As the adrenaline began to ebb, he could feel pain just about everywhere in his body. His ankle felt like it was in bad shape, his boot beginning to feel like it was constricting any blood flow to his right foot, and his thigh was on fire.

He continued to move with caution. It was quite possible that whoever these people were, they had returned to wherever they came from. It was just as likely that they knew where he would be headed and move to intercept him before he could warn everybody of this new danger.

He glanced over his shoulder more than once the rest of the way until he could see the walls that signaled his safety. When he reached the massive and open clearing that was strictly and very well maintained, Chad began to wave his arms above his head in an obvious sign of distress and danger to get the attention of the tower and gate guards.

He had only covered half the distance when the closest set of gates opened and a team of five horses came out at a full gallop. Chad stopped walking and let them close the remaining distance. As they approached he could see that they were searching the tree line past him for any signs of danger.

The leader yanked back on the reins and came to a stop. The

others stopped just beyond and the riders were obviously looking for trouble.

"Thank goodness another one of you made it," the man (Chad was almost certain that his name was Marcus) said with obvious relief.

"What do you mean?" Chad asked. "I know I got hit and the riders who came to divert the herd of zombies rode into an ambush, but—"

"Two other mounted patrols were hit and only three of our twenty rovers have returned…counting you," Marcus explained.

Chad was pulled up onto the back of one of the horses and they returned to the relative safety of their walled community. As they did, Chad had to wonder if there was anyplace left in the world that might be safe.

***

"Who the hell are you?" Jody asked, climbing to his feet, but maintaining a wary posture.

The man across from him was not incredibly imposing. He seemed average height, and his mop of curly, sandy colored hair was a filthy mess. He wore wire-framed glasses without any lenses, and his eyes were sort of a muddy brown. If Jody passed this guy on the street, he would forget him almost instantly (except for the wire-framed glasses, maybe).

"My name is Gable Matczak. I met your friend Tracy. Tracy Sasser I think was his name? We can talk later about your choice in squad members." The man shot a glance down at the dead body lying a few feet away. "We don't have time right now, you still got a couple of these folks lurking."

Almost on cue, a man let out a yell and dove from the top of the RV. Gable side-stepped with an incredible elegance and the would-be attacker landed gracelessly on the ground. Gable stepped in just as quick and dug his booted heel down into the back of the neck of the man. There was only a moment of struggle before an audible 'crack' ended it.

"You go that way, I'll go this way," Gable whispered, point-

191

ing out the way he wanted Jody to go.

"B-b-but—" Jody stammered.

"No time! Later!" the man barked as he took off at a fast trot. And with that, Gable was gone.

Jody turned and headed for the corner of the last RV. He heard running footsteps and halted, ducking low. A person could get a knife in the chest catching somebody by surprise. Getting low almost guaranteed that any reflexive action would catch nothing but air.

Sure enough, the person rounded the corner almost at a run. They almost collided with Jody and ended up on their back as they tried to leap backwards and escape. A large knife swished through the air a good few inches above Jody's head.

A second later, Jody was up and on the man. He smashed the butt of his knife into the person's head with the intent that maybe he could take one alive and get a few answers. The man's eyes rolled back and Jody quickly searched the body for cuffs. He found them on a belt pouch and flipped his captive onto their stomach. He pulled the man's arms around behind his back and slapped on the cuffs. As a secondary measure, he pulled off the belt the man was wearing and wrapped it around the head, cinching it tight as a gag.

Confident that this person was out of the game, he scrambled up and took off at a jog. He did not hear anything and was only slightly surprised when he passed one of the RVs and caught a glimpse of this Gable person getting to his feet. Another man was down; another neck had been snapped. Jody was no idiot; that took a degree of strength to pull off. Snapping a neck was not as easy as it looked in the movies.

"Where is the girl you were with?" Gable asked as he approached.

"Wait!" Jody hissed, holding his hands up. "I appreciate the fact that you more than likely just saved my ass. But I don't know who you are or where you came from. Not to sound ungrateful, but I would not just tell you something like that."

The man paused and seemed to consider Jody's words. He pressed his lips tight and then gave a curt nod. "I understand where you are coming from, and if we had all day to shoot the shit, I could tell you all kinds of stories and give a proper introduction. As it is, I have no idea what you are doing here and could have just as easily killed you if not for seeing you take down a couple of these assholes. Somebody very dear to me is in that house and I plan on getting her out. We obviously have similar interests, or at least it seems that way. When we are done, we can exchange names and all that crap."

Jody saw the man's point. Time was of the essence. He had no idea what was going on in that house, but he had a pretty good idea that this guy could help him get his daughter out.

"They have my little girl in there," Jody blurted.

"So then you see how us standing here and wasting time with all this talking nonsense is a stupid thing." Gable pushed past Jody and moved to the end of the RV where he could get a good look at the house.

"She is on the other side of the house," Jody whispered, despite being far enough from the house that it was unlikely that anybody could hear if he spoke in a conversational voice. "There was one guy on a balcony. She was going to try and get close enough to take him down. She is a pretty good shot...and her name is Jan."

"Fine," Gable muttered, but Jody knew the man was paying him almost no attention. He was focused on the main entrance.

Suddenly, the front door opened and a figure stepped outside. Jody knew instantly who it was and felt like he had obviously missed something; otherwise, how could he explain the presence of Margarita?

"Hey, Jody?" she sing-songed. "Come out, come out wherever you are."

***

Entry Thirty-six—
I am waiting. I am hunting.

When it comes right down to the cold, hard facts, it is not like I have anything else to do. Otherwise I probably would have quit doing this a long time ago.

As I sit here with my journal, I wonder if anybody ever reads the ones that I leave behind. I am sort of sneaky in that I usually go someplace where they have books and such for trade and then slip mine in amongst the others.

Guerrilla marketing at its finest.

I should also admit here that I don't always catch my target. In fact, more have managed to elude me than I have captured. It is the nature of things. I do my best, but the reality is that, unless the person is actually pointed out to me on the spot, I have to search. People can fade into oblivion now. No more Amber Alerts to aid in these sorts of things. Also, and this is the part that I do struggle with from time to time, I am taking one side of a story and buying into it completely.

There was one guy who denied what he'd been accused of right up to the very end. He died with "I didn't do it" on his lips. Maybe he was just made of stubborn stock. Or…maybe he was not lying.

There is no court of law these days. Sure, some settlements have their own version of law and order; but I have seen people ended based solely on hearsay. Again, that is the world we live in. Not that it was all that different before, but it is even more lax in actual justice and quick to condemn. It reminds me of stories of the Salem Witch Trials. Point and scream and you got a conviction.

All that said, I don't have any doubts this woman has done what she is accused of doing. And now that I am hot on her trail and confident that she no longer has the baby with her, I am eager to catch her and put her down like a mad dog.

But on nights like this when I can hear the screams of a man being broken on the wheel (who thought of that nasty little sentence?), I wonder if I am part of the problem, or part of the solution. I tell myself that I am some sort of avenger, but I am really nothing more than a contract killer. What is worse, I don't even require payment in many cases. Does that make me evil? Am I the one who people should be hunting?

Entry Thirty-seven—
She slipped my grasp again.

I was right on her heels. In fact, at one point, I bet we were within fifty feet of each other. Only, this time, I feel like it is just a matter of time before I have her. She made a big mistake. It is also obvious that she has no idea that I am on her trail; unless she actually wants to be caught.

Early this morning, I was sitting down to breakfast when there was a huge commotion. I walked out onto the street, my senses tingling. Sure enough, this lady drops to her knees in the middle of what passes for a street in this little community. She starts screaming and crying about how her baby is gone.

Naturally, everybody is all twisted up and unsettled. One guy even spins on me. Newcomers are always the easiest target. That is also why I sleep in a public place most times when I stop over for a spell. It ensures that I am not unaccounted for at any time.

I gave a description of Mary and asked if anybody recalls seeing somebody that fits the bill. Sure enough, the mother said that Mary stopped at her home just before sunset. She said that she was just passing through and wanted to know if there might be a wagon for sale. The woman had directed her to a neighbor.

That man picked up the story from there. He recalled Mary and admitted to selling her a small cart as well as one of his old mules. As it was, she could barely afford either, but he felt so sorry for her seeing as how she was just trying to escape the clutches of a terrible man who beat her regularly. He did not re-call at any point seeing a child.

Runners were sent to each of the gates. (This particular community covers an area of about ten square blocks.) The north gate came back with an affirmative. While we were waiting, I managed to let a few of the calmer folks know who I was and what I was doing. As soon as I knew which gate she left from, I was on the move.

I bent my rule about not accepting any form of pre-payment when one of the people who had heard everything made the offer of lending me a horse. I swore that I would return it if at all possible. The man told me that it would be mine to keep if I brought the baby back. As I started to ride away, he amended his offer in a harsh whisper that it would also hold up if I only managed to bring back the head of this evil woman.

I am certain that I will catch her tomorrow. Currently I am just waiting for the ferryman to return to take me across. I can actually see the wagon on the flat-bottomed barge that is just now halfway across this river. The man who took my fare affirmed that a woman fitting Mary's description was the driver of that wagon. Also, she was in the company of a very fussy little boy who could not yet be a year old.

It is still a few hours until dark. There is simply no way that I can imagine her escaping me.

14

The Geek's Wife Makes Waves

"I think maybe we should send for Elliot," one of the guards managed to choke out.

"How long have you been in this place?" Catie said with a scowl. "And lay that body down. You don't need to hold him any longer. He won't be putting up any more resistance."

The two security guards laid the body of Clarence Carson down on the floor. The hole in in his temple was still oozing dark blood that smelled almost as bad as the cell.

Catie had demanded that the two guards hold Clarence Carson so that she could put him down. One of them had laughed, thinking that she might actually be joking. She ended that notion when she grabbed the young man in a wristlock and slammed him against the wall. She told him he could either help, or she would break his wrist and then make him do it anyway. Only, with an injured wrist, it might be possible that Mr. Carson would get loose or perhaps land a few good licks.

There had been no further argument after that display. The two men had opened the cell door. Oddly enough, Clarence Carson did not put up a fight. He stepped forward and looked Catie in the eyes as she held the spike in her left hand. She asked him if he had anything he wanted passed along to anybody in particular.

The man looked at her in open disbelief. Something harsh came to his lips, but he bit it back. His eyes changed just a little, going softer. It was not anything to do with the tracers; no, his glare retreated, and there was actually something warm and human in them for a moment. It was in that instant that Catie had to brace herself for what she was about to do. It was also then that she was hit with the largest wave of doubt that she'd had so far in regards to if she was on the side of good.

"There ain't no more good and bad," Kevin had said one *night when they talked about some of the things that they had seen, done, or said. "Now it is all about the shades of gray. You just have to choose how black you will allow your gray to become."*

"I have a son back at Montague. His name is Kelly. If you guys go in there and you are able to find him, don't let him do anything stupid. Tell him that I want him to at least find out. And if he is one of you people, try to make sure that he does right."

Clarence said all of that while he looked directly into Catie's eyes. Then he glanced down at the spike and back to her. He gave a nod and stared straight ahead. When she brought the weapon up, the man had one last thing to add. "We ain't so different, you and I. And of all these punks that I have met since being brought here, you got more balls than any of 'em."

It took all of her effort to finish, but Catie drew her hand back and then plunged the long, thin metal spike into the temple of Clarence Carson. The man went rigid for a moment, and then he began to shudder violently as his brain apparently fired off one final barrage of information to the body. At last, Clarence's eyes rolled back in his head and he slumped, going completely limp. Neither guard seemed prepared for the sudden amount of dead weight that they were holding and had to struggle to keep from dropping the corpse.

Catie turned and went back up the hall. She waited for the two young men to join her. Now she would see what came next. Maybe she would talk to Elliot first. She wanted to be the one to tell him that Clarence was, in fact, dead. She also wanted to warn him to never put her in a position like that again. But that was one option, and not likely the direction she was headed.

"I've been here three years," a voice said, snapping Catie out of her ruminations.

"What?" She turned to see both men standing a few feet away.

"I said I have been here three years," the man with the skin problems spoke after clearing his throat.

"You act like that is the first time you have been around death," Catie said as she folded her arms across her chest and leveled her best military inspection gaze at the young man.

"No, ma'am...err...well..." the kid stammered and stumbled, his face turning a bright and very embarrassed red.

"First time around a living person dying?" Catie amended.

The young man said nothing. He simply stared at the ground. His head might have given the slightest of nods in affirmation.

"That bother you back there?" Catie stepped close to the man and hid a smile when the other guard actually stepped a few paces back.

Once again she did not receive a verbal confirmation. However, at least his head bobbed a bit more perceptibly this time. Catie put a curled index finger under the young man's chin and tilted his head up so that his eyes were no longer glued to the ground.

"Good. It should always be a struggle to take the life of a living person. If that ever becomes too easy, then you might want to consider the possibility that the next life that needs taking is your own." She saw his eyes widen and his mouth opened, but Catie fixed him with her own look that was equal parts compassion and command. "Killing is not something you should ever take lightly. So if you feel bad right now, that's okay."

"Do you feel bad?" the fresh faced guard asked.

"Jeez, Trevor, what do you think?" the other scolded.

"Let her answer, Jimmy."

Catie eyed the two young men for a moment. She took a deep breath and then searched herself for the truth. That was the problem; in the past couple of days, her truth had shifted. She was still trying to pin it down.

"I feel bad that I had to take a life." She once more fixed first one of the young men and then the other with her gaze, trying her best to ensure that she got her point across. "But killing Clarence was a mercy. He would have suffered otherwise. There was no need for him to endure that slow change.

"Also, Clarence is a soldier in this new world. Soldiers die. That has been the truth for an eternity. That does not mean we don't mourn their loss, but it is something that they face each day knowing of the possibility that it may be their last. In the Old World, I think too many people forgot that simple truth."

Catie recalled a few times right after all of that terrible madness of September 11, 2001 before she had enlisted; she recalled an instance in particular when she saw a man in uniform get off the bus as it stopped in her town on its journey to wherever. People started clapping. Sadly, that sentiment of appreciation faded just like anything else. But until the day she had signed those papers for herself, she always made it point if she crossed paths with one of the men or women in uniform to walk right up to them and say "thank you."

"Now, I want both of you to go find something to wrap the body in so it can be disposed of properly," Catie said with a sigh that was partially coming off the adrenaline of the situation and partially from a deep fatigue that threatened to never release its hold on her soul.

Catie turned and made her way outside. She reached the street and decided to take a walk around before returning to Elliot. Eventually she passed a massive building that showed signs of a great deal of life. Despite most of the exterior sign having fallen off over the years, she still recognized the remnants of a Marriott logo. Unlike the other buildings, this one looked like the bottom three floors had been cleared. None of the windows remained on those levels. Armed individuals could be seen roaming the length of the open floors. One actually waved at Catie as she stood looking up at the building. A large section of the sidewalk in front of the building was heavily stained as if perhaps some great battle had taken place.

"Thinking about staking your own quarters?" a voice said from behind her.

Catie had mixed feelings about not immediately reaching for her weapon. She had let some of her guard down; or perhaps it was an effect of being tired and a shade wrung out. Still, she turned to face the owner of the voice.

"What are you doing out here, Marty?" Catie asked.

"Melvin is more of a book guy than I am. He was walking around in a daze with drool coming out of his mouth as he roamed the aisles at the library," the big man said with an easy smile. "Just passed one of the boys that you traumatized and he said that you headed this way."

"There are some surprisingly naïve people here for as open as this place is." Catie turned back to the hotel-turned-housing complex. "For all their freedom, they are very isolated from what is out there."

"Maybe they prefer to kill zombies. Maybe they are not the boogeymen that Dean has been preaching."

"That is fine until you consider the kidnappings."

"How do you figure?"

"They are snatching kids from their families," Catie pointed out the obvious.

"I hear that some of those kidnappings have been arranged. There were a lot of parents not happy with things at Montague. They wanted their kids to have a shot at a better life. Pretty normal stuff if you ask me."

"Are you telling me that these kidnappings are simple relocations?" Catie turned back to the large man and planted her hands on her hips.

"Not all of them," Marty said with a shake of his head, "but well over half. And where do you think they are getting their information?"

Catie opened her mouth and then shut it with a snap. That fact had never once raised itself as a question in her mind. She had assumed that it might be the bracers that the immune wore. Yet, even with markers to identify the immune, a kidnapping has to be targeted in advance for what was going on here.

"Okay," Catie finally pushed that bit aside, "let's say I give you that one. But here is my big question. You know what Elliot has planned for the people at Montague, right?" Marty nodded. "And are you okay with that? We would be killing innocent women and children."

"And do you think that they will just line up voluntarily and take the shot?"

"So we infect people on purpose? You can paint it with any pretty color you like, but genocide is still genocide. We would be exterminating people for no other reason than they are not like us."

"Or we can live under their heel? This takes the 'what if' out of the question. The more we can get on our side, the more people we have in place to stand against these communities that hunt us down, the ones that would just as easily kill us without any of the debate that you and I are having."

"And that makes them the bad guys? Will we ever be able to call ourselves good or righteous after we commit this act?" Catie had to struggle to keep the tears at bay. Her emotions were all bubbling to the surface again.

"You have been alive too long to think that way," Marty muttered with obvious discomfort; whether it was the topic or the fact that he could see Catie's emotions seething just below the surface, she didn't know. "It is as simple as survival. I'm glad that you are struggling with this. That sort of brings me to my next point."

Catie had to sniff hard to continue holding back the tears. She looked up at Marty and saw something now in his eyes that suddenly helped her regain her composure.

"What?" she asked once she cleared her throat and was con-fident in her ability to speak without her voice cracking or sounding strangled.

"Elliot is way too gung ho for this. He wants to just hit these people and damn the consequences. He shows no reservation for what we are about to do."

Catie let that hang between them for a moment. She actually

looked around; almost like she was afraid that somebody might overhear them. Since the closest person was two stories above their heads and not paying them the slightest bit of attention as he or she walked the edge of the cleared out hotel floor, it was highly unlikely that anybody could discern anything they were saying.

Still, when she spoke, Catie made it a point to lower her voice and keep her lips from moving as much as she was able. "Just what exactly are you saying?"

"I am saying that he either needs to be neutralized or eliminated." Marty's eyes showed almost no emotion as he spoke. This was simple fact for him, and it was obvious. "If he won't step aside willingly, then we kill him. You are the one who put this plan into motion. It is too late to change it now."

"Wait!" Catie fought to keep from raising her hands for added emphasis. "We just got here. We are either guests or prisoners depending on how you look at it. There are a good number of people here. Do you really think we can just kill their leader and take over with nobody raising a fuss?"

"You were out for a while. I haven't slept since we got here. I have walked around and seen these people for myself. Most of them are drones. They have either managed to escape being hunted and are just happy to be alive, or they are kids that have been snatched up. In any case, you saw it for yourself today. These people are not fighters. There is a core group of about ten that do all of the nasty work. We might have trouble with them, but other than that, this place is like a Hollywood set. If you look behind that curtain, you will see it is mostly smoke and mirrors. Why else do you think that they haven't launched an actual assault on Montague? They don't have the manpower. This place is built for defense."

Catie looked around. She readjusted her appraisal of this area. She had absolutely noticed that this place was big on holding a defensible position; but until this moment, she had not considered that it might be simply because they were not combat ready. Seriously, this far into the zombie apocalypse she just did not see how any culture could survive without having a certain degree of warlike ability.

Was this some sort of post-apocalyptic Athens? A society capable of functioning, but not adept in the fighting skills so necessary in this world of lawless chaos? And perhaps the whole Beastie Boy thing was nothing more than an image. Once again, she was looking at a *Wizard of Oz* sort of scheme. As long as nobody peeked behind the curtain, then those in the surrounding area were kept at bay by a façade maintained by a select few.

"Are you certain that I should remove Elliot from power and take over?" Catie asked softly, her mind whirling with the possibilities.

"I think my brother and I are as bad of a choice as Elliot. We would let this place go to our heads. Pretty soon I am sitting on some throne made of skulls having naked serving girls feeding me grapes or some shit."

Catie stifled a laugh. "Given this a lot of thought, have you?"

"Probably more than is healthy," the big man admitted with a shrug. "I was a huge fan of the classic *Conan* movie. I always wanted to be like Ah-nold. That would be me, only, he was sort of the good guy in that movie. I would be what happened a few years later. That ending image of him on that throne? My brother said that the books were even better, but I enjoyed the version my mind came up with over having somebody ruin it for me with words and stuff."

"We will have to have a talk someday about how you need to expand your mind, but for now, I have to think on this." Catie headed for the former Marriott. While she saw activity scattered about in a few of the downtown Chattanooga buildings, this one had more than the others by far. If this was indeed the truest example of the citizens of this community, then she needed to take the pulse.

Marty fell in at her side and Catie stopped him. "I am going on my own little fact finding mission. Having you along would probably taint the results." The big man cocked his head to the side in obvious confusion. "A woman by herself can get people to talk in ways that somebody like you might not. This place looks like the residential area. It will give me the truest read."

"So where do you want me to go?"

Catie explained in minimal detail about Clarence and how she wanted his body disposed of. Also, since he was going to be in the area, see what he might be able to find out about the jail. Many of the best revolutions came on the backs of released prisoners who felt that they had nothing else to fight for except their lives. Then he needed to go tell Melvin that the plan was a go.

Once Marty was headed back towards the TVA building that had been converted into a jail (or at least had that as one of the functions), Catie headed to the massive gate that secured the residential building. She was directed to the side where a rope ladder was in place and soon found herself in the stairwell. When she reached the first floor that was actually occupied— the fifth—she was almost run over by two children between the ages of seven and ten (she could not really tell) who exploded from a doorway in a rather spirited game of tag that was more of a tackle version.

"You cheated, Stephanie!" the smaller of the two hollered as he picked himself up from being shouldered rather hard into the left-hand wall.

"Did not, Danny the dummy!" the girl, Stephanie apparently, crowed as she skipped backwards down the hall and darted down the first intersection and disappeared from sight with little Danny doing his best to give chase.

Resuming her journey down the corridor, she glanced into the still open door on her right where the children had burst from to discover a toddler making unsteady steps for the open door without a stitch of clothing. The little girl was almost to the door when a young woman rushed around the corner.

"Sarah Jean, get you—" the woman's voice choked off abruptly when she saw Catie standing there. "Oh, sorry."

Without another word, the woman grabbed the child into her arms and shut the door with a slam that reverberated up the now vacant hallway. Catie considered knocking on the door to tell the stranger about the two that had gotten away and then decided against it.

By the time that she had made a full circuit of the floor, she had only encountered one other person. A man who looked to be in his forties exited one room and walked past her in the hall, giving a polite but brief nod of acknowledgement as he passed. She had mostly the same experience on the next three floors minus the two children and their spirited little chase. She had no reason to expect anything different when she opened the door to the ninth floor.

"Can I help you, hun?" an elderly lady said from her doorway—the first door on the right as she entered.

"I'm just sort of taking a tour." Catie tried to paste on her most harmless and friendly smile.

"You are just sort of scaring the crap out of everybody," the woman retorted.

"Excuse me?"

"You have prowled each floor below this one, pausing to look into any open door that you pass and generally putting folks in a tizzy."

Catie made it a point to look at this woman instead of trying to see past her into the room beyond. Easily the oldest woman that Catie had seen in a long while, she honestly would not be surprised if this person claimed to be a hundred years old. Her dark skin was laced with wrinkles that looked more like crevices. She was wearing a simple white frock with short sleeves and her bare arms were showing the effects of a lost battle with gravity as the flesh hung down and actually swayed when the woman made a point of folding her hands in her lap. She was in a wheel chair, her bare feet resting in the foot plates with some of the most hideous yellowed toenails that Catie had ever seen.

"Drink it all in, Tootsie Roll," the woman cackled. "You might be a pretty thing today, but we all end up like this sooner or later."

"Sorry," Catie apologized when she realized that she had gone from observing to openly gawking at this woman.

"Psshah!" the woman made a dismissive wave of her hand. "You part of them folks was brought in late last night?"

"Yes," Catie admitted.

"How come you are the only one scoping out for a room? The rest not survive the needle?"

"No, there are others. I guess I am just the first one to be interested in where I might be calling home."

"Don't normally see newcomers allowed to just mosey about by themselves." The old woman leaned back in her wheel chair and gave Catie a full up and down appraisal of her own. "And you look like you belong more with the ruffians than you do here in the general housing. But what do I know? I'm just an old woman." Suddenly, her face lit up in a toothless smile and she smacked her lips together and gave her forehead a light slap with one hand. "Where the blazes are my manners? My name is Abagail Jones."

The hand that took Catie's and shook it was cool and the skin was as dry as it looked. Still, despite her age, Abagail's grip was plenty firm.

"Catie Dreon, pleased to meet you."

"Yeah...we'll see about that," the old woman cackled and pushed back from the door and into her apartment.

Catie looked around. It did not seem that much different than any hotel, although she doubted the Marriott would ever allow the furniture and linens to fall into such disrepair. The window was open and let in a nice breeze as well as plenty of sunlight. There was also a crossbow on the table with a case beside it that she had to imagine contained bolts for the crossbow.

There was a little portable grill on the table as well, and something wrapped in what looked like aluminum foil was on it at the moment. When Catie got closer she could smell something laced with garlic.

"Just sittin' down for my lunch. It ain't much, but I seldom eat it all anyways." The woman rolled over and removed the foil pouch with her bare hands and opened it to reveal some sort of fish.

Catie sat down and allowed the conversation to flow wherever Abagail took it. She heard exactly what she was hoping to hear and thanked the gods that, just this once, Abagail Jones proved to be a movie stereotype: the "town" gossip. It seemed that there was very little that this woman did not know when it came to the personal lives of the tenants of this building. Even better, she enjoyed sitting at her window at all hours of the night to see people coming and going on various errands.

She is right out of the movies, Kevin, Catie thought as she nibbled at the dry, bland fish while sipping tepid water.

"...and those three boys weren't carrying nothin' but a few metal garbage can lids, but with the ruckus they was makin', you'd a thought there were fifty men in armor stomping down the street," Abagail finished this last tale with her dry cackle and a clap of her hands.

"So you say the last herd came through about three weeks ago and those three re-directed it straight through your own town on the way to one of the other communities nearby?" Catie was pretty sure she had heard it all correctly, but she just wanted to be certain.

"Folks been terrified to set foot in the downtown area since this whole thing began. Lotta bad thing happened, not too many folks that was in this area managed to survive. This is hiding in plain sight. None of them other communities send people out to these parts, and we make sure to lead a few hundred of them things through town every so often just to make it look like they are still around. Truth is, ain't been many of them in these parts since after about the first year or so." Abagail's voice grew distant. There was a haunted quality to it now, and Catie knew the woman was reliving some past horrors.

"I got stuck right here. Been in this very room since it all began. Was in town for my grandson's wedding. He did his grand mama right and put me up in this swanky place. Told them desk folks to feed me good and treat me like I was their own. The boy had just signed his big contract with that pro basketball team and he was one of them good ones they didn't like to talk about as much. Did good in school, didn't have no tattoos or police problems. Married his childhood sweetheart..."

Catie sat quietly. It wasn't that this story was any different than most, it was simply that she had the feeling Abagail didn't tell the story often. A person who told the old stories from the early days with any regularity could just spit it out like reciting the alphabet.

A single tear carved its way down the old woman's face, defying the fact that the skin probably wanted to suck that moisture in to salve its parched surface. It reached one saggy jowl and hung in the air, Catie's eyes transfixed on that tear almost as intently as she was the story.

"...stood outside my door and clawed at it for probably three or four days. The whole time he was making that awful sound like a baby crying for its mama. More than once I wanted to go out and just take the boy in a hug. Finally, he wandered away. Never saw him again."

Abagail brushed at her face with both hands and smeared the trail of moisture across her cheeks. "Look at me rattling on and on. You most likely want to find a place to settle. I can tell ya that the rooms facing out to this street are mostly taken, but there are still a couple on this floor. I'd be more than tickled if'n you was to stay around, maybe come visit. I see you gonna have a young'un soon enough. Grand mama Abagail makes a good sitter as long as the Good Lord intends to keep me alive and kickin'."

"I will keep that in mind," Catie said as she got to her feet. She was just opening the door when Abagail called out from where she still sat at her table.

"Felt good to squeeze some of that poison from my heart. Any time that you are ready to do the same, I promise to listen just as keenly as you just done. Might wanna do it soon. Babies can carry that sort of pain in their being if you keep that blackness swirling around inside ya the whole time you carryin' it."

Catie pulled the door shut and resumed her wandering of the once grand hotel. She saw more of the same; frightened people who were probably afraid of their own shadows more than they were zombies. She saw a few folks that had some hideous disfigurement from zombie bites. However, she passed more that seemed to show nothing.

And then there were the children. By the time she had finished her tour, she was estimating the population to be close to five hundred. Over half were below the age of eighteen, and at least a hundred of that two hundred-plus were likely under age ten.

"This isn't an army," Catie muttered as she exited the building. "It's a day care."

She headed across the street and made her way back to the library. She was just reaching the building when four men came around the corner a block away. Even at this distance, she recognized one of them as being with that group that she had hidden from the day that she met Kalisha. Now that the situation was different, she took the time to really observe these Beastie Boys.

The first thing that came to mind was a bunch of jocks at a frat party out for a night of pulling little pranks. They were pushing and shoving at each other, and one of them was easily identified as the lead instigator and likely leader of this band of miscreants.

Catie was going by the seat of her pants now. An idea had come, and it was sort of like the days when she sat around the barracks playing cards. You reached a point where you either shoved all in, or you could tell yourself after the fact how you "shoulda, woulda, coulda" pulled off something epic.

She changed course to intercept the band of young men who were hooting and hollering like they did not have a care in the world. They were paying her absolutely no mind at all, and she hoped that continued to be the case until she was right on them.

At last they were less than a few strides away. Catie had stopped walking and now stood planted in the very center of the sidewalk. One of them finally noticed and elbowed the others.

The group slowed, but they did not actually show signs that they intended to stop.

"Afternoon, ma'am!" one of the young men finally said, knuckling his forehead and acting as if he might be tipping the hat he was not wearing.

"Who is the leader?" Catie asked. She folded her arms across her chest and widened her stance just a little.

The group of four finally stopped, and the one that had been carrying on the loudest (as well as being the one that she had guessed to be the leader) stepped forward from the bunch. He shot a look of warning over his shoulder to the others and then made a show of wiping the huge grin from his face.

"That would be me, ma'am." He had a tooth missing in front and a nasty scar that looked like it came from a blade running across his face. She could actually see where the weapon had jumped a bit when it hit his nose.

"And how was that decision made?" Catie made her voice as pleasant as possible. This only seemed to confuse the young men; more specifically, their leader seemed at a total loss.

At last he found his voice. With a slight smile that was actually made all the more charming somehow by his scar causing his left eye to crinkle around the edges, he replied, "I called it and nobody else argued."

"So you didn't have to fight the old leader or anything like that?"

"This ain't *The Lion King*, lady. We aren't a bunch of Old World gang bangers or anything like that."

"So what are you then?"

That seemed to confuse the young man even further and Catie pressed. "Do you choose when to go out, or are you sent?"

"Who the hell are you, lady" one of the young men blurted. "Ain't no more newspapers, so you ain't a reporter."

"You need some help with your grammar, kid," Catie shot back, taking her eyes off the leader for just a second to address the one who spoke, but then she went right back to her informal stare down of the young man seemingly in charge. "So...how do you guys decide what you are doing?"

"You're that lady we carried back last night," the leader said, smacking his forehead. "Hey, we didn't do nothin' but what we was told. And nobody in my group had anything to do with dosing your team. We just cuffed them all up. Them two big fellas actually did the injections."

"Hell, I woulda got the shot a second time if one of them guys would have turned and shoved that needle my way," another of the men said with obvious awe leaking from his words.

"What if I told you that I wanted you to do something for me?" Catie asked casually.

"We'd have to clear it with the boss," the leader answered matter-of-factly. "As it is, we gotta at least tell him about this little meeting."

"And what if I told you that there might be a new boss giving orders soon?" Catie let the silence last for as long as she dared. The longer she gave these guys to process what she was saying, the more likely that one or all of them might do something crazy. "Are you guys happy being the only ones having to go out? The only ones who have to take the risks while everybody else sits here safely in their little homes?"

"We get taken care of," the leader said stiffly. "And we can even turn down a mission if we think it is too hairy."

"But you are still the only ones doing all the dirty work."

"And like I said," the leader began to emphasize his words, "we get taken care of very well for our troubles."

"I think the lady is trying to say that you guys don't have to go it alone anymore," Melvin said as he stepped around the corner.

Catie shot the man a questioning look and he made a sad shake of his head. Catie's eyes flicked to the large bag on the man's belt. The stain at the bottom was wet and a drop fell to the sidewalk and left a small red circular splat.

"But..." the leader started. His mouth clicked shut when Marty came around the corner to join his brother.

Catie took in the full vista of her surroundings. So far, nothing was any different than it had been ten minutes ago; at least not outwardly. However, in that span of time while she visited with Grand mama Abagail, a great deal had changed.

"You boys have a choice," Catie locked down her emotions and affected her best imitation of a drill instructor from boot camp. "You can either climb on board and take choice seats at the new table...or..." She glanced at Melvin who was already reaching inside the bag.

15

Bringer of Death

I could hear those amazingly loud noisemakers in the distance. Glancing up the road a ways, it was obvious that the army of undead on my heels could hear it as well. They were still advancing, with me having long since slipped from sight. This was the first real test and it had passed. The zombies were rounding a corner and now they were orienting on the direction the sound was coming from.

Kayla had sped away on her bike several minutes ago. Her report was that a patrol had spotted Cricket's mob a little later than expected and that had forced them to react in haste. The patrols were being called back by the use of a series of flags. That might prove to be a small problem.

Nat had spied the three person group moving along a ridge about a half a mile or so away. If they spotted our zombies too soon, then it was possible that both groups could be diverted and our work would prove all for naught. We had made it over a fence and ran through what looked to me like a car graveyard. I recognized the vehicles for what they were, but somebody had actually taken the time to stack them up; several cars on top of each other—and in fairly neat rows. It was actually kind of creepy looking.

When we reached the other side, we could hear the patrol

talking amongst themselves as they rode along. One of them was saying something about staying alert since they were "veering close to the Island City settlement where people kept turning up missing." That statement struck me as odd since, if they were indeed missing, then how were they actually turning up?

Nat held up a hand in the universal sign for us to stay put and then climbed up one of the stacks of defunct automobiles. She reached the top and then pointed to me and then to the stack to my left. At first I thought she was perhaps crazy and thought I was going to climb one of those towers of scrap just as she had done a moment before. I stood there for a minute, just staring up at her until she made the same gesture much more emphatically.

I was reluctant at best as I began my ascent. Everything was going fine until I looked down. It is one thing to be on a ladder or something that is designed for you to climb; it is quite another to be holding on to some rusty bumper from whatever the hell a Ford Taurus is and be twenty or so feet off the ground.

Once I was able to open my eyes again, I got up on top of the cursed piece of junk and laid down flat on the hood or roof, or whatever the hell they call it. I shot what I hoped was a nasty look over to Nat, but she either did not take it as intended or could care less that my eyes were sending toxic daggers at her from across the open expanse.

She had her crossbow ready and signaled to me that she was shooting at the one on the left. Either that or she was swatting at a fly. I took a deep breath and tried to focus my energy on aiming at the rider on the right. Whoever killed her target first could deal with the one remaining.

That was my thought all the way until Kayla came racing around a corner about a block in front of the riders. They were pretty damn quick to react despite appearing to be in conversation as they were heading back to camp. Suzi would probably have been pleased with their reaction all the way up to the point where two of them took a bolt in the middle of the back. Mine fell from the saddle and landed awkwardly. Even from up on my perch, I could tell that a neck should not turn quite that far.

Kayla saw the horses coming and did the smartest thing she

could do; she dumped the bike. Her feet were moving even before they hit the ground and she bounded towards the fence to a back yard that looked like the owners had been really into palm trees.

I was pleased with how fast I was able to reload despite my fear of sliding off and plummeting to my death. Still, Nat was faster. Her bolt caught the third rider just ahead of mine. The second rider fell, but unfortunately, the one that Nat shot first was still in the saddle and obviously aware that he or she was under attack. The horse had taken off and did not even slow as it passed by where Kayla had just vaulted that fence and landed in the back yard with impressive grace.

I reloaded, but it was pointless. The rider had taken a corner, and even if he or she had continued straight ahead, there would have been little to no chance I could have hit the target. The effective range had been surpassed by then.

Nat was already scrambling down her tower of cars. My trip down was not nearly as quick or graceful and I had to run to catch up to where Nat was already talking to Kayla who had climbed back over the fence to meet us in this little alley or whatever was running between the junkyard and the row of houses that bordered it.

"…got away, but that won't matter at this point," Nat was saying as Kayla kept glancing over her shoulder in the direction that the zombie horde was coming from.

Their moans were carrying on the breeze and I could tell that she was more than a little bit nervous. I had to remind myself that she was not used to being outside the walls. Not that I was some sort of seasoned veteran, but I still had flashes of Platypus Creek before it had become the walled community that we knew as our home. Not to mention the fact that the last several days had numbed me considerably.

In the distance, I could hear the noisemakers being employed to distract the herd that Cricket had led. I looked back the way our smaller group was coming from just as they rounded this last corner. From here, we would be leading them down through what was once the heart of La Grande. Most if not all of the buildings had been stripped, and many were either collapsing, burnt down to a charred skeletal frame, or outright leveled over the years of neglect and harsh weather. Once we reached the end of this old junkyard, the zombies were on their own, so to speak. We were now supposed to break to the right and hook back up at the walls of Island City where Cricket and his group were going to meet up with us. That was where my plan differed from the norm. I hope that Kayla played along; we hadn't really had the chance to discuss this next part.

"You guys go on ahead, I want to stay here just a bit longer and be sure," I suggested.

"That isn't the plan," Nat said with a dismissive wave. "The herd is moving right for them, and by the time they realize this group is coming, they won't have enough time to deal with it." Nat turned and looked back towards the tent city that was Suzi's camp and planted her hands on her hips. "I just do not understand why they never made the move to occupy Island City. There are a lot of living people in that camp, but no more than four or five thousand at the most. The zombies will be too much. They will have no choice but to run. And that is going to cost them in gear, because they aren't ready to move. This just does not make sense."

That last part of her monolog was more to herself than anything. In fact, I don't know if she was even aware that she was saying it out loud.

"Yes, well, as I said, I will catch up to you in a bit."

I started to walk away and choked back a grimace as Kayla hurried to fall in beside me. It wasn't that she was not welcome. She had proved to be a solid companion up to this point, but what I had planned next was going to require me moving fast and not being able to take even a second to watch over her.

"We are in this until the end," Kayla whispered. "Don't even think about going off by yourself."

"Okay," Nat moved around us in a hurry, "what is going on?"

"I don't have time for this," I said, pushing past the woman.

Or, at least that had been my intention. Nat grabbed my arm

and spun me back to face her.

"You have kept whatever this little secret is of yours long enough. Cricket likes you. He trusts you. He put his ass on the line for you. Now, you can go on and do whatever it is that you have in mind, but you are going to tell me what it is before I let you go. He deserves that much. We all do for that matter."

I glanced at Kayla who only shrugged. I turned back to Nat and explained about Jackson. I did not go into a lot of detail, but I at least explained that not all of us had escaped. I had to try and see if there was any way that I could rescue him.

"That is pretty stupid," Nat said when I finished.

I expected any number of responses, but that had not been one of them. Not that I completely disagreed with her assessment. I knew what my limitations were as far as this little rescue mission was concerned. I hoped that I had the sense to know it was entirely hopeless before I slid past the point of no return. I wasn't entirely confident of that possibility, but I could still hope. It wasn't like I wanted to die. I knew that going after Jackson had almost no chance, but if I would have just given up on him like the others, then his slim chance would become none.

"I'm not throwing my life away, sorry, kid," Nat said.

I was okay with that response. Apparently Kayla wasn't.

"Nobody asked you," the girl snapped, shoving her back. "You go back to your little gang and keep hiding in the shadows while that army comes in and takes the town that your people worked hard to create. You let those piles of dead bodies rot and become fertilizer without trying to do anything in response."

"We've done plenty," Nat shot back. "We've killed thirty or forty of their patrols so far, not that I have to explain myself to you."

"Can we do this later?" I asked, stepping between the two before somebody threw a punch.

"Doubtful, since it is unlikely that either of you will survive this little escapade."

Nat spun on a heel and started away. She reached the fence for the junkyard and was over and gone. Kayla and I stood in the alley alone; well, except for the hundred thousand or so zombies coming our direction.

"We need to get moving." I grabbed Kayla's arm and pulled her along.

We were content that the zombies were on a solid trajectory that would lead them into Suzi's camp. Now I just had to try and find my way in without being noticed. If Suzi caught me, it was all over except the dying.

We reached a small stream and I was pretty sure that this one would be the one I needed to follow to make my way into the camp. I was at least ninety percent sure that it had been the same one that I had followed when I was attempting to escape. That all seemed like a lifetime ago now.

We slid down the embankment and did our best to move from one clump of tall grass to the next as fast as we could. I saw the sentries before Kayla, and had to pull her back so she would not walk out into a small clearing and be seen. Now is when it would get dicey.

I was still thinking about how to approach these guys when Kayla slipped past me and walked right out into the very opening where I'd prevented her from doing so just moments ago. I could not believe it. Then...she turned into Kayla.

I was actually a bit mesmerized myself as she peeled off her jacket and slung it over her shoulder. She did not seem to be paying the two sentries any mind as she stopped under a tree and hung her jacket on a branch. She was still plenty far enough away that they were just now noticing her arrival. I actually saw one of the sentries nudge the other when Kayla reached down and pulled her shirt off. She gave it a dunking in the rather cold water. I was impressed considering how my feet felt like they were actually turning into ice cubes. Kayla did not seem to notice at all now that she stood in just her bra while repeatedly dunking her shirt.

It took me a few seconds to realize that the girl was using one of the old tricks from the manual. Not exactly as it was written, but the best way to deal with a situation is to turn the strength of the enemy into a weakness. Sure enough, the men were now heading right for her, neither had a hand near his weapon.

I brought up my crossbow and sighted on the one who was actually a few steps behind his comrade. I waited for Kayla to bend down and then come back up with her shirt because that was when she was making the most noise. In that instant, I fired. I did not take time to see the full effect of my shot and reloaded as fast as I could. I almost had it cranked back and ready to fire when I heard a shout.

I looked up just in time to see the man I had not shot turn to see his partner floating by flat on his back with a bolt jutting from his chest. He was smart enough to realize what was happening and his hand went for the large blade at his hip. I fired my second shot and caught the man in the shoulder. He staggered back just a step, but that was only a momentary setback. He resumed his charge and actually tackled Kayla, both of them landing with a loud splash.

I knew that there would be nothing I could do with the crossbow at this point and rushed in to help. I arrived as arms and legs thrashed in the water, making it almost impossible to tell who was who until I was right up on them. By then, I had my knife free. I was raising it to strike when the man came up sputtering, a mouthful of blood pouring from his lips.

Kayla emerged, shoving the body away and spitting out a mouthful of water as well. She gave the body a hard knee and grabbed a handful of the man's hair.

With one quick movement, she brought her knife across his throat and slit it, ending the last of his feeble struggles. Honestly, I hadn't even seen her draw her knife.

"Wow." Seriously, that was all I could say. I was at a loss.

"Grab my coat, please," Kayla said as she wrung out her shirt one more time and then put it back on. I did as she asked, not bothering to hide how impressed I was by the outcome of this little skirmish.

After we dragged the bodies to the grass to hopefully keep them from being discovered, we picked up the pace and hurried along the bank of the stream. We could actually start to hear the sounds of the camp now that we were closer. They had no idea what was coming, or, if they did, they were underestimating things severely.

I urged Kayla to follow me out of the creek. We were so close now that, if we acted like we were sneaking around, we would probably be spotted and treated like enemies. If we merged with some of the people that were coming and going, then perhaps we could get in easier. After all, with this many people, was it likely that everybody knew everybody else?

I saw a group of five carrying wood. That seemed like the best way in. I hurried over to the one that was lagging and moved in beside him. "Let me help," I offered.

"Thanks." The guy did not even give me a second glance as he allowed me to take a few of the sections that he'd been carrying.

Kayla made no such overture and simply stayed beside me. She was keeping her eyes peeled and I wanted to elbow her and ask her not to look as obvious, but I was too busy keeping my own eyes scanning for anybody who might recognize me. I guess I was glad that I had spent most of my time as a prisoner here inside my tent.

It only took me until we reached the drop off for the fire wood before I managed to spot a few familiar landmarks. I dropped my load onto the growing pile and started away.

"Hey!" a voice said from behind, causing me to freeze. I noticed Kayla's hand drift towards the hilt of her belt knife.

I turned to the person that had spoken. It was the guy I'd taken some of the wood from. He was smiling. "Thanks."

"No problem." I really hoped that I sounded cooler than I felt. At least Kayla had taken her hand away from her hip and was now pretending like she was inspecting her fingernails out of boredom.

"Are you on one of the teams tonight?" the guy asked just when I thought that we had managed to get away clean.

I opened my mouth, but once again, Kayla was proving to be more than just a little useful.

"Can we go? I promised Billy I would be back in time for our little *meeting*."

Her words dripped with innuendo, leaving no doubt as to what she intended. Even though it was pure fiction, I could not help but blush. That might have actually helped sell our ruse. In any case, it covered our exit as she started pulling me by the wrist.

We hurried away and I waited until we were out of sight to pull free. As soon as I did, I turned to Kayla. "I apologize for ever underestimating you," I said with all sincerity.

She actually beamed at my compliment. We blended in with another group and I had to backtrack twice to get us in the area of where they were keeping Jackson. When I finally spotted the tall, metal boxes, I felt my heart sink. I knew which one had been his.

It was wide open and empty. There were no guards posted. In fact, all of them were open. That had me curious. Maybe this was shower time or something. I needed anything I could find to cling to in order to keep my hope alive. The churning feeling in my gut was telling me that this was not going to turn out well. I shoved the voice of rational reason aside and clung to my raft of faith with all my might.

Maybe that was why I did not hear the shouts until Kayla grabbed my arm and yanked me back so hard that I almost hit her out of reflex. I turned and saw the look of pain on her face. My gaze followed hers and I found Jackson.

He and five other men and women were hanging from a long gallows. Each of them were still thrashing about, their bulging eyes easy to see.

"Let's go," Kayla whispered.

My feet were planted. This was yet another thing that made no sense. Jackson was dead, and it was obvious that he had been so for at least a while. Suzi had never meant to release him. That was the only thing that came to mind. But if that was so, then why had she let us go at all?

Kayla continued to tug on me, but I was not ready to just walk away from this. There had to be answers. I was missing something.

A hard slap to my cheek snapped me out of my daze. Kayla's own face was inches from my own.

"We have to go. Now!" she hissed.

I was about to join her when I heard a series of gongs. The camp as a whole seemed to freeze. Everybody turned with looks of confusion on their faces.

"How could that be?" somebody nearby said.

"That is from the north watch!" somebody else exclaimed.

"That has to be a mistake," a woman insisted.

Then, it was like watching a large flock of birds being startled. People began to run in every direction at once. It was still not a mass hysteria, but more of a sense of purpose. If nothing else, these people were proving that they were very adept at handling a crisis. There was an urgency, but no signs of panic.

We used the people all moving with haste to our advantage. I was numb and allowed Kayla to sort of take me by the hand and lead the way. This entire trip had been all for nothing. Jackson was dead.

My mind was trying to come up with even a shred of reason for all of this and continued to draw a blank. I was still in shock when Kayla suddenly came to a stop. I had to look around to figure out why.

We were out of the camp. I had no idea how long we'd been running, or even a clue as to what direction. It took me a few more seconds to realize that we were west of the encampment for some reason. If there was any direction that we did not need to go, it was west. That took us away from not only Cricket and Island City, but it also put the zombies that she and I had helped lead in between ourselves and home.

I guess I had given up at some point. I wanted to go home. I was certain that I would be in trouble, but I didn't care. I was just tired.

"Why are we going this way?" I asked.

"Because of that," Kayla said, pulling me down into the brush.

I followed her finger. We had started up a small hill and were in tall grass, bushes, and a few scraggly trees. Somebody would have to be actively searching for us to even have the slightest chance of spotting our position. This hill provided an excellent view of the ruins of La Grande, Island City to the northeast, and Suzi's camp to the south. I could see our wave of zombies trudging onward in the direction of the encampment. It was obvious that they had spotted the zombie equivalent of a picnic. Noisemakers would be useless at this point.

However, I also saw a group of about fifty people on horseback. They were emerging from the ruins of one of the other settlements that had supposedly been razed by Suzi's army. Then I saw a group of riders emerge from the encampment. They had two people with them that were wearing dark hoods and had their hands tied behind their backs.

I watched as the two groups approached each other. We were not exactly close enough to be able to overhear from this spot. If we moved to our right about a hundred yards or so, then we should have no problems. I motioned to Kayla and she shook her head. Now was not the time for her to be a pain in my ass.

"I want to hear what this is all about," I insisted.

"Then you go. I will wait here."

I scowled at her, but if she wanted to miss whatever this was, that was her problem. Staying low, I moved through the grass with as much stealth as I could manage. It seemed to take forever, but I absolutely did not want to give away my location.

As luck would have it, I reached my place and got situated a good few minutes before the two groups reached each other. When they stopped, I had to stifle a tiny gasp. I recognized one of the riders from the encampment. It was the guy who had first brought me to Suzi. I was pretty sure his name was Randy. He had belted me a good one and Suzi had sent him on Outrider duty or some such thing.

I was only forced to wait for another moment to see who were under the hoods. I did not know the one woman, but I sure as hell recognized Suzi. If I was curious before, I was positively itching to know what the hell was going on now.

"Took you guys long enough," Randy said to one of the men as he yanked Suzi's hood off.

16

Vignettes LXVI

A tremendous roar echoed across the clearing where the cabin sat. Juan was frozen in place; too frightened to do much more than just await his impending doom. The grizzly rose up on its hind legs, and its mouth opened once more to let loose with another guttural roar that caused any of the remaining birds that might still be perched nearby to take flight in a rush of flapping wings.

"So this is how I go out?" Juan actually found enough moisture in his mouth to allow him to laugh.

He considered the machete at his belt and then recalled a few things that he'd heard about bears. One of the biggest (besides the whole ridiculous ploy of pretending to be dead to make the bear lose interest and walk away) was the fact that their skulls were incredibly thick. Even if he could get his feet under him enough to allow for a decent swing, he doubted his ability to cause enough damage to kill a grizzly bear.

"Hey!" a voice barked.

The bear wasn't the only one to turn towards the sudden and new distraction. Juan was actually surprised that his eyes had been able to be pulled away from the giant bear. He was in a position that put the person who yelled with his back to the sun. That had cast all his features in darkness, but the outline gave away the identity.

"Gerald!" Juan would have been embarrassed at any other time in his life to hear his voice crack and sound so weak and relieved, but his emotions were at the breaking point as despair collided with relief.

The big man took a step forward and raised his hands over his head. "C'mon, you over-stuffed teddy bear," the man hollered.

The bear seemed to take a moment to consider its options. Juan was certain that he looked to be the most appealing of the two. After all, he was on his knees and basically defenseless. The bear turned towards Gerald and let its head fall back in another rumble of sound that Juan swore was deep enough to cause his insides to shift.

The bear dropped to four feet and began to approach Gerald. For the briefest of moments, Juan had this idea where the man was going to ruffle the bear's fur and scratch it behind the ears telling him he was a bad bear for scaring the nice Hispanic man.

When the mountain of a man brought up a massive maul, that fantasy went out the window. Gerald seemed to wait until the last possible second before bringing the heavy steel weapon around in a tremendous swing. There was a solid sound like the head of the maul striking granite.

"Son of a bitch!" Gerald yelped, his hands letting go of the weapon.

Thankfully, the bear was, at the very least, seriously dazed. It staggered a step, but did not fall. It was equally fortunate that Gerald seemed to be the first to recover. He pulled a huge knife from his belt and came in from the side, driving it into the beast's throat.

Apparently the bear was made of stronger stuff. It rose up, although not quite managing to come to its full and massive height. Gerald managed to duck the first swipe with one of those vicious paws, but the follow-through of the second sent the man sprawling like he was a child's plaything.

Juan pulled himself to his feet. He glanced at Gerald who was busy trying to shake loose the cobwebs. Also, in the exchange, the man had lost his knife.

"Hey, Winnie-the-Pooh," Juan called, "I thought you were in the mood for Mexican food!"

The bear did not seem to even notice the challenge and continued to lumber towards Gerald. Juan knew he couldn't run, but if he did nothing, he was equally certain that the man who'd once again saved his life was going to be ripped apart. With nothing else handy, Juan hefted his crutch and threw it like a javelin; a very poorly designed javelin to be sure judging by the way the thing wobbled and spun as it flew through the air.

By the time it reached its intended target, the crutch had turned almost sideways. It bounced off of the bear's body and landed impotently on the ground. The bear paused and turned for the briefest of moments, but apparently it wanted to dish out a little get back to the man who'd caved in the side of its head and cut a gaping hole in its throat.

It took another two steps toward Gerald and then started to rise up on its hind legs again. Sadly, for the bear at least, the massive blood loss along with the trauma to the brain finally proved to be more than the beast could withstand.

With a low growl, the bear rocked and then fell forward in a graceless face-plant. There was a tremendous exhale, and then the grizzly was still.

Both Juan and Gerald remained stock still for a few more seconds before each man let out his own exhale; theirs being ones of relief rather than a final death rattle. Gerald had managed to make it to his knees. He turned, and Juan could not help but wince. The man looked like he'd just gone the distance with the champ.

He wanted to express his thanks and gratitude, however, what came out of his mouth was, "Have you seen my girls?"

"No," Gerald answered hesitantly.

Just that quick, the relief of having been spared evaporated. Once more, Juan felt grief seep into every crack in his being.

***

Vix sat around a roaring fire with one of the strangest groups of people she could ever recall having met. Besides Paddy and Seamus, there was Algernon, a bookish looking man who looked like he belonged at a library checkout counter instead of dripping from head to toe with a variety of blades that he was able to throw with amazing precision. He had milky white skin and wore his long red hair in a series of about a dozen braids. Next came Gable, the American. He was as black as Algernon was white and kept his coarse ebony hair in a topknot. At well over six feet tall, he was built a lot like Seamus, but his muscles were well defined instead of just hiding under a lot of bulk. Gable always smiled, but it was that sort of smile that you might expect on a shark. Last was Randi. The only woman of the group, and of obvious Middle Eastern descent, Vix doubted that was her real name.

Randi had probably been a beauty once. The parts of her face not puckered and twisted from the horrible scars gave hints. She kept two cudgels on her hip, each tipped with a misshapen hunk of some sort of silvery metal. She did not talk. If she had something to say, she leaned over and whispered it to Gable who spoke on her behalf.

As a bottle of something that felt like it was carving its way down her throat was passed around and the contents shared, there was singing and laughing. Vix almost forgot the entire reason for why she'd ventured away from home. Stories of a rising faction that apparently modeled itself after some twisted version of the already deplorable Nazi regime were almost forgotten.

As more drinking continued and stories from the past were shared, this began to feel more like an old night out at a local pub. Sure, she hadn't been sitting around with an American, a few Irishmen and a Middle Eastern woman, but then, maybe she should have tried it. She kept finding herself laughing at one tale or another like the one Seamus was just finishing.

"…and there is Algernon in his birthday suit, running down the middle of the Westminster Bridge with a giant stuffed panda under one arm and one of those plastic Big Ben baubles that they used to sell to tourists, screaming at the top of his lungs the bloody Canadian National Anthem!"

A roar of laughter followed and even the edges of Randi's lips curled slightly. Chaaya had long since passed out after having a good sick that smelled like rotten apples and something yeasty.

Vix sighed and wondered if these people would be able to help at all or if they had simply coaxed her into walking away from her people and leaving them to their fate. In her alcohol induced stupor, she could not recall anybody talking about this Dolph person and his little army.

A half dozen rabbits were roasting over the fire, and every so often, somebody would go over and tear off a piece and flop down to eat. She had to admit, after the past couple of days, they smelled very appealing.

"You gonna keep eyeing them bunnies, or are you gonna have yourself a leg?" a voice said from beside Vix.

She had to concentrate to see only one, but eventually she was able to focus and recognize Paddy. He was no longer dressed in the outlandish garb and was instead in a brown jerkin and trousers made of some sort of animal skin. He wore hobnailed boots and studded gloves with wicked spikes across the knuckles.

"Is this some sort of trick?" Vix slurred.

She was having a terrible time staying upright. She would think everything was fine, and then she would discover that she had leaned over to the point where her head had dipped below Paddy's. She recognized it had gone to an extreme when she realized that she was actually on her side with her head in the little man's lap. He was looking down at her with a smile on his face that was perhaps the warmest and most genuine that she had seen in a long time.

"You have a lot of pain bottled in your soul, lass," the man said with amazing kindness and understanding. Vix briefly forgot that he was almost half her height...and Irish. "Maybe if you shared some of that, then some of the wounds can heal. Keeping all of that poison bottled inside is going to be the death of you."

At first, Vix had no idea what on earth the man could be

talking about. She even tried to sit up, but after the world began to spin faster and apparently tilt sideways, she decided that there were worse places in the world than lying on this log with her head in Paddy's lap.

Then, the strangest thing began to happen. She started telling her story. She told of losing Ivor, her ill-fated plan to raid the museum display, and her up and down relationship with Gemma. She told about poor Harold and his terrible fate. Then she told of New England. Yet, as she shared that piece of the tale, she began to realize that she had isolated herself for the most part from the residents of the community. Sure, she helped those in need, but in all those years, she had not become close with one single soul.

She told of her discovery in regards to Gemma and how she finally thought that she was bringing the girl home. When she recounted how the girl had simply thrown herself into the water and vanished from sight, the tears flowed. It had been, in her eyes, her greatest failure.

At some point, Vix felt her eyes become heavy. She stopped being aware of her surroundings. She did not even notice that, at some point, Randi had taken one of her hands and was holding it, stroking it softly, patting it whenever Vix began to sob, unable to speak any longer as all the grief of more than a decade seeped from every pore.

Vix eventually drifted off to sleep and dreamed of a time before. She dreamed of coming home to her cats and her husband. She dreamed of trivia night at the local pub.

"Wake up, lass," a voice whispered. "We have an army to stop."

***

The threat proved mostly impotent. A small band of seventy, that had no idea the size of the community that they had picked a fight with, fell in short order. Chad missed out on it with a severely sprained ankle and an arrow wound in his thigh. He also ended up with six stitches in his chin.

Services were held for those who were lost the day of the attack. It was little consolation that not a single person was lost when they went out to deal with the potential threat. Even more anti-climactic, it was really only one of the five groups of forty riders that were sent to scout that happened upon the camp of the raiders.

The fight was over almost before it began. The few personal effects of some of the fallen found and serving as the final damning evidence that these were the ones. Four prisoners were brought back that day and questioned with a veracity that ensured they had given up every bit of information (confirming that they were indeed just this single small band). After the interrogation, they were taken to the square and executed.

Chad sat that out as well. It was not because he was against it, or had any reservations about such swift measures, he was simply not feeling well that day; most of his body was feeling the effects of his journey downstream.

As the spring yielded to summer, Chad watched Ronni truly start to show happiness and contentment. He and Caroline became closer friends and were able to admit that romance would never be a factor, but that their friendship was stronger than any they thought possible.

Chad was pulled from exterior patrol for the duration of his healing and rehabilitation. When winter came, it was the first that Chad could recall in a good long while where they were not even the slightest bit miserable or uncomfortable the entire season.

Once he healed, he was asked if he wanted to return to patrol duty with the mounted division. He was surprised that he had no such desire. During his rehab, he came to the conclusion that his biggest reason for wanting to be involved was because he did not feel that anybody else could keep his daughter safe.

When he was pronounced healthy, Chad was hit with the realization that everything was fine. Even more important, he and his daughter had begun to gel in a closer relationship. Going out was a needless endangerment. As it was, when he had first volunteered, he was the oldest on the roster by almost a decade.

Taking a job as a field worker, Chad found the work hard

but rewarding. Not to mention that he was in his bed every night and able to enjoy evening meals with Ronni who had been given her own classroom of second graders to teach.

As the seasons once again passed, Chad began to hear about people going on honest-to-goodness vacations. The concept seemed absolutely foreign at first. When his supervisor called him over one day to tell him that he had accumulated a week's worth, he had no idea what to say or do.

That evening, he sat down to dinner with Ronni and Caroline. He told them and was surprised when Ronni began to gush about some cabins she'd heard about from another of the teachers. Apparently they sat on a lake and that people from this community and a neighboring one had come together and built a sturdy wall.

After only a little convincing, Chad agreed that it might be fun. He could scarcely believe that he was willingly venturing outside the safety of the town walls. It was a simple act to arrange for him and Ronni to have the same period of time off.

There was even a package that was put together by the general store with all of the supplies they would need. They were even provided horses for the one day journey that had three armed checkpoints along the way for them to stop.

As he and Ronni rode out of the gates, Chad could not help but be swept up in the surreal feeling of going on vacation in a zombie apocalypse. The day was bright and sunny. Perfect in every way. It took Chad almost an hour to get over the idea that it would all come crashing down at any moment. He simply could not wrap his mind around what was something far too normal in a world overrun by the undead and dotted with bands of raiders and outlaws.

They arrived at the gates to the cabin getaway a few hours before sunset and were greeted by an armed detachment at the main entrance. Letting his eyes scan the scene, he was amazed to discover that this location had a security detail that numbered higher than some of the communities he'd encountered over the years.

"Is this real?" he asked the woman who accepted his voucher that was issued when he and Ronni had left that morning and stamped at each of the checkpoints along the way.

"Between the two communities, we number close to five thousand now," the woman said with a laugh. "This is actually a duty assignment for members of each communities' army."

"You gotta have seniority to draw it, though," a man called from his station at the gate house. "Took me five years to get here."

"Five?" another quipped. "I just hit my seventh year. One of the first enlistees at our camp. Who'd you blow to get this gig?"

"Who'd you piss off?" another crowed.

Chad and Ronni were directed to their cabin. The gates were closed at dusk, and the bell was rung at the dining hall signaling the evening meal. That evening, Chad sat across from his daughter, doing everything in his power to fight back the tears.

As they walked back to the cabin, Ronni put an arm around him and that was all he could take.

"What's wrong, Dad?" his daughter asked, coming to an abrupt halt.

"I just never expected to be happy like this. Not before the whole zombie thing, and certainly not after."

Ronni wrapped her arms around him and they stood there for a moment, hugging each other. Chad looked up, half expecting to see a shooting star. Instead, it was just the vast and twinkling expanse of a normal night time sky.

Everything seemed absolutely common. That scared him deeper than any herd of zombies or group of lawless raiders.

***

"I take it they know you," Gable muttered. "Good. Maybe we can use this. You keep them busy. I will go around to the other side where your other friend is…Jan, right?" Jody nodded. "I will go around and see if she is making any progress. If not, I will give her a hand."

Just like that, Gable Matczak turned and jogged away. Jody watched him slip around the corner of the RV and vanish. That made him think of the kids. He'd been so caught up in things that he had forgotten them. He stepped back, ignoring Margarita who was calling his name once more.

He reached the door of the RV he was beside and tried the handle. It opened and he could see a pair of legs. Dread filled him as he poked his head inside and took a look. He was actually relieved when he discovered that the four residents of this particular RV were simply bound and gagged. He gave a shushing motion with one finger and pulled the gag free from the closest person. The girl spat angrily and chomped her teeth a couple of times to get her jaw working right again.

She looked up at Jody and whispered, "Aren't you Mister Rafe?"

"Yep."

"I heard your name more than once while they were doing all of this...the jerks."

"And I would love to hear about it, but I don't have time." Jody reached down and flicked his blade to sever the twine that bound her wrists. "You get the others in here free, but stay inside."

"You gonna kill them?" the girl asked with a surprising lack of emotion or concern.

"Yep."

"Good. And when you save Mister Pitts, I'm sure he will be really thankful."

Jody had just stepped down from the RV and was about to close the door when he heard that last statement. He spun. "Pitts isn't part of this?"

"Are you kidding?" The girl sounded equal parts incredulous and offended.

Jody shut the door and crept back to the corner of the RV. Margarita was still standing on the porch. She was looking his general direction, but Jody could tell that she didn't know his exact location. Taking a step back into the shadows, he fought the urge to just charge in and kill this woman; and, if he was certain that George was the only other person inside, he might have actually considered that as a viable option.

"I figured you and your boyfriend would be long gone by now and causing havoc for some other community stupid enough to put up with your crap," Jody called back.

"You never did get it. This is not about being nice or any of that other garbage that you were trying to push. If that community is going to survive, then we needed to make sure we were the meanest dog in the park."

No," Jody countered, "it was you two who did not get it. What is the point of trying to save humanity if we can't act human?"

"Weak!" Margarita bellowed. "That has always been your problem. You are far too weak. You want the good life and want to raise your family behind the assumed protection of a few walls. The zombies have long gone by the way as being the problem. We need to be prepared for other communities—"

"And people like you!" Jody shouted, cutting Margarita off. "People who kidnap children, people who murder innocent women or beat them until they give the answers that you want to hear."

"Always comes back to that, doesn't it?" Margarita replied with a sarcastic laugh. "And it was so easy for you to believe some stranger and her version of things."

"There was a body in the fire pit!" Jody really did not feel like engaging in this circular argument again. He'd had quite enough during the trial.

George and Margarita had insisted that they were simply trying to get Jan to come clean about how her group had come to the tower with ill intent. That the women had been used as bait to draw out the men who were subsequently ambushed. The part of the story they wanted to ignore and gloss over was how the woman, Angel, had been basically abducted and used as a sex toy until she either slit her own throat (as was one side of the story) or had it slit for her.

During the trial, it was revealed that George was not only aware of this happening at a few of the towers, but had come out with Margarita a few times to engage in God knows what. The entire thing made him sick to his stomach. Part of him wanted to enact a much more final sentence regarding the dysfunctional duo, but the charter of the community was such that it was forbidden unless a unanimous verdict was reached; where only a majority would result in banishment.

"It doesn't matter anymore," Jody shouted. "You have violated your banishment. That is grounds for execution, and now I don't need a unanimous vote."

"Good luck with that," Margarita's voice dripped venom. "We got more people in our pocket than you realize. Maybe even enough to get your ass tossed out...or executed. I don't think we'll need some silly unanimous decision."

Jody was fuming at this point. He had no idea how much longer he could keep this up. Where the hell was this Gable person?

"Then how about we all just head back to town and let it get sorted there?"

"That is where you have lost the handle. There are other places, other communities. And a few of them have had their eyes on this little strip of land for a while. You just—"

Margarita's tirade was cut short as she yelped and then started to scream. That scream was silenced almost immediately. Jody peeked around the corner to see Gable standing over a downed body. He had a curved sword that looked like something from a Sinbad movie in his hands. He was raising the weapon over his head, preparing to come down with a final strike.

Jody was reeling. What did she mean other communities? He had to know.

"Gable, no!" Jody yelled as the blade came down in a blur.

***

Entry Fifty-eight—

I want to make this very clear. I take no pleasure in doing what I do. I certainly took none in this latest kill. I fear the day when that may change, but it is not today.

Yes, I caught the woman. No, her name was not actually Mary. Again, I will offer her the equal lack of courtesy that I give the men I normally hunt. I will not allow her real name to be used so that it can become some sort of legend or myth. That you think of her as "Mary" is already more than she deserves.

I do not know what happened in her mind that allowed her to tread this path. Honestly, I do not think I actually care. Am I curious? Sure. Just as I am sure that whoever reads this might be curious how I can live my life hunting the living and seeing to their extermination under less than humane conditions.

It felt like forever for that blasted barge to return. It did not help that I could have requested the attendant to wave the emergency flag to expedite its return, but I did not want to do anything that would give away that I was in pursuit of the previous rider. When, at last, enough people boarded on the other side so that the barge pushed away, I felt the butterflies begin to churn in my belly. As I rode my horse onto the barge and then waited for our own departure, those butterflies became eagles. By the time I set foot on the other shore, they were jet airliners.

I rode as hard as I dared, knowing that the woman might veer off of the main road at any point. Fortunately, there was enough residual moisture from earlier rains to allow me to see the perfect grooves that were cut into the muddy road by the wheels from the cart.

I lost them only for a short time at an intersection and had to climb down to actually crawl around and trace one groove with my finger until it was clear of the mess. As soon as I felt confident, I climbed back on the horse and rode all the harder.

At last, I was rewarded. I could see the cart ahead, the same figure seated on the bench that I recognized from being on the barge.

I galloped up from the rear and had to pretend to ignore her when she cast a glance over her shoulder at the sound of my approach. I was hunched over and looking past her so that she might mistake me for just a courier or somebody in a hurry.

The moment I was alongside, I brought my left hand up and gave a huge backhanded swing with the handle end of my tomahawk. She never saw it coming. Blood and teeth flew in a chunky red slurry, and the woman toppled from her seat and hit the ground hard. Unfortunately for her, the cart ran over one leg and crushed it.

Before you get too worked up, I had plenty of time as I approached to see that child was in a bundle in the bed of the cart. I would have never done anything to intentionally endanger the little one.

The woman was unconscious from the pain—and likely my shot to her mouth. I was able to get the horse to stop and then I led the cart off the road. The first thing I did was to secure and gag the woman. Once I was done, I actually took the child home to the mother. People wanted to make a big fuss, but I simply told them it was the right thing to do. When asked about the captor, I just said that she died in the struggle.

After being re-supplied (this time I was willing to accept the fresh baked bread, the block of cheese, the dried meats, and even a bottle of handcrafted blackberry brandy), I was ready to go. I also kept the horse. The man who had been so generous actually wanted to give me a better one, but I told him I was fine with the one he'd originally provided.

I rode back and reached the woman sometime after dark. I settled in for what was to come, but found that I simply did not have the taste for it. Yes, she had committed terrible acts; and yes, she would pay for them with her life. However, I could not bring myself to draw this ordeal out as I had with men in the past. Call me weak, or whatever else you like. (Although I do not suggest you call me compassionate.)

Once I had her awake (the method is unimportant) I explained to her who I was and what I planned. I was not surprised that she made no attempt to beg or plead. Honestly, that usually only happens after a considerable amount of trauma has been inflicted.

I did ask her if any of the children she stole were still alive. I hoped that maybe she would tell me that she had indeed sold them or something along that nature. Sadly, it was not the case. While she would give no details, she did nod in agreement when asked if each of them were dead.

It would have been nice to at least hear what ever sick and

twisted reasoning she might offer as an excuse for her actions. That would not be the case.

When I brought her to the stream and pushed her face down in the water, she did not even kick. The only indication I had that she was dead was when she went completely slack.

I gathered my things, climbed on the horse, and rode away. She might still very well be face down in that stream to this day.

17

The Geek's Wife Plants a Flag

"Jesus Christ!"

All four of the young men jumped back as the severed head landed with an ugly sounding thud on the sidewalk. Marty and Melvin both stepped in beside Catie in the momentary confusion. Catie hid the wince she felt inside. This was the line, and it had officially been crossed.

She took a second to shoot a quick glance over at the head that had come to rest on one side. She looked into the glazed over and dead eyes that actually showed no signs of surprise. Maybe he had not seen it coming.

She could hope.

"You killed Elliot!" the man who had admitted to being the leader of this little band said with a strangled cry. "Why would you do that?"

"You are aware that he injects people with a serum that either kills them and turns them into the undead or else proves that they are immune?" Catie replied. She was proud of how calm her voice sounded. If she was going to pull this off, she knew full well the need for appearances to be just so.

"We are only trying to protect ourselves. In case you are new around these parts, there are actually groups of people out there that hunt the immune. We have been run out of every community except one, and that one treats us like animals!" the young man shot back.

Catie was actually impressed. The other three young men were a mix of confusion and open fear. They had the right one in charge as far as she was concerned.

"Listen…" Catie paused, "I don't know your name. I don't want to just call you 'Kid' or 'Hey you' so maybe we should start over. My name is Catie Dreon. I am immune just like you, and I want to make some changes that require your help."

"Braden Riley," the young man said. He cast a nervous look over his shoulder at his three companions. "This is Chuck, Mario, and Luigi."

"My name is not Luigi!" one of them snapped, stepping forward and extending a hand to Catie. "My name is Louis."

Catie shook the offered hand and gave a tilt of her head to each of the men at her shoulder. "This is Marty and Melvin. And since you haven't run off in fear or tried to attack us, can I at least assume that you are interested in what we have in mind?"

"We haven't run because those two look like they would have no problem shooting us with those crossbows they have on their shoulders." Louis jutted his chin in the twins' direction. "As for an attack, I think I would rather them shoot me than rip me apart like a daddy longlegs. Those two look like what I imagine when I read stories about huge ogres."

"Wow, don't hold back, kid," Marty mumbled.

"First, I will tell you that we are in agreement that this community needs to be free to exist, and we also believe that the immune at Montague Village should be free as well. What we disagree with is the method." Catie glanced back at the twins who nodded in consent. "I don't think forcing people to be injected is the right way to go about it. I did not agree with biological or chemical warfare before the zombie apocalypse and I sure as hell don't think it is the way to do things now. We just prove that we are the evil that those who hate us profess."

"That is all good, but Dean Stockton made it clear a long time ago that he would not let the immune go. They are his best source of free labor. He can use them outside the walls as he sees fit without endangering one of the unknown," Braden protested.

"That is because you have been going about this all wrong. You have let this man hold the high ground by kidnapping children," Catie countered.

"We took the ones that we were asked to take by the families inside Montague," Louis said with an openly defensive tone.

"But that is not how it is being sold to the people of Montague. Also, what you now have is a heavily slanted population that needs to be cared for versus one that can hold its own. And can I ask why it is that nobody else seems to be engaged in these missions that you boys have been running?" Catie elbowed Marty and indicated for him to retrieve the head and return it to the bag. The point had been made and there was now no longer a reason for it to be out in the open for anybody else to see.

"Who would you send?" Braden laughed. "The doc? Any of the medical people? Those folks are way too valuable."

"What about some of these people that we see standing sentry positions?" Catie asked.

"Standing guard someplace safe is one thing," Braden replied with a shake of his head. "Going out there where stuff can get real nasty in a hurry is another thing entirely. Elliot liked to keep it to just us and a few others."

"Less people to worry about possibly defecting?" Melvin asked.

"You old people watched too many movies when you were young," Braden snorted. "The truth was that this post was one hundred percent voluntary. Nobody was made to leave the community. He said that forcing people to act against their will was Dean's way, not his."

"And I am surprised that you all have survived this long." Catie's voice came in a harsh tone that made all four of the young men wince.

"Why?" Louis challenged. "Because we are not out trying to conquer our neighbors? We just want to be left in peace."

"And how is that going for you?" Catie shot back.

"Fine until you showed up!"

Catie stepped right up to Louis. Her voice was little more than a low growl as she spoke, but all four of the young men could hear her very clearly. "This is not the world where you can just stick your head in the sand and wait things out. There are bad people out there who rape and murder for fun because nobody is out there to stop them. There are people who want to kill you because you are different, and you think parading a few hundred zombies down Main Street every so often is going to be enough. I just left an army behind that was led by a lunatic that makes Dean Stockton seem like an angel. If she would have turned south instead of north at some point, it might have been you and your people that she came across."

"Sh-sh-she?" Louis sputtered.

"Did you think that only men could become evil, self-serving pieces of crap?" Catie scoffed.

She suddenly stepped in and grabbed Louis by the throat. With a single sweep of her foot, she swept his legs out from under him and was straddling his chest while his mouth opened and closed and he wheezed in a pitiful attempt to bring air back into his lungs.

"I could kill you right here and now before your buddies could take so much as a step closer to try and help you," Catie said flatly, her nose almost touching Louis' as she leaned in close.

Hopping to her feet, Catie wiped her hands on the seat of her pants and turned her attention back to Braden. The young man started to take a step back and then stopped, making a point of actually planting his feet. He shot a nervous glance at Marty and Melvin; neither who so much as flinched or batted an eye as they stood with their arms folded across their massive chests.

"But you won't kill him or any of us," Braden said, his voice giving away just a slight tremor that belied his fear despite the brave face he was wearing.

"You are exactly right." Catie gave a slight nod. "I need you boys on my team."

"And what about everybody else?" one of the other young men asked; Catie thought that it was Mario. "We are not the only people here. This place has a population of seven hundred and thirty-seven. How are…" he made a point of doing an exaggerated head count, "…seven of us going to just take over. I don't know what you think you knew, but the people here loved Elliot. He let them have a sense of peace and calm. You are talking about turning this place into an army and becoming the type of people that we were trying to stay away from."

"Elliot was going to inject people! He was going to mount a war of his own. The only difference is that he was going to do his in a sneaky, dirty way that is wrong on every level." Catie had to fight to keep her voice down. She was already surprised that nobody seemed to notice when she had thrown Louis to the ground.

"Last I checked, killing is killing," Braden offered.

"This whole time, have I said anything about having to kill anybody?" Catie raised a single eyebrow and let her eyes drift from one of the young men to the next. Eventually, she saw a slow shaking of heads.

"That is because we don't actually have to kill anybody if this works." She saw all four of the young men open their mouths with the questions each had, but she raised her hands and stopped them as she went on to explain the basic idea of her plan.

"You have been running around this place making the Beastie Boys something that people actually fear. All of that with just four of you? You have caused enough havoc to have people think that there is some band of heartless animals out in the zombie wilderness preying on innocent children. In a way, it is genius. It helps us take your little masquerade to a whole new level of deception."

Catie saw looks cross the faces of the four as they listened. She hurried on with the explanation of the basics regarding her plan. As she spoke, she began to see eyes go wide and lips curl into smiles. She was winning them over even easier than she believed. She also watched Marty and Melvin. This was not exactly the plan she had laid out to them. In the one she used to bring them on board, there was no bluffing. Of course that plan had been made when she was one of those who thought that Elliot's Beastie Boys were an army, a force to be reckoned with as opposed to the reality.

In truth, these people were ripe for the picking. She could make bigger changes once they had secured their safety. It would start with Montague, but she would deal with the less tolerable communities as well. She had found her place. This is where she would plant her flag and make a home for her and Kevin's unborn child.

She had no doubt that there was going to be a fight ahead. She did not think this would be able to be pulled off without casualties. It would be the first ones that made or broke her fledgling band, but she would see this happen now. As if to signal that she did in fact need to hurry, she felt something shift in her body.

The baby had kicked!

18

So Few Answers

"Ladies and gentlemen, may I present to you Commander Suzi McFarlane," Randy crowed.

"I am just going to go out on a limb and guess that there is no mutated plague virus inside the walls of Island City," Suzi spat as her gag was removed.

"Nope." Randy handed the reins of her horse over to one of the riders that had come from the ruins.

"So then where are my people?" Suzi asked. "I have lost at least thirty of my scouts on missions in and around that place."

"Honestly, I couldn't tell ya. We were not kidding when we reported that your Outriders were disappearing." Randy did not seem the least bit bothered by the icy stare that Suzi was directing at him.

"And it wasn't the college kids or some rebel faction from Island City that tampered with and contaminated our vaccine?" Suzi pressed.

"Correct again, *Commander*." Randy did not try to hide the derision in his voice and the mockery he was making of her title.

"I take it you have failed to locate the Haynes faction?" one of the riders asked Randy.

"If she knows, she isn't telling me," Randy replied, giving a nod of his head to indicate Suzi. "You have people better suited for that kind of thing. I got no problem if you want me to just kill her, but I am not the torturing sort."

"Since I am about to be tortured…apparently," Suzi shot a withering glance back to Randy once more before continuing to address her new captors, "perhaps you can finally let me know what your real reason for wanting this Billy Haynes might be. After all, we at least got you in the ball park. And had your idiot child here not just up and killed the one prisoner we still had in our care, it is likely that he would have eventually come down and spoken with me."

"You let the other two go!" Randy spat. "I would almost wager that they are behind those two herds that are causing so much trouble."

"So much trouble?" Suzi lost her cool at that moment. She was starting to struggle against her bonds and her voice was audible death. "You would not let the alarm be sounded and the word given for my people to enact the emergency evacuation procedure. By the time somebody figures out that I am gone and gives that order for my people to move, it will be too late. You will be allowing thousands of men and women to die needlessly."

"You only have yourself to blame." Randy wheeled his horse around in a complete circle and came up beside Suzi. "Hunter was making headway, that stupid girl was starting to trust him. She would have spilled her guts before much longer."

"Then I guess I am glad that I used your own serum on him. I suspected that he was doing something sketchy when it came to that girl. I only wish that I could have broken him in time to reveal your names so your head could have joined his on that trip. I am willing to bet that this Dr. Zahn would have been able to understand the message."

I had to cover my mouth with my hand. While I was almost gaining some sort of understanding on some of the things that had evaded me for the most part, I was now getting a whole new batch of questions dumped in my lap.

Suzi knew Dr. Zahn? And what was this about rumors of a mutated version of the zombie virus inside the walls of Island

City? All of this was now a lot more than I was ready or able to handle. I needed to get back to Platypus Creek and give this to Billy and Dr. Zahn. As much as I tried to be all grown up and try and handle things like an adult, I was not up to the task of dealing with something this big.

I was going to hate myself, but I started to retreat back to Kayla. I would try to swing through Island City on the way and make good with Cricket, but my priority was to make it home. Even if they abandoned Platypus Creek, this was not going to go away. For whatever reason, this group wanted Billy, and by the sounds of things, it was not going to be a happy or pleasant meeting.

I reached Kayla to discover that she had actually fallen asleep! I leaned over and shook her. She did not move at first and I felt my heart skip a beat. I put a hand to her chest and it took me a second before I felt it rise and fall very slowly. All I could think was that she had somehow gotten nipped or infected while she led me to safety from the encampment.

When her eyes fluttered, I pretty much expected to see dark tracers. When I saw regular old whites, I grabbed her and hugged her.

"What's wrong?" Kayla mumbled. I could hear the fatigue in her voice and realized that she had simply been asleep; all of this adventure had taken its toll on her.

"Nothing." My voice was muffled as I had yet to release her from the hug.

I finally put myself at arms' length and gave her one more quick inspection; never can be too careful. After I was reassured that she was not infected or in any way injured, I related what I had heard. I don't think that I was ever happier to see such an expression of cluelessness on somebody's face. If I was stumped, Kayla was even more lost than I.

"Look, I doubt we are gonna figure this out," I finally said. "What I am sure of is that we need to get home and tell Billy, Dr. Zahn, Jim, and Paula. If somebody is going to make sense of this mess, it will be one of them."

"I wouldn't be so sure," Kayla sighed.

"We have a long haul ahead, so we need to get going."

I got to a crouch and looked back down the hill. The meeting was still going on. Also, apparently the person that had been captured along with Suzi had been deemed unnecessary. I could just barely make out the form of a body on the ground.

Kayla and I stayed in a crouch until we were over the ridge of the little hill. Only, now we had a new set of problems. There was a sea of zombies down below. They had reached the encampment and, now that I was not solely focused on what I'd heard at that meeting, I could hear the screams and cries as people below died terrible deaths. I could also see that, while some were trying to fight, most were running for their lives with whatever they could carry. A very fortunate few had managed to reach the area where the horses were allowed to graze and galloped away. Sadly, most of the horses had been on the fringe of the camp and gotten engulfed by the undead swarm.

Seemingly a million miles away to our left was Island City. I tried to find a way around that mob, but it seemed unlikely unless we wanted to move parallel to it and move around the tail end. That would not be a problem except for the fact that it would put us on a wide open stretch of land where we would have no cover and easily be seen. I was impatient, but this was no time to be careless. We would have to wait out the zombies.

***

"Let's go."

Kayla shook me awake. I had not thought that I would actually be able to sleep. Between everything bouncing around in my head, my desire to get to Billy, and the screams that seemed to never end coming from the encampment, I honestly thought that I would just lie in the grass under the interlaced branches in this grove of trees and churn things over in my mind.

Apparently not.

I'd let Kayla resume her nap while I took the first watch. When she woke and promptly scolded me for not letting her do her part, I'd relented. The next thing I knew, she was waking me up and it was almost dark.

"We have wasted the better part of a day," I said around a yawn.

"Yeah, but that herd has finally cleared out for the most part. I think we can move right down into that old neighborhood area and stick to the shadows. We could make it to the walls and then use Island City as our cover as we make for the pass road that will take us home."

That was as good of a plan as any. I got up and slung my pack over my shoulder.

"Oh," Kayla said as she climbed over the fence that enclosed the junkyard, "I sharpened your blades. Also, you have my crossbow. Yours got messed up somewhere along the line. You are the better shot, so I figured it would be best if you were the one with the working crossbow."

"Thanks," I grunted as I landed on the ground and in the near perfect black of the shadows of one of those towers of old automobiles.

"I tell you because I think you should probably load that thing."

It was then that I realized Kayla was talking in a whisper. A second later, I heard the rumble of a zombified dog. I saw a shadow that oozed along the ground and was just a bit darker than the shadows already being cast.

I was thankful for the bright moon just overhead; otherwise we might be in for a bit of trouble. I backed up a few steps and looked over at Kayla who was already up on the rear bumper of a car and trying to keep her eyes on the zombie dog while still doing her best to get out of range of its muzzle.

I lined up my shot and fired. There was a noise, and I thought for a second that I'd scored a kill. Then I realized I'd actually pinned the pathetic thing to the ground. Hopping down, I hurried over and ended its suffering—if zombie dogs suffer, that is.

"That is odd, don't you think?" Kayla asked as we sort of jogged across the rest of the junkyard.

"What?" I was scanning for any more signs of trouble, so I

was not really doing much in the way of thinking.

"Did you run across any zombie dogs when you came this way the first time?" Kayla asked, although I could tell she was starting to struggle with running and talking, so I slowed my pace just a little. Also, she made a good point.

We rounded the corner of a long row of those stacked cars and emerged in a relatively bright swath of ground that seemed to almost suck in the moonlight. I only took a few steps when the low moan of a zombie caused me to pull up short. Kayla actually skidded to a halt and ended up on her butt from trying so hard to not only stop, but reverse directions as well.

"Where the hell did they all come from?" Kayla asked.

Looking around, I saw zombies coming out from all over the place. Also, I could see a section of the junkyard where the wall had fallen. Zombies might be like electricity and take the easiest path, but when they are stuffed into a space too small to contain them, they have no problems making a new path.

"Just run, Kayla," I urged, grabbing her arm and pulling her along.

She drew her belt knife and seemed to gather herself with a few deep breaths. We ran along together, making no style points at all as we pushed, shoved, and spiked our way to the other end of the junkyard. We finally reached the fence on the other side. It was no problem to jump, hook my leg over and be free and clear.

I turned and saw Kayla as she struggled to pull herself up and over as well. She just got one leg over and her face was an expression of triumph; then she vanished. It was like seeing somebody get pulled under water.

"No!" I screamed. I ran back and pulled myself back up just in time to see Kayla disappear under a pair of zombies.

She screamed and I threw myself over, landing on my feet and plunging my knife into the back of the head of one of her attackers. A trio of undead were all reaching for me and I only had a split second to think that it was lucky for Kayla, otherwise she would be under a pile of five instead of just the pair, one of which I had already ended.

I heard Kayla shriek and my blood chilled. That was not the sound of fear, it was a scream of pain. I kicked at the closest zombie of the trio approaching me and then grabbed the one that was on top of Kayla by the back of the neck. With a quick jab, I stabbed it in the side of the head.

Kayla shoved the body off of her and scrambled to her feet. I could hear her crying and I kept hearing the word "no, no, no, no" being almost chanted as she threw herself at the fence. I had to shove another of the trio away, this time angling my push so that it collided with the remaining one that was still coming.

I looked up to see maybe a hundred more of the undead advancing towards all this commotion. Turning, I leaped and caught the top of the wall and hauled myself over for the second time. Kayla was on her knees and I could see dark liquid dripping from her left arm and onto the ground in front of her.

"C'mon, Kayla," I panted, finding myself out of breath after the repeated trips up and over that tall fence that had once sealed off the junkyard.

"Just go," she whimpered.

"Umm, no."

"I'm bit, Thalia." She held up her arm to emphasize the point.

I was about to say something when more moans carried from close by. We needed to get to the relatively safe walls of Island City. This was not the time or the place for a debate.

"That does not mean a thing until we get you someplace and wait for a symptom to show." I grabbed for her and she scrambled back and out of my reach.

"Don't touch me!" she cried. "If I am infected, you can catch it."

"I know how it is transmitted," I huffed. "And I will not touch you, but you need to get up. If you are infected, I promise to take care of you."

"You need to get back to warn the others, you don't have time."

"I can wait until we get someplace where I can get a better look."

"But—" Kayla tried to protest.

"Shut up and get on your feet!" I barked. "You came this far. You have shown that you are not just another pretty face and that you can handle yourself. Don't throw it all away now by acting like a...a...a girl!"

Kayla sniffed and stood up. I blew a sigh of relief since I could now see zombies converging from all over. That herd had broken up quite a bit coming through here. I felt like an idiot for not realizing that this possibility existed.

I unzipped my coat and cut away a piece of my shirt, handing it to Kayla to use as a bandage. She wrapped her forearm quickly after she used her own knife to cut away the ragged section of the sleeve. It only took a moment, but in that amount of time, the hundred zombies coming our way had more than doubled.

We ran for the oasis that Island City represented. When we reached it and had gotten safely behind the walls, I sought the first house and hurried inside. Lighting a lantern, I did not really care if I gave away our location. I held my breath as I turned to face Kayla.

I staggered back and I saw her expression crumble. I had to shake off my emotions right away.

"No!" I said in a rush. "I am actually just relieved. No squiggles!"

"Really?"

She stood up and walked over to a mirror mounted on the wall and peered at her own reflection. She used her thumb and index finger to peel her eyes open as wide as possible as if she expected to discover something hidden that would reveal her to actually be infected.

Her face slowly broke into a smile and she turned to me. Her mouth opened as if she were about to say something, and then she simply collapsed.

"Kayla!" I ran to her, my heart suddenly in my throat. She had looked fine. What could have caused her to just drop like that for no apparent reason?

I reached her side and was relieved to discover that she was still breathing. I held my breath as I peeled her eyelids back again and re-inspected her eyes. They were still clear. However, I did notice that she felt warm to the touch.

I was at a loss as to what to do. For the most part, she appeared normal and healthy. I was beginning to feel myself fray at the edges. Seriously, I'd heard the stories of the old days when it was one stretch of bad luck after another. Hearing the stories, you did not understand how anybody had survived, much less been able to bring people together and create communities.

I felt it build, and then it was as if a dam burst. My eyes flooded with tears and I began to cry. I clutched Kayla tight and sobbed so hard that I started to feel dizzy. I guess I was making quite a racket. That is the only reason to explain how somebody (or a group) had made it to the porch.

When the door flew open with a crash, I was crying so hard that I couldn't even scream as the lantern toppled from the table and landed with a crash on the floor. Flames raced up the curtains of the living room window and the splatter pattern from the oil in the lamp had caused the large couch to add to the conflagration.

Over everything, I heard the moans of the undead. Somehow, they must have been able to get inside Island City as well. They had followed me, and then, between my having lit a lantern in the first place, and then all my crying, I had led them right to us. Now I had to make a choice.

Die by zombie.

Or die by fire.

DEAD returns for
the finale
October 30, 2015

DEAD: End

But turn the page for a
sneak preview of

*That Ghoul Ava and
The Queen of the Zombies*

That Ghoul Ava and
The Queen of the Zombies

1

Same Ol' Situation

"Do you have to play this crap so loud?" Lisa said with that petulance that only teen girls can truly master. It's so sad. When we get older it just comes off as whiny or bitchy.

I pretended not to hear her. Not one thing that she could say or do was going to ruin my mood tonight. I was behind the wheel of my very first brand new car. No little tushies had planted themselves in this seat but mine. I had been assured that I was the very first person to test drive this little baby: A candy-apple red 2013 Corvette.

Now I'm not one of those girls who knows a lot about cars, so most of what the very cute salesman said just didn't stick. I think he even had a fancy name for the color red that my car was painted. Don't care.

I flew down the on-ramp that deposited me onto I-5 and went through the gears like I imagine those racecar drivers did when they zoomed around in circles. By the time I actually hit the freeway, I was on the high side of ninety miles per hour.

"Got your seatbelt on?" I asked. I wasn't planning on getting into a wreck...but who did? Safety first!

"Try to remember that only one of us is guaranteed not to die if you wreck this thing," Lisa yelled over the strains of the luscious Brett Michaels who was currently begging me to talk dirty to him. Trust me when I tell you, *that* would be the least of his worries.

She was referring to the fact that I am a ghoul. Now let me assure you, being a ghoul is absolutely nothing like being a zombie. As if. Zombies are nasty creatures that eat the living. I only eat the dead. See? Big difference.

Lisa Jenkins was a teenage runaway. However, I doubted that her parents would come looking for her any time soon. In the six months that she had lived with me, I learned enough to know that it was unlikely that they were even aware that she had left home. Her father was long gone, and her single mother was busy sleeping with every bus boy, waiter, and bartender at this dirty little all-night place in Southeast Portland.

I'd popped in once and the woman was letting some slob put his hands up her skirt every time she came to the table. When she brought the actual meal to the table and cleared away the five empty beer bottles to make room, I almost lost my pro-verbial lunch. It was fried chicken, and I know for a fact that he didn't wash his hands before picking up that drumstick. And considering where that hand had just been...

But back to my dear friend and boon companion. (I don't actually know what a 'boon companion' is, but I heard that term used on some show on the local Public Broadcasting channel where everybody spoke with English accents. It sounded smart, so I claimed it.) I met Lisa one night shortly after my transfor-mation. She had been in a seedy hotel after just giving birth. Her "boyfriend"—a pervy forty-something that actually convinced her to dump the child in the garbage right after giving birth—made the mistake of answering the door when I knocked. Long story short, baby was rescued and eventually given a home, perv was killed *and then* eaten, and Lisa became my roommate.

It was around the time that I met Lisa when I was intro-duced to a whole part of society that most folks don't realize exists under their noses. Call it supernatural or whatever you like, but things like ghouls, and ghosts, and vampires—like that snarky little bitch Belinda Yates—exist.

Some have gone on to sustain themselves through books like the one you are reading right now. You see, the best way to hide is in plain sight. You'd be surprised if I told you which of the other books in your collection are real; or at least based on real events in the lives of some of my fellow monsters. Yeah, most of them don't like the "M" word, but I like to consider my-self a bit more progressive.

I actually decided to join the ranks of the writer-types after my first little "adventure" where I was hired to deal with a rogue vampire that had designs on the aforementioned Belinda. Well...not really Belinda, more specifically, her Kiss. (A "Kiss" for the uninitiated is what vampires call their little groups or clubs…whatever.) I didn't actually have to write, but Lisa thought it would be fun. She worries about the finances like nobody I have ever met and keeps telling me that the payday I got for taking care of Belinda's "little problem" won't last forever.

After I saw this car, I finally agreed that we needed an additional source of income. The only problem now was waiting for the next "job" from Morgan. For those of you who didn't catch my first little attempt at telling a story, Morgan is the psychic for my region. Unlike the ones on television that lie about being able to tell your future, Morgan is for real. Apparently true psychics are able to detect any supernaturals in their district. I don't know all of the details—mostly because she tells me very little—but I guess they act as some sort of mediator and boss for their given district.

The day I became a ghoul, I received a visit from Morgan. She kind of told me the rules. Mostly she went on about all the stuff I couldn't do. Of course, it was good old Ava's door that they knocked on when that vampire came in and started mucking things up.

By the time Billy Idol had told me all about what a great day it would be for a *White Wedding*, and the Go-Gos encouraged me to take a *Vacation*, we were home. And here was the reason we needed Morgan to show up with another job…or people needed to start buying these books. Home was no longer the dirty little apartment that I'd rented while I was a busty waitress with raven-black hair. Now we lived in a sweet little two-story looking down on Lake Oswego. (I never knew there was actually a lake here! Just thought it was a cute name for a town.)

It has four bedrooms! Now I wasn't ever going to hear the pitter-patter of ghoulish feet, but maybe Lisa might give it a go when she is actually old enough and meets a nice guy. I have a feeling that I will be living vicariously through her.

And there you have it—my word for the day: *vicariously*. Take that Morgan. She always talks to me like I am the idiot child. Well now that I have hired a ghost writer—literally, I seriously have this ghost that comes in and helps, she possesses Lisa when it is time to sit down and put the story together—I get to hear all sorts of big words.

Chantal, my ghostly pal, likes to chat sometimes during the day. She sometimes slips in to Lisa while she is dozing and will chat with me about stuff. At first it was weird having these conversations that Lisa has no memory of, and I have to get it straight who I am talking to or what I have said to Chantal-Lisa and what I have said to Lisa-Lisa.

Hmm, that reminds me. I fiddle with my iPod docking station and thumb to a song. One of my favorite features of this home was the sound system. You can have music—or whatever you are watching on television—piped throughout the whole place. *Head-to-Toe* by Lisa Lisa and the Cult Jam starts, and I head for the basement door.

"Back in a few minutes," I call over my shoulder. I catch Lisa's face in the reflection of the kitchen window. Her nose wrinkles. If I wasn't so secure in our friendship, my feelings might be hurt. Hey…a girl's gotta eat.

My basement is the other feature that really sold this house to me. A serial killer would blow his…well, whatever it is that they blow. You can bet my basement would be the thing that would send said serial killer over the edge.

It is absolutely sound proof. I tested it out early when I brought my ex-husband's guitar amplifier down here. My actual goal was to check out the real estate agent's claim that this basement was, in fact, sound proof. If I just happened to blow up his amplifier in the process, that would be icing on the cake.

I plugged in the pretty green guitar that was still in my closet despite the fact that we had been divorced long enough for that cheating bastard to remarry and have a pair of twin snot factories…err…I mean a lovely set of boy and girl twins. (I can never remember which is fraternal and which is maternal…not like I actually care.) Anyways, I plugged that guitar in, turned every single knob on the amplifier to "10" and strummed. I forgot all about my super-sensitive ghoul hearing.

For almost a week I was absolutely deaf. Thankfully I have the ability to heal. Supposedly, I can take a shotgun blast to the chest and not die. I'd just as soon not test the theory, but it is kind of nice to think that that little bit of insurance is in my tool box. To actually kill me, you need to either sever my head, or pierce my heart with a weapon made from cold-treated iron—

whatever the heck that is. I feel comfortable sharing that with you because you will either dismiss this as just another one of "those" stories that are so popular right now, or you just won't ever feel the need to go out and hunt down a ghoul that is trying to make the world a better place.

So once I could hear again, Lisa assured me that she did not actually hear a thing. She was really glad when my hearing came back. I guess I am one of those women with a naturally loud voice.

So back to my basement. As I told you, I am a ghoul. I eat the dead. To be clear, they have to be "unprocessed." I don't know if you are aware of what they do to a person before spray painting them and stuffing them in a box, but no ghoul would ever touch a body after a mortician got ahold of it. I keep about a half dozen corpses on ice for those times when I can't go out and hunt down a fresh meal.

This is another of the perks from that job I did for Belinda-the-vampire-bitch. She occasionally has one of her minions bring by a thrall that might have been snacked on a bit too heavily or the chance human version of a monster that they might stumble across. I had no idea that so many icky beasties maintain human form and transform under whatever weird circumstance is their trigger: full moons, high tides, the opening day of football season.

Opening the walk-in refrigerator, I pull the first body out and set him on the huge table. Already the smell is causing my mouth to water. I know it will just be a moment—

"Mrrgl."

Oh yeah. Sharkmouth makes the scene and I dig in. I can't really explain it better than that. When I smell a dead body—something that you would probably find repulsive—it is like being in Martha Stewart's kitchen on Thanksgiving. The smell is beyond delicious.

My mouth does this thing that sort of defies biology. It stretches out several inches and these three razor-sharp rows of needle-like fangs drop. I become the human equivalent of one of those wood chipper thingies. I can down a whole body in less than ten minutes. The only part that is a bit icky for me is re-gurging up the clothes. To my credit, I strip the bodies that are put in my fridge. However, I don't exactly have control over my appetite. When I encounter a dead body out and about, I just can't help myself.

The best thing I can equate it to is what used to happen with those spray cans of whip cream. I couldn't open my fridge when one of those things were in there back when I was alive without grabbing it, popping the top, and shooting a mouthful of tasty, sweet whipped cream into my mouth.

So anyways, I got my Sharkmouth going, and made short work of my dinner. I think we found this one under a bridge. Probably not the solution to the homeless situation that they were thinking of with *Comic Relief*; but, in my defense, he was already dead. Being out in the elements is really not something that we are designed for in our human form.

When I was finished, I went back upstairs. Lisa was already asleep. She was sprawled on the couch, the remote slipping from her fingers. I glanced at the screen long enough to decide that if I ever got the chance, I might break my rule about eating a live human if I ever met the 'Sham Wow' guy. I turned off the idiot box and pulled the blanket that was draped over the back of the sofa across Lisa and headed upstairs.

My room is a marvel. It has shutters that allow in absolutely no sunlight. That way I didn't have to stay in a rickety closet like I did back in the apartment. One of the drawbacks of being a ghoul is the vampire-like aversion to sunlight. For some reason, it burns like acid if it touches my tender, gray skin. (Although I do keep it airbrushed a golden bronze most times when we are going out in public.)

"Is this your idea of living a low key life?" a familiar voice whispered from the darkness.

I did my best not to shriek. However, I have this thing that happens when I get scared. My toenails and fingernails turn to three-inch claws. I've ruined more shoes in the past several months...

"Morgan, I wish you wouldn't do that," I managed to say. Sometimes I went all sharkmouth, too, depending on how scared I got.

So that brings me to another of my abilities. I can totally see in the dark. And not Paris Hilton sex-tape vision. I can *see* in the dark like a normal person can in the daylight. However, for some strange reason, Morgan is invisible to me when she chooses. It is like she wraps herself in the darkness and vanishes. Also, I can hear. I'm talking footsteps of a fly on the other side of the wall type stuff. It is like having a radio tuner in my head. I just scan the area, and I can pick up on things as far as a few blocks away. (I know this because Lisa and I played this game one night where she kept walking and talking in a whisper until I couldn't hear her.) However, like her ability to evade my sight, Morgan can also be so quiet that I can't hear her so much as breathe. (And she does, because I watched her chest one time to see if it rose and fell…it did.)

"And I will remind you that I am the authority in these parts and keep my own council."

Bitchy mood, I thought. *Great, just what I need.* What I said was, "So what brings you to my house tonight? I know it isn't to hang out and do each other's hair and nails." To emphasize my point, I kicked off my newest pair of ruined Nikes.

"It seems that there has been a disturbance." Morgan moved into view. Now when I say that, what I mean is that she went from being invisible to standing three feet away from me in the blink of an eye.

"In the Force?" I scoffed and sat on the edge of my bed to pull my shredded socks off my feet. Bummer, these were the ones with the cute little roses on the toes. I kind of liked those socks.

"Your attempts at humor have not gotten any better." Morgan walked to my door and pulled it shut.

"Neither has your attitude," I shot back. "You sent me on a job with the high likelihood that I would die, but that I would do enough damage so your precious little vampire could come in and finish the job."

"Not true," Morgan countered. "We gave you a fifty-fifty chance."

"You still sent me in underprepared and with the thought that my death would be an acceptable loss."

"We paid you very handsomely for your services." Morgan gave me a dismissive wave. I wondered, and not for the first time, if I could take her in a fight.

"Lot of good that would have done me if I were dead."

"You *are* dead."

I have no idea how long I stood there with my mouth open. I desperately wanted to fire off a witty comeback. Sadly, that is not really my strong suit. Instead, I went to what I felt I did best. I glared.

"I suppose you came here with a purpose?" I finally said after a few seconds of uncomfortable silence that was probably worse on me than on the emotionally stunted Morgan.

"I have." Morgan took a seat in the over-stuffed easy chair. She settled in and went so far as to grab the handle on the side and recline! Talk about making yourself comfortable. "There has been an incident just outside of the city in a little town called Estacada."

I had grown up in the Portland area. There are several little towns on the fringe that are mostly full of loggers, and, as of late, meth cooks. Back in the Seventies, there were always stories of people growing marijuana out in the forests. Supposedly they had the farms booby-trapped and if they caught trespassers, they just killed them and left the body for the animals. It was the Pacific Northwest's equivalent to moonshining, I guess. If you believe the stories, that is.

"When you say incident…" I let that hang in the air and become my question.

"I have been…" Morgan paused. For just a second, I thought I saw something flit across her face that *almost* looked like an emotion. Seriously, this lady could make Mr. Spock look like a Jerry Springer guest when it came to containing emotional expression. "I have been *informed* that there may be zombies in the woods."

I looked at Morgan, and then I pulled out my phone and tapped the screen to wake it up. Yep, it was the middle of March. That would rule out April Fool's. I tucked my phone away.

"Zombies?" I tried not to sound like I thought she was full of it, but I'm not sure how well I managed to hide my skepticism. "Like *Dawn of the Dead* zombies, or like *Serpent and the Rainbow* zombies?"

I was so proud of myself. I was never into the whole scary

movie kick when I was human. Honestly, I was a giant scairdy cat. Those sorts of things gave me nightmares. Now, heck, I'd done battle with an honest-to-goodness vampire. I'd spoken to a few ghosts, and I live with a teenage girl. Movie monsters had nothing on my reality. Since Morgan had let it slip that a lot of what most people would consider popular fiction had some basis in reality, I decided that I would do some homework. Turns out Lisa was a big fan of the stuff. So I let her pick the selections for movie night.

"We aren't sure yet," Morgan said with all seriousness.

"Wait! What?"

"There has only been one report and it was made by a witch that has a propensity for sipping a bit too much hemlock tea."

I was pretty sure that hemlock was some type of poison, but I could worry about that later. Morgan was talking about zombies. Worse, when I asked what type, her answer leads me to believe that there is more than *one* type of zombie! That tops poison drinking witches in my book.

"So what am I supposed to do? Do I go out there with a shotgun and blow their brains out?" I said with as much of a laugh as I could muster.

"I imagine that would be one way to deal with the situation," Morgan said with her usual lack of emotion.

"You can't be serious."

"I am absolutely serious. Do I strike you as somebody who jokes?"

I tried to imagine Morgan even smiling and it gave me a bit of a chill. It would probably be like a shark's smile...the last thing you ever saw before you became a snack. There was something about this woman that was just the most pure form of scary. And she was a tiny little thing. And then it dawned on me who she reminded me of: Carol Kane in that Bill Murray movie, *Scrooged*. She was that ghost or fairy, or whatever the heck she was supposed to be. But when she hit Bill Murray with that toaster, I laughed so hard I think I peed my pants just a little bit. She even had a voice very similar to Ms. Kane. Of course I would never tell her that. The only reason that I am sharing it with you here is because I know that she will never stoop to reading any of my books.

"So what in the world would zombies be doing here? And what am I supposed to do if I find one?"

"If I had all of these answers, do you think that I would be here asking you to investigate? That is what you are going to be paid for, Ava."

"So am I supposed to just investigate, or am I supposed to kill something?"

"I imagine that will be determined once you go check things out," Morgan said with a sigh as she unreclined (is that even a word?) from the recliner and stood up. "Perhaps I have overestimated your abilities. Maybe I should find somebody else."

I thought about that last seven figure paycheck. Considering the fact that I had worked as a waitress, and a good night was when I walked out with a hundred bucks, I decided that I wouldn't have a problem taking a drive out to Estacada to look for zombies. My only concern was Lisa.

"You might want to leave your pet human at home," Morgan said.

I know she told me that she isn't a fortune teller or a mind reader, but that was just too spooky. I think she had a good point, though. If these were the *Dawn of the Dead*-type of zombie, I would feel just terrible if Lisa got bit and turned into one of those things. Of course that brought me to another question.

"How come this isn't ending up on the news? If there are zombies, wouldn't that be something that the humans would want to report?"

Morgan was silent for a moment. I think that worried me more than anything else. She was keeping something from me and I didn't like it one bit.

"Somebody is keeping the zombies under control for now," Morgan finally said.

Now I was even more confused. There was so much wrong with that sentence that I had no idea where to start. I decided to just wade in—not that I expected much in the way of answers.

"Some*body*?"

Morgan's face actually seemed to melt into something resembling an emotion for just a split second. At least I think so. It might have been a trick of the shadows or something, but I was almost positive that I saw one eyebrow knit ever so slightly.

"There may be a person behind this," Morgan admitted.

"So if it is a person…" My mind tried to make what I considered to be a logical jump. "Then it must be some sort of voodoo thing, right?"

I had to consider that voodoo was real. After all, just scroll back a bit to that whole part where I mentioned meeting vampires and ghosts. Oh yeah, and the part about me being a ghoul. So if those things were real, then why not voodoo?

"Not necessarily," Morgan said with a slight movement of her head that may have been a shake in the general direction of "no."

"But if somebody is in control…" I heard that sound in my voice that was dangerously close to a whine. This was not going to get me any answers. I took a second and regrouped. Maybe if I tackled something else.

"You said something about 'for now' when you said that these zombies are under control."

"Bravo for catching on," Morgan said. The only problem was that I was not sure if she was being sarcastic or not.

"Does that mean this might be some sort of beginning of one of those zombie apocalypse thingamajigs that everybody seems so excited to read about?"

Personally, I didn't get the whole infatuation with that genre. Anybody with half a brain would know that a zombie apocalypse would eventually mean that there would be no more *anything*! Things like hot showers and stuff would be gone. It would be like the camping trip that never ended. I don't know about you, but I like to maintain a certain degree of personal hygiene. Soaps would stop being made…and that would be the least of our problems. You think you have trouble with feminine itching…or the lack of "feeling fresh" now? Try living without the local drug store or supermarket.

And for you men…I wouldn't start feeling so smug just yet. There are certain things that a woman may or may not do in these modern times regarding "your little soldier" that I can promise would come to an immediate halt when you stop being able to keep that area clean.

I knew this one guy, and he was just so dreamy; broad chest, dazzling smile, and strong swimmer's legs that were attached to buns that you could bounce a dime off. We met one night in a little club downtown and I swear that he was so well-groomed that I was certain he had to be gay. When he whispered in my ear that he would like to buy me a drink, I had to go check my make-up.

I am a very busty gal with my 38DDs, and I play to my strengths. I also have Elvira-black hair that comes to my waist. If I get a bit too carried away with the make-up, apparently some people have suspected me of being a drag queen. Now I don't want to get into the whole thing about whether or not that is a bad thing. Let's just say that when that revelation was made to me a few years back, I learned to tone down the face paint.

Anyways, we get back to my place and he is one of those guys who likes to do a little bit of taste-testing before he gets down to business. *Yay for me!* is what I was thinking. Me being the kind of gal who is into reciprocity, I went to return the favor. I got to his naval when I noticed what I first believed to be just a case of bad feet. I was prepared to overlook that…until I got to the actual source of that sweaty stench.

So, fellas, if you think that whole zombie apocalypse thing is gonna just-freakin'-rock, let me tell you that there are some major downsides.

"…would take a lot more than that." Crap, Morgan had been saying something important. I knew that she was going to be annoyed, but I didn't have much to lose since she already thought I was an idiot.

"Excuse me?" I tried to make it sound like I wanted her to elaborate. She is far too smart for that.

"I should have known when you had that vapid look in your eyes that you were off on some sort of mental picnic," Morgan said. The thing is, she said it with as close to no emotion as possible. It was like my Speak-and-Spell using a female voice.

"Sorry, just trying to wrap my mind around how bad a zombie apocalypse would be."

"So you didn't hear a single word that I said." I couldn't swear to it, but it almost sounded like Morgan was annoyed.

"Okay, I'm listening." I even cupped my hands to my ears for effect.

"I said that all those books and movies are preposterous. Do you really think that one person infected with some sort of zombie virus could cause a chain reaction that would wipe out the world? It would take something a great deal more widespread."

Morgan headed for the door and started downstairs. I guess she was leaving. I followed her down and even edged around her to open the door. I doubted that it would raise my standing in her eyes, but perhaps a little politeness would gain me a little something.

"I want to repeat," Morgan turned and stood in my doorway, "that I believe it would be a very bad idea to take your little human pet with you on this assignment."

"She'd not a—" I began to protest, but she was gone. I could say that she vanished in the blink of an eye…but I hadn't blinked.

"What assignment?"

I jumped. If my heart still beat, it would have been pounding like a Rikki Rockett drum solo. Instead, my fingernails and toenails went switchblade. Lisa took a step back and had the decency to look apologetic. *How had she snuck up on me?* Hmm.

"Morgan just came by with a job." I shut the door and headed upstairs to my room. It would be daylight soon, I could feel it. "She thinks I can handle it by myself and didn't want you getting involved." I guess that was at least part of the truth. I wasn't all that sure that Morgan believed that I could handle anything by myself.

"What is the job?" Lisa moved past me into my room and plopped down on my bed. I could tell by the look on her face that she wasn't buying any of what I was selling.

"Just something up in Estacada. I will head there tonight and be back before morning most likely."

"So is it werewolves?" Lisa said that with way too much enthusiasm. I guess this was all just a big adventure to her. She still was not really in tune with the whole "we are monsters" part of things. If she knew how close she'd come to being a late-night snack to Belinda back when we first started hanging out together…perhaps she would be a little more concerned with her own safety.

"No." I closed my bedroom door. A little bit of dim gray

light was starting to spill across the floor of my hallway.

"Then maybe you can let me know what it is, and *I* can decide if it is too dangerous for me or not." Lisa folded her arms across her chest and cocked one hip. That was teenage girl body language for 'I ain't budging until you talk.'

"Zombies," I said.

Seriously, what could it hurt? In fact, we'd watched a bunch of those movies. Even went to some author's book signing. Marvin, or Mark, or Mel Tufo...something like that—he had some series that she was just crazy about. She got home that night and wrapped the book in plastic like it was a priceless artifact. I was certain that when I told her it might be zombies that she would see the logic in sitting this one out. After all, I am a ghoul. I was pretty sure I am off the menu.

I could not have been more wrong.

DEAD returns for
the finale
October 30, 2015

DEAD: End

But turn the page for a
sneak preview of

DEAD: Snapshot—Portland, Oregon

DEAD: Snapshot—Portland, Oregon

Ken ducked instinctively and felt something swish through the air where his head had been just a second ago. Kicking backwards, his foot struck something solid and was greeted with a loud "oof".

Turning, he saw the punks from inside the store. The one that had reached him first was already doubled over, but he had no chance to defend against the next and took a booted foot to the shoulder. He slammed into the rear of the truck and ended up down on his knees. He could hear the dog barking from the cab of the truck.

"Get him!" Jinks yelled, obviously not the one to lead the charge.

Ken saw the boot coming and moved his head just enough to take little more than a grazing blow to the cheek. His hand was going for his gun as the rest of his attackers arrived. He rolled under the rear of his truck, pulling himself into the fetal position in order to do so.

A set of legs appeared just past the rear tires and Ken brought his gun around. He fired and winced at the loud report. A body fell, the person clutching their wounded leg and rolling back and forth. If not for the ringing in his ears, he would have heard the wail of pain.

Looking to the rear of the truck where the attack had begun, he spied the person that he'd kicked as he or she struggled to reach their feet. Lining up his next shot, he fired again; the person flopped backwards and was still. Scuttling back just a little further, he saw another set of legs. The owner had obviously decided to give up on the attack and was turning to leave. Once more Ken fired. He saw the body sprawl in a pool of blue radiance from one of the parking lot lights.

Waiting a second to ensure there were no other attackers, Ken slowly emerged from under the pickup. His hearing was still hampered, but he heard the cries of the person he'd shot in the leg. He walked over and looked down to discover the young lady with the crewcut.

"P-p-please don't shoot me!" she wailed, holding up her hands.

Ken looked around to see if anybody might be paying any attention. When he realized that nobody was coming to investigate, he leaned down to the girl and examined her more closely. She was filthy and smelled like it had been a good long while since she'd had a shower.

"I'm not going to shoot you...again," he added that last word as he tucked his gun back in his belt.

He saw the other two that he'd shot lying where they'd fallen. He also saw a few figures moving with that slow, awkward walk in his general direction. Reaching down, he scooped the girl up. She yelped and struggled weakly in his grasp.

"Shut up, I'm not going to hurt you. You need to see a doctor," he hissed.

"Just let me go!" she insisted.

Ken looked back at the advancing figures. Turning slightly, he pointed them out. "You want me to leave you to them?"

She seemed to consider her choices and then leaned into his side. He walked her to the front of the truck and opened the door. He cast a look of longing over his shoulder. There was still so much inside the store that he could use, but he needed to check on his mother and get this girl some help. He knew that Legacy Hospital was not too far away. He could drop the girl off at the emergency entrance and then head to his mother's.

Moving around the car, he heard a scream and, as he unlocked his door, he saw three figures falling on the prone body of one of his attackers. He actually felt sorry for the person. He'd heard that scream from Gina Glendon and could only imagine what was happening to whichever of the male attackers he'd shot.

Climbing into the cab, he was instantly met by the snuffling face of the retriever. He eased in and nudged the dog back into the extended part of the cab behind the front seats. The scream rose in pitch and then went silent in an instant.

"What was that?" the girl asked, sounding for the first time like a frightened young lady.

"Something bad," was Ken's reply as he started the truck and headed for the exit. "Now buckle up. I am taking you to the hospital."

***

Rose backed away. Frank stood, his insides spilling from a rip in his belly. Before she could take another step, Rose heaved, the contents of her stomach making a splash on the hardwood floor of her living room.

Her mind struggled to process what she was seeing, but nothing made any sense. As she fought to get her mind to wrap around what was happening, the two men began to draw closer. Standing in the entry hall, the sounds of frantic barking came from her bedroom where Imp and Circe were shut away.

The two figures, Frank and the neighbor, took step after agonizing step towards her. As the intensity of the barking increased, Frank's head turned in a jerky movement that was almost inhuman in the way it twitched; very nearly like that of a bird. Rose could not allow them to head down the hallway to her bedroom. She had no idea if they could open a door or not, but she needed to get these two men out of her house.

"Hey!" Rose yelled. Frank's head came back around and he started towards her once again.

Rose backed to the front door, reaching behind her to open it. She had to actually step closer to the advancing monstrosities for just a second as she pulled her door open. At last she was able to slip around it as the neighbor's hand swiped at her and missed by just a few inches.

Stepping outside, Rose backed down her stairs and looked around. The entire neighborhood was strangely quiet. It was only late afternoon, and not even children could be seen playing outside or walking down the street. It was as if she were the only person actually at home.

Reaching the bottom of the stairs, Rose backed down the path once the neighbor and Frank both exited her house. The neighbor reached the first stair and stumbled, landing with a sickening crack as he struck the concrete and tumbled down the three stairs. Frank did not seem to notice and followed in the neighbor's footsteps. The only thing that was different was that Frank landed on the neighbor who was struggling to try and roll over.

As the two men became disentangled, and the neighbor crawled free, Rose noticed that the man's arm now had an obscene break in the forearm. Bone jutted through skin, but he took no notice and actually tried to use the arm as he struggled to his feet. Rose had to battle with her rising gorge as she saw the broken forearm bend at the midpoint and then snap in half. The arm was, at this point, totally useless, as the lower half of the forearm was now barely connected by skin and ruined muscle.

Rose walked out into the street and waited as Frank and the neighbor, through some miracle, managed to make it to their feet and continue to pursue her at their slow, awkward pace. Once they reached the end of her driveway, Rose was actually at a loss as to what to do. It wasn't like she could continue to act as some sort of Pied Piper. She had to figure out a way to ditch the pair and get back to her home.

Then what? she thought as she backed down the middle of the street.

Almost on cue, her phone rang. She knew by the ringtone that it was her sister. Grabbing the phone from her pocket, Rose thumbed it and answered.

"Hello? Violet?"

"Rose!" Her sister's voice was frantic. But there was something else about it that sounded off. She couldn't place it, but there was definitely something off.

"Violet, Frank is here, and there is something wrong—" she began, but her sister cut her off.

"Don't let him in, Rose. This is every—"

And then the line went dead.

***

"*Dios mio,*" the voice sighed.

Jason had hit the brakes and spun to look in back. Juanita was climbing up from the floor where she had tumbled. He was pretty sure that zombies didn't talk. Sure, some of the more peculiar books had that going on. He didn't much care for those, but who knew where the line was drawn between fact and fiction. He would have laughed at the idea of zombies as early as this morning, but events were proving that perhaps truth was as strange as fiction...or something like that.

"Juanita?" Jason asked tentatively. One hand was opening

and closing in a tight fist; the other was gripping the door latch. He was pretty sure that he could escape before she bit him.

"Where are we?" the woman asked, rubbing her head tenderly and wincing.

"The hospital." Jason paused before making his admission. "I thought you might be dead. I was bringing you here to be sure."

Juanita was silent for a moment before she finally spoke again. "Then you must not have seen what I saw."

"You mean about the zombies?" Jason blurted. As soon as the word left his mouth he wished that he could get it back. He had already given Juanita enough reasons to ditch him. Showing that he was nuts in the head would not do him any favors.

"So you have seen them," Juanita whispered.

"Don't tell me that you think…" His voice trailed off as a woman walked past the car.

They were parked so that they could see the sidewalk that ran along the front of the parking lot where the street went past. The streetlights were all coming on as the light sensors activated them to push back the gloom of the growing darkness of night.

The woman was a bloody mess. There was a strand of what could only be intestine trailing behind her. and as she passed directly under the light, the knife jutting from her chest drew the focus from the missing flesh of her cheek. Her walk was a sort of drag step that reminded Jason of an old man he knew in prison that had suffered a massive stroke. One side of him was partially paralyzed, so his walk was this incredibly awkward gait. Unfortunately, inside, that made him not only a target of ridicule, but also of the general population's bullies.

"But when I listened to your chest, I didn't hear a heartbeat," Jason said weakly.

"Well, I can promise you that I am not a zombie," Juanita replied as she climbed over the seat.

"So what do we do?"

Juanita thought it over for a moment before turning to face Jason. "I don't think going into the hospital is a good idea."

"But your head."

"I'm fine," Juanita brushed aside his concern.

"It wouldn't hurt to be sure," Jason insisted.

The two craned their necks around to look back at the hospital entrance. Despite the fact that the lot was packed and three ambulances sat in the entry bay with lights on and back doors open, the warm glow of the entrance did not seem to bode ill.

"I will stay right by your side," Juanita said, patting Jason on the arm.

Together, they took another look around to ensure that there were no more zombies walking past. Once they were fairly certain that the coast was clear, they exited the car, both taking special care to shut the door as quietly as possible.

Without realizing it, they clutched each other's hand and started toward the entrance to the hospital emergency room. They were just crossing the last crosswalk where the main entrance allowed access to the parking lot when the roar of an engine sounded and the bright headlights of an oncoming vehicle chased away the darkness in a blinding flash. The tires screeched as the driver had to slam on the brakes to avoid hitting the pair.

So this is what a deer feels like, a muted voice said from somewhere in the back of Jason's mind.

MAY DECEMBER
Publications

**The growing voice in horror
and speculative fiction.**

Find us at www.maydecemberpublications.com
Or
Email us at contact@maydecemberpublications.com

TW Brown is the author of the ***Zomblog*** series, his horror comedy romp, ***That Ghoul Ava***, and, of course, the ***DEAD*** series. Safely tucked away in the beautiful Pacific Northwest, he moves away from his desk only at the urging of his Border Collie, Aoife. (Pronounced Eye-fa)

He plays a little guitar on the side...just for fun...and makes up any excuse to either go trail hiking or strolling along his favorite place...Cannon Beach. He answers all his emails sent to twbrown.maydecpub @gmail.com and tries to thank everybody personally when they take the time to leave a review of one of his works.

His blog can be found at:http://twbrown.blogspot.com

The best way to find everything he has out is to start at his Author Page:

You can follow him on twitter @maydecpub and on Facebook under Todd Brown, Author TW Brown, and also under May December Publications.